FROM NEW YORK TIMES BESTSELLING AUTHOR KATY REGNERY,
WRITING AS K. P. KELLEY,
COMES HER FIRST DUO OF PARANORMAL ROMANCES!

ONCE UPON A TIME…
the most beautiful boy in the world kissed me.
I've never been able to forget.
Perhaps it was his jet-black hair,
or the changing copper-color of his eyes,
the intense way he looked at me…
or the fact that he awakened my passion for the first time,
at once otherworldly yet heartbreakingly real.
But after that kiss, I never saw him again.

His name was Jack Beauloup.
Jack, my "Beautiful Wolf."

Twenty years passed. He has returned. For me.

www.BOROUGHSPUBLISHINGGROUP.com

IT'S YOU, Book One
Copyright © 2017 Katharine Gilliam Regnery

ISBN: 978-1-541174-96-2

Interior Format
© KILLION
GROUP, INC.

It's

BOOK
ONE

You

KATY REGNERY
WRITING AS
K. P. KELLEY

For Grandma.
Your gift gave me the freedom to do what I love.
I am so very grateful.

Part 1:
Darcy

Chapter 1

DARCY TURNER FIDGETED UNCOMFORTABLY IN the stiff waiting room guest chair, flicking her eyes to her wrist. The "doctor" was running seven minutes late. Shooting a quick look at the receptionist, she wondered if the petite blonde would chase after her if Darcy suddenly got up and walked out the door without a word. But, then what? She'd still need answers she didn't have.

As a rule, Darcy didn't believe in holistic practices like hypnosis, which she regarded with a boatload of skepticism. So the fact that she was sitting in the waiting room of the most well-regarded hypnotist in New England meant that she was far, far away from her comfort zone. It also meant she was desperate.

She needed answers.

She needed to go back to that night in her mind and figure out what had happened, because it didn't make sense that it was still haunting her on a near-daily basis.

"Mrs. Turner?"

"Miss," said Darcy, standing up and gathering her purse and jacket from the chair beside her.

"Miss Turner. Doctor Canard will see you now."

Darcy took a deep breath, offering the perky receptionist a tight smile, and stepped toward the office door. She hesitated for a moment, but heard her best friend Willow's voice in her head. *What do you have to lose, Darce? I made you an appointment. Go for me. Just go and see what happens.*

I'm only doing this for Willow, she thought, turning the knob and entering the dimly lit office.

"Darcy." A tall, dark-haired woman stood up from an easy chair, holding out her hand. "I'm Doctor Canard."

Darcy almost replied that one of them was a doctor and it certainly wasn't *Doctor* Canard, but Darcy rarely made use of the academic title conferred on her from Harvard almost ten years ago. Instead she offered "Doctor" Canard a weak smile and shook her hand before sitting down on the couch across from the hypnotist.

"You're a skeptic?"

"I'm a doctor. A scientist," Darcy said, by way of explanation. "Of botany."

"I see." Dr. Canard crossed and uncrossed her legs, offering Darcy a warm smile. "That doesn't matter, you know. We'll gauge your suggestibility before we begin."

"Gauge my suggestibility?"

"Mm-hm. And don't worry about feeling anxious. It's easier to hypnotize an anxious person."

"Is that right?"

"Mm-hm," said Dr. Canard in her low, soothing voice. "That's right."

"Well, then I should be a breeze for you."

"Why are you anxious?" Dr. Canard chuckled lightly. "I mean, besides the fact that you're here with me and hypnosis is outside of your comfort zone? Why are you here?"

Darcy took a deep breath, moving her jacket and purse from her lap and settling them on the couch beside her.

"My best friend insisted I give this a try."

"Okay. Why?"

Darcy shook her head lightly, knowing what she was about to say had the potential of sounding crazy or pathetic and she wasn't comfortable with either. Then again, whom did she have to impress? "Doctor" Canard? She let her defenses drop and started at the beginning.

"When I was fifteen, there was a boy I knew in high school. He was..." Darcy felt her face soften as she remembered Jack Beauloup's intense brown eyes looking into hers. *It's you. It can't be.* The words came from nowhere, taking over her brain for a few seconds before she started speaking again. "He kissed me once. One time. During a school play. And I never saw him again after that. I never saw him again, period."

"It made quite an impression on you."

"It's been twenty years," Darcy murmured. She looked at the hypnotist's kind, sympathetic face and cleared her throat before continuing. "I've dated. I've even been engaged. But, my mind always—*always*—returns to that kiss. I can't shake it. I can't—"

"You can't get past it?"

"I guess I can't. And I was thinking—well really, my friend Willow thinks that maybe if I could regress my memory, maybe I would see something, find something, remember something from that night that would explain my…obsession."

Dr. Canard nodded. "I understand. Do you have *any* substantial memories of that night?"

"Oh, yes! I remember the night very well," she explained. "In fact, I feel like I remember every detail. I've watched it all happen in my dreams thousands of times like a movie. My brain just won't let go of it. Honestly, even if you're able to regress me, I don't feel like there's anything new I'm going to find there that I don't already remember in minute detail. But, maybe there is. Maybe there's one little thing I'm forgetting that will explain its hold on me. I just don't want to be trapped—not trapped, but, it's like it's holding me hostage or…or…"

She couldn't think of the right words to explain the strange grasp that night still had on her, but the connection was like a fetter, keeping her chained to it despite the passage of time. She didn't understand it and she couldn't explain it. She only knew she wasn't free from it, and one kiss, one moment, with one boy who she should have forgotten years ago had taken up way too much real estate in her head for way too long.

"Well, I have all the information I need," said the doctor in a calm, soothing voice. "Are you ready to go back, Darcy? Are you ready for whatever's there?"

Darcy looked up at Dr. Canard's kind eyes, knowing she didn't really have a choice, feeling she had nothing to lose. "I'm ready."

"Then let's get started."

THIS WAS DARCY'S FAVORITE PART of the entire play.

She knew if she stayed inconspicuous, concealed behind the thick curtain of velvet, she would be left alone to watch in the darkness. Leaning her cheek against the soft, musty fabric, she closed her eyes.

The moment the high school auditorium house lights went dim, the hum of intermission conversation dissolved to a murmur. She heard the pitter-patter of actors taking their places on the century-old high school stage: the girls in their silly dancing poses that would elicit light laughter when the curtain opened, and the four guys in red, pinstriped barbershop jackets walking out in unison and taking their places downstage next to a papier-mâché street lamp—a quartet that included the most beautiful boy she had ever seen.

As she thought of the tall, dark baritone standing just a few feet from her, butterflies filled Darcy's stomach, beating their wings against her pounding heart. All was silent now. She clutched at the velvet and willed every bit of longing in her fifteen-year-old body to focus on him— pleaded wordlessly with every bit of magic in that old high school theater to find him in the darkness and to let him somehow know: *Jack, I wait here every night for you.*

She opened her eyes when the curtain parted and she heard the audience chuckle. Darcy smiled and eased her grip on the musty fabric, distracted by the action on stage and delighted by the audience's response. She was proud of the play, but on the heels of triumph was a fast approaching melancholy; she tried to chase away the bittersweet thought that this was the final performance.

Darcy regretted that she had never mustered up the courage to speak to Jack Beauloup directly during the weeks of practices and performances. She first noticed the handsome transfer student in the library during the school year and had secretly watched him over the ensuing weeks, desperate to know if he was brooding or just reserved. Sometimes she felt him watching her too, but when caught, he would look away so lazily as to suggest she was merely in his line of sight, not the object of his gaze.

Jack had paid her no special attention during the sweltering months of summer stock rehearsals, but he often left the theater at the same time she did. Crackling with awareness, she felt him following her, though he never spoke to her or otherwise sought her attention, except for one time when he grabbed her arm. She was distracted that day; walking and reading at the same time, she had missed a car coming sharply around the parking lot curve, headed for her.

"Be more careful," Jack had graowled at her, his face sharp with anger as he held her eyes with a searing gaze. She'd glanced down at his hand on her arm and he'd dropped it instantly before stalking away.

The next day, right after "It's You," Darcy held her breath as he exited to stage right, walking decisively to the wing where she stood, fully composed and ready to thank him, only to be disappointed with a terse nod that made her swallow her words. Seeking hidden meaning in these brief encounters was pointless and painful, but her longing for him would not be so easily cast aside, despite his seeming indifference toward *her*.

Not that any of it mattered after tonight. He was two years older than she and leaving for college tomorrow, while she still had two more years of high school left to go. She was a ridiculous, love-struck toddler with a crush on a boy who was leaving Carlisle in the morning, a boy who barely acknowledged she was alive.

The "ladies" finished their silly dancing routine and Darcy giggled and clapped quietly from her place in the wings. Her delight was fleeting, though, and her smile faded when the music director played a short note on the harmonica. As the quartet hummed the first chord of "It's You," preparing to sing the sweet, old-fashioned love song, her heart clenched with yearning. It was the final time the boys would sing the song on stage, and she felt—desperately, unreasonably—that time was going too fast, that there should be a hundred more performances, that she needed more time to make him see her, notice her, want her. The boys took a simultaneous deep breath and she closed her eyes to savor their voices, picking through them for Jack's strong baritone.

It's you in the sunrise; it's you in my cup.
It's you all the way into town.
It's your sweet "Hello, dear" that sets me up
And it's your "Got to go, dear" that gets me down.

The harmonies were so pure and true, tears pricked the back of her eyes and a lump rose in her throat. She stood hidden in the shadows, riveted on his strong, handsome profile, watching his lips make the sounds that heated her young body until she wanted to cry out to him. She felt an urgency to memorize this moment so she could relive it forever—so that tomorrow night, alone in her bedroom, cold with gnawing emptiness, she could close her eyes and hear Jack Beauloup sing for her once again.

It's you on my pillow in all my dreams.' Til once more the morning breaks through What words could be saner or truer or plainer Than it's you, it's you. Yes, it's you. Oh, yes it's you.

The audience broke into applause, and Darcy swallowed, licking her painted lips and smoothing her dress. She took a deep breath, her shoulders rigid with anticipation. It was almost time for the next number.

The quartet took their bows and separated to the four corners of the stage. As Jack approached her, she tried to catch his eyes, smiling at him as she did every night when he made his exit to the wing where she stood. Most nights, short of simply ignoring her, he seemed to *avoid* her as she would avoid something painful that she couldn't bear to see. Purposely looking over her head or down at the floor as he approached, he would pivot to take his place beside her for the few minutes before their entrance. Then he would offer her his elbow, without looking at her, so they could skip onstage together.

Something was different tonight, though, as he crossed toward her in his candy-cane-striped jacket and slicked-back hair: for the first time, he looked directly into her eyes. Darcy's breath caught and her smile froze on her face. He approached her so purposefully that she blinked in surprise and stumbled back, anticipating him. He stopped where she had been standing a moment before and they stood toe to toe, just a breath away from each other. He was taller than she, and her eyes leveled at his throat for a moment, adjusting to his nearness. She was surprised to feel the warmth of his body on the skin of her cheeks, like standing in the sunshine on a chilly day. She watched him swallow twice before she lifted her eyes to his face.

His eyes seized hers, serious and direct, shiny in the shadowy darkness, flecks of copper catching the dim light like smoldering coals, changing color before her from indistinct brown to something warmer, feverish even, like embers stoked into fire.

It was as though a spell had been cast, drawing her into the vortex of his gaze and stopping real time entirely. The stage, the other actors, her parents and brother in the audience…suddenly they were all a lifetime away. Everything but Jack faded into a vacuum of cold, grey nothingness, and in an instant her entire world was unbearably vibrant, made up wholly of the mesmerizing boy standing so still and serious in front of her. Here was Darcy and there was Jack, and—for this moment—they were the whole world.

He brought his fingertips to her throat and pressed lightly on the pulse point that raced and pleaded beneath them. His eyes followed his fingers to her neck where they rested, narrowing transiently with unspoken emotion, then widening and furious as he met her gaze again. She watched his mouth breathe her name, "*Darcy Turner,*" while his eyes searched hers for a tight moment, almost blazing now with licking flames and primitive intensity. As he dipped his head smoothly to brush his lips against hers, her eyes filled with tears and fluttered closed, her small fingers curling by her sides into fists. He drew back for a moment, and then she felt his lips on hers again. Stronger and more urgent now, he claimed her lips again, tilting his head to seal his mouth over hers. It ignited an unexpected warmth that bubbled up from the depths of her body, radiating out from her middle until her clenched fingers relaxed. She leaned closer to him, her heart drawn like a magnet to his, seeking and finding peace in its rhythm.

I belong to you.

A wave of requited love overcame her and a small, strangled sound rose from the depths of her throat, rousing him from the throes of enchantment. As quickly as it happened, and with as little notice, it was over. She opened her eyes in confusion and doubt, and saw he was out of breath, his chest heaving as though he'd just run a marathon, staring at her fiercely, astonished, uncertain.

"It *can't* be," he whispered, anguished, shaking his head as his eyes searched hers. "It's *you*."

Then, in one agile motion, he moved to her side and stared straight ahead.

In the darkness of the velvet curtains, she felt his trembling hand reach for hers. Another pulsing thrill shot through her young body at the touch of his hot, taut hand. She ran her fingers gingerly over the wiry hairs on the back of his fingers and glanced up at him, but he was still staring straight ahead at the stage, clenching his jaw with measured determination. He shifted to lace his fingers through hers until their palms were flush and, so entwined, finally still.

And you belong to me.

A moment before their entrance, he gazed down to meet Darcy's imploring eyes. Jack's were a soft brown now, unaccountably grieved, holding hers gently, desperately, almost as though he would never see them again. He kept his fingers woven through hers until the last possible second, only moving her hand to his arm as they skipped onstage in character.

For what is bound cannot be broken.

"DARCY? DARCY, ARE YOU WITH me again?"

Darcy's eyes fluttered open slowly and she looked up at the light directly on the ceiling where the doctor had told her to concentrate as she'd achieved a trancelike state, remembering that night in blistering detail.

"Darcy? Can you sit up for me?"

Darcy took a deep breath through her nose and sat up slowly, bracing on her elbows for a moment before sitting up straight and turning toward the doctor until her feet gently dropped to the carpeted floor.

She swallowed once, the strong images, smells and feelings fading—like waking up from a dream—as she stared back at Dr. Canard.

"So?" she asked, looking at Darcy searchingly once she'd had a moment to compose herself.

"I think hypnosis works," Darcy said softly.

Dr. Canard nodded and chuckled lightly. "Yes. But what about your memories? Did you see anything new? Anything to help explain why you're holding on to that night so tightly? There must have been something?"

Darcy's shoulders slumped and she shook her head.

"There wasn't," she replied, the trancelike version of that night a carbon copy of the one that had claimed her dreams for almost twenty years. "Nothing at all. It's the same night I've relived my whole life."

Dr. Canard cocked her head to the side. "*For what is bound cannot be broken.* You repeated that over and over again before I woke you. What do you think that means?"

Darcy gathered her jacket and purse onto her lap, scooting forward on the couch to say good-bye. "I have no idea, doctor. But no matter what? Someday I'll find out."

Chapter 2

T HREE DAYS LATER DARCY ADJUSTED the multicolored-flower ruffle of taffeta that exploded out of her shoulder strap into her neck and chin. It looked ridiculous and itched like crazy. She readjusted the bustle in the back of the bridesmaid dress and pulled up the embarrassingly low-cut décolletage up for the tenth time, clasping a bright orange bouquet of tiger lilies in her gloved fist, wishing she was anywhere but here.

"Maybe someday, Cousin Darcy." The bride, Honoria, sighed loudly, giving Darcy a sympathetic glance before touching the diamond comb in her blonde hair and fixing a photo-ready, can-do smile on her erstwhile cheerleader face.

Darcy ground her back teeth together, holding her tongue, checking out the huge meringue that was her cousin. Covering a swelling baby bump was one thing, but covering it in yards and yards of white tulle was something else. Honoria looked ludicrous, but it was little comfort against the humiliation of her words in front of all of the other bridesmaids.

Maybe someday? Darcy was thirty-five years old. More and more it felt like maybe never.

Darcy turned back to the doors in front of her that swung open into the packed sanctuary, as the organ played the first few notes of the *Wedding March*. She took her steps slowly—*step-together-pause, step-together-pause*—well practiced after two decades of acting as a bridal attendant for various cousins and friends. She had even been a bridesmaid in some of her cousins' second weddings, as she was today.

Seconds afore every'un else been served. Ain't fitting. Ain't fair. She could hear Miss Kendrick's voice in her head, and almost grinned.

Step-together-pause, step-together-pause.

She caught her brother Amory's eye in a pew toward the back and he winked at her, and then he raised his eyebrows and cringed at her dress. She stared straight ahead, biting the sides of her cheeks to keep from smiling.

Her great-aunt Lucy waved at her cheerfully from beside him, and took a quick photo with a disposable camera. *Great. There's a shot to remember.* The stuffed quail on the old woman's hat bobbed up and down, nodding at Darcy, as if it might coo, "Maybe someday. Maybe someday," with its singsong call—if it could only escape Lucy Turner's chapeau.

Step-together-pause, step-together-pause.

Her best friend and roommate Dr. Willow Broussard had her lips curled tightly inward between clenched teeth, and her eyes danced merrily, taking in Darcy's "Sunset Delight" gown in varying shades of hot pink, fluorescent orange, shiny gold and metallic lavender. Darcy could see her shoulders quaking with laughter under the straps of her simple dress. It was Willow's favorite: soft black jersey with a scoop neck, empire waist, and a hem that barely allowed her always-black-lacquered toes to peek out from underneath. Darcy crossed her eyes momentarily at Willow during a *pause* then resumed her serene pace up the aisle.

Step-together-pause, step-together-pause.

Darcy's mother, Cassie, sat in the second row and twisted her neck to see her daughter—her still-single daughter—then rolled her eyes, covering her mouth with a delicately embroidered handkerchief. Darcy could see the disappointment in her mother's eyes, almost feel the heaviness of her mother's heart... *There's my good girl. Always a bridesmaid...*

As she approached the altar, Darcy breathed in through her nose, only to be assaulted by the thick scent of gardenias. Huge bunches of the pungent, sweeter-than-honey blooms had been arranged in large vases in the front of the church and Darcy's stomach rolled over, offended by the strong smell.

You cannot get sick, Darcy Turner. Breathe through your mouth, for heaven's sake.

She turned left into the empty pew in front and stepped lightly to the end, thanking God that she was sitting closest to the long floor-to-ceiling windows that had replaced the centuries-old lead glass windows in the old Second Congregational Church of Carlisle, New Hampshire. Some parishioners had taken offense at the newer, simpler plate-glass windows, whose bottom halves could be opened to allow fresh air into the ancient church. Great-Aunt Lucy and her sister, Darcy's great-aunt Mildred, had refused to attend services for an entire year after the installation of the new windows, protesting by holding weekly Sunday Bible study in the front parlor of their Victorian house on Main Street, dressed in their Sunday best.

Since there was a snowball's chance in hell that she'd ever wear this dress again, Darcy slid back to settle comfortably into her seat, crushing her bustle and closing her eyes. Still wary of her churning stomach, she tried to focus on the fresh early-spring air coming in from the window.

Her cousin Theodora snapped her gum—*classy*—and elbowed Darcy in the side. "Saw your girlfriend."

Darcy rolled her eyes at Honoria's nineteen-year-old sister, took a deep breath and sighed. "Don't. Be. Ridiculous."

Theodora chewed her gum like a cow with cud and Darcy wondered how distracted her Aunt Bess must have been not to notice her gum-chewing youngest daughter. *Then again, I guess a knocked-up daughter and a shotgun wedding are pretty distracting circumstances.*

"At least you have each other. Willow the Witch and Darcy the Spinster. Thirty-five may as well be a hundred. Kill me if I'm not married by then."

"Gladly."

Theodora's eyes widened and she turned away quickly, just in time to see her older sister take her place at the front of the church: a big, poufy, pregnant bride that took up most of the altar space in a mockery of a white dress, practically dwarfing the skinny groom beside her.

The minister took his place before the couple. "Dearly beloved, we are gathered here today..."

Darcy closed her eyes again and tuned him out, propping her elbow on the side of the pew and leaning her head toward the window.

And then it happened, as it always did when she least expected it.

She "went inside."

That's what Willow called it when Darcy shut out the world for a little while and escaped inside her own head. Either that, or she referred to it as "soul flight" in the manner of the Métis people, a Native American tribe located north of Carlisle near Quebec. Like dreaming without sleeping, Darcy would close her eyes and mentally wander away from wherever she was. When she opened her eyes inside, she'd find herself somewhere else.

Sometimes her soul flight took her to a pleasant clearing where she'd fan her fingertips against tall grasses that shuddered lightly in an afternoon breeze. Sometimes she found herself in a cathedral of pine trees, dwarfed by the greatness of the forest around her. Sometimes she wandered high into the mountains, eventually gazing down at the woodlands with wonder.

Two things were consistent when Darcy went inside without exception: she *always* found herself in the woods, and without exception, the illusion *always* ended the same—with *his* voice from long ago, and the whispered words

It's you

as hot as flame, as still as breath, in her ear.

This time, when she opened her eyes, she was kneeling in a clearing on a thick mattress of long pine needles at dusk. She could feel the soft needles piled high under her knees, so she spread out her hands by her sides to run her fingers over their hay-like texture. Looking around, she realized she knelt in the middle of an intersection of pathways, smoothed trails flattened to tidy dirt paths by years of tread, one to her left and one to her right. She breathed in and smelled the fresh pine trees all around her. A loon called from the distance, its sad howl drenched with longing. As she sat back on her heels, the simple white cotton shift she was wearing settled around her in a perfect circle of brightness in the dying light. To her left she heard a noise, like a foot snapping a twig, and turned to see, but there was nothing there. Still she felt she wasn't alone. No, she *knew* she wasn't alone. *Are you here?* she wondered.

It's you...

Theodora nudged her. "Wake up, Darcy. Geez! Ruder! It's almost over!"

Darcy's elbow slipped off the side of the pew, banging painfully into the sharp, elaborate molding below. She winced and opened her eyes, reorienting herself. She didn't need to put her hands to her cheeks to know they would be flushed bright pink with heat. She could still smell the pine needles, but it was fading like mist, its welcome freshness being mercilessly replaced by the nauseating gardenias.

Back in real time, she turned to the window again, sucking in a cleansing breath, squinting her eyes against the bright sun that bathed her face in light.

She froze.

That's when she saw him.

On the edge of the woods, in the shadow of the ancient pines, with his back to her. He was a good bit over six feet, and had his hands in his front pockets. He wore a pressed long-sleeved blue dress shirt tucked into the waistband of belted black pants. His dark hair was thick and wavy, peppered with gray, and Darcy's fingers twitched with the irrational desire to run her fingers through that hair. Having lived in Carlisle for most of her life, it surprised Darcy that she couldn't place this man—even without seeing his face—within the families she'd known forever. Was he a late wedding guest? Someone Honoria met at college in Portsmouth? Her heart beat loudly in her chest for no good reason as she gazed out the window, widening her eyes despite the bright light, unable to tear her gaze away from the tall, dark stranger. Wishing she could ignore the insistent feeling that she knew him, that he was significant to her, that he might even be—

"What's *with* you? Are you *okay*? *You. Are. So. Weird*," Theodora hissed again, standing up with the rest of the bridesmaids, staring down at Darcy's flushed face.

She looked up at Theodora and stood quickly, bracing her hands on the pew in front of her, holding the bright white wood with a claw-like grip.

"You may kiss the bride."

The congregation broke into applause as the recessional music played cheerfully.

When Darcy looked back at the edge of the woods, he was gone.

"**W**HAT DO YOU MEAN, YOU think you saw Jack Beauloup? When you went inside?" Willow held her champagne glass at an awkward angle, leaning her head toward Darcy at their assigned table, and speaking in an urgent whisper. "You've never seen *anyone* in there. You know what I think, kid? You and weddings don't mix."

"Tell me about it. Honoria was kind enough to remind me of my unmarried state and Theodora implied we're lesbians."

"Your family's the *best*." Willow shook her head and the little silver feathers hanging from her ears jingled. "Honoria Turner is a rhymes-with-stitch and Theodora Turner is a moron. No. You know what? That's unfair to morons."

Darcy was accustomed to the snickers and low-toned gossip surrounding her and Willow. They had been roommates for ten years, sharing the old Victorian house left to Willow by her grandparents. Two adult, unrelated women living as roommates for a decade simply wasn't acceptable for the simpleminded, straitlaced, New England sensibilities of Carlisle.

"Wait. Are you trying to change the subject? Where did you see him?"

"Not when I went inside. Through the church window. Standing at the edge of the woods."

"He hasn't been in Carlisle for twenty years. You saw him *here*? In Proctor Woods?"

"No, Willow. In the Vienna Woods is Austria. Yes, Proctor! What other woods are there?"

"Are you sure it was him?"

"No. He was tall and dark and had his back to me."

"His back. You saw his *back*. So…you're basically saying it could have been anyone."

"I had a *feeling*. A strong feeling. Of recognition or something…"

"We're basing this wild assumption on a *feeling*?"

"And I had just *gone inside*. I had just heard…"

"…his voice," Willow supplied. "You are *really* losing it, kid."

"Maybe." Darcy took a sip of her champagne and rubbed her eyes. "Maybe you're right. It's probably just weddings. Always a bridesmaid."

"So defeatist, Darce. It's not like you have one foot in the grave. You're still young. I mean, *someday*—"

Darcy turned to her friend sharply, giving her a warning look, and Willow stopped talking. Willow knew full and well that "someday" was just about Darcy's least favorite word.

Distracting herself, Darcy pulled at the fabric flower that was crushed against her neck, making her itch. "Isn't there anything I can do with this awful dress? It's scratching the heck out of my skin."

She tugged at the stiff taffeta, pulling at the seam until she ripped the odious puffed flower off entirely, and with it, a bit of the already scant décolletage. Willow gave Darcy's chest a quick glance.

"Well, well. Carlisle will just *love* that."

"I didn't choose this monstrosity of a dress."

Darcy pulled a light, cantaloupe melon–colored cardigan sweater out of her bag and unrolled it, shrugging it over her bare shoulders and buttoning the top three buttons.

"That's more like it. Matches your hair. By the way, where'd you go this time? When you went inside? Where were you?"

Willow was the only person who knew about Darcy's occasional visions, her escapes to the enchanted forest when she went inside. Darcy had started having the visions the fall after her fifteenth birthday. At first they would just appear out of nowhere; a dizzying, swirling feeling would overtake her and if she closed her eyes, she'd feel as though she was transported somewhere else. She'd be enveloped in the welcoming warmth of the forest, soothed by nature's sounds, know the pleasure of belonging somewhere, and best of all, she'd hear Jack Beauloup's voice from that night whispering softly in her ear once again.

But she'd also been frightened by the trancelike state that would last anywhere from thirty seconds to several minutes, no matter how good it felt while she was there; by Christmastime, she felt like she was going crazy, losing her mind, and fearfully confided the visions to Willow.

Thank God, because Willow, who was one-quarter Métis on her father's side, had taken the news in stride, impressed and intrigued. Pouring over Métis books on trances and hypnosis for their entire winter break, they agreed that Darcy had somehow tapped into the gift of Soul Flight. Willow encouraged Darcy to master her special talent, control the length of her stays, when and where she welcomed them, and how to fend them off at inopportune times. Darcy had never actually been able to control them, but with the exception of the last few months, their frequency had diminished to two or three times a year. She didn't mind them. She was grateful, even, to turn herself over to the embrace of the forest now and then, to the warm heaven of Jack Beauloup's low, urgent voice from long ago.

In the past few months, however, the frequency had increased again. She was going inside more and more often, unable to control the arrival and length of the visions. While it wasn't exactly frightening her, after a decade of only occasional episodes, it was unsettling. And for the first time, the forest visions didn't seem like a private world. For the first time she understood something, or someone, was there with her.

"Darcy and Willow." Honoria and her skinny, bald husband, Bob, approached their table for the duty-greeting.

For the first time, Darcy realized that the table was practically on the outskirts of the outdoor, tented reception, and only sat four people, as opposed to the tables of eight and ten closer to the dance floor. It was definitely the spot farthest away from the head table where the rest of the bridesmaids, led by Honoria's twin sisters Theodora and Aurelia, were doing a good job getting drunk on shots of clear liquid.

"I just *knew* you two would want to be together, so I didn't put you at the head table, Darcy."

"How thoughtful."

Willow stood up to greet the bride, her slim figure, black dress and gamine, jet-black hair a striking contrast against Honoria's blonde chignon and cream puff of a gown. Willow gestured to Honoria's belly with her champagne glass. "No drinking, now. Doctor's orders."

Honoria's eyes widened then narrowed as she gave Willow, Carlisle's only local physician, a tight smile. "Wouldn't dream of it, Doctor Broussard."

"Congratulations, Bob." Darcy stood up and opened her arms to her cousin's new husband. Bob glanced quickly at Honoria, who answered his silent question with a curt nod as if to say *Oh, for God's sakes, just hug her and get it over with so we can get away from these two!* before stepping into Darcy's embrace.

"Welcome to the family," she whispered into his ear. "Good luck with Honoria. You're going to need it."

Bob stumbled back, staring at Darcy, who smiled at her cousin's new husband with amusement. "Why, Bob Fellows, you'd think I bit you."

Honoria glared at the two women, and then gestured to Darcy's altered neckline and cardigan. "Always have to be different, right, Darce?"

Darcy met her cousin's blue eyes with cool defiance. "You know me."

"Unfortunately." And then Honoria flounced away, dragging poor Bob behind her.

Without missing a beat, Darcy turned back to Willow to continue their conversation. "You asked where I was this time? A bed of needles. There was someone nearby. Watching me. Near me."

"That's happening more and more lately, isn't it? Someone else in there with you…"

Darcy nodded, sitting back down and refilling her own glass from a bottle of champagne set on the tables for toasting.

"You know that I straddle the line between the medical world and the natural world, but I'm starting to worry, kid," said Willow, refilling her glass as well. "I'm wondering if we should get an MRI on that head of yours."

"Don't worry, Will. It doesn't feel any different than it ever has. Nothing's changed…except when I'm in there."

"Okay. But, I can arrange it in North Conway or at Dartmouth whenever you say the word. No one needs to know." She paused and placed her hand over Darcy's. "Who do you think it is? Who's inside with you?"

Darcy had no answer for her friend, so she shrugged. In twenty years, she had never seen another person when she went inside. Her mind amended the thought: *Maybe you haven't* seen *another person, but you've certainly* heard *one.*

And lately, she *felt* someone. She knew someone was there, watching, waiting.

Darcy gestured to the two empty chairs at the small round table. "Who do you think these chairs are for?"

"For us."

Darcy and Willow looked up simultaneously to see Darcy's brother Amory standing over their table. Darcy smiled at her brother, shielding her eyes from the bright sun then noticing— for the first time—the figure standing beside her brother, who stepped in front of the sun like a solar eclipse, blocking the light, but somehow not the warmth.

Darcy's heart stopped beating and her breath caught in her throat as she stood up, slowly, disbelievingly.

It was the man from the edge of the woods.

For the first time in twenty years, Darcy Turner was face to face with Jack Beauloup.

Chapter 3

DARCY STARED AT JACK LIKE he was a dream or a ghost or an impossibility.

What do you say to the man who was the beautiful boy who kissed you once twenty years ago and changed your whole world, consigning you to a lifetime of relentless longing in the space of a single moment? What in the world do you say?

"Darcy Turner." He breathed her name the same way he had that night.

She nodded vaguely, focused on his face. Her breath came out in a whoosh as she grabbed the back of the chair she had been sitting in.

I think I'm going to faint, she thought, staring into his eyes.

No, you're not.

Wait! What? She wrinkled her brows in confusion. Had he spoken? Had he just said that out loud?

His eyes widened and dilated as he searched her face, devouring her with his gaze, the brown of his eyes glinting with shards of molten copper. Suddenly, he turned away sharply, looking over her shoulder, back into Proctor Woods. He rubbed his jawline between his thumb and forefinger, as if to collect himself, then turned his eyes back to her, and she noted they were warm and brown, all trace of fire gone.

"Let's sit down. It's—it's been a long time." He moved his hand to hers and peeled her fingers from the back of the chair. The heat of his hand was almost unbearable and she flinched, pulling hers away, sitting down as he sat across from her.

Vaguely, she heard Willow mutter something about getting a drink and some answers, but barely noticed as her friend grabbed Amory's jacket sleeve and pulled him away to the bar.

Darcy swallowed, trying to calm her racing heart. Of all the things she thought might happen today at Honoria Fellows's bright and sunny spring wedding, seeing Jack Beauloup again had not come close to making the list.

He was a touch taller than he had been at eighteen, maybe 6'4" or 6'5", a good half-foot taller than she. His hair was thick and wavy black, but, as she had observed watching him from the church, lightly peppered with gray at his temples. His face showed a five o'clock shadow, altogether more gray than a peppering, which gave him an older, more mature, more masculine appearance. Not that he was short on manliness: his chest was massive and looked hard and toned under his simple blue dress shirt. He didn't wear a tie, and she stared at the open neck of his shirt for a moment, swallowing again, almost hypnotized by his tan skin against the light blue combed cotton.

His eyes were the same brown that she remembered, with little copper flecks that caught the sunlight as he grinned at her, surprise and amusement written all over his beautiful face.

You're checking him out like he works at a strip club! she thought, grateful that he couldn't read her mind; her cheeks colored pink and her ears buzzed with embarrassment.

"You've grown up," she said.

He nodded slowly, holding her eyes for a long moment before dropping his deliberately, to take his time to look at her too. She could have sworn she saw his fingers twitch as his gaze rested on her neck where he had pressed his fingers against her pulse in the dusky light of the Carlisle High School backstage curtains. His eyes dropped lower and his nostrils flared, staring at her chest. The hunger in his face made her feel hot and faint, even though the early afternoon breeze was cool. Suddenly, his lips turned up and his brows furrowed; he was staring with confusion and amusement at the multi-colored mess of taffeta sunset exploding below her conservative cardigan. His eyes snapped up to meet hers in question.

"I didn't choose it!"

His smile exploded into laughter, deep and rumbling, crinkling the tanned edges of his eyes. "Didn't think so."

Her face grew stony as she regarded him.

It's not like you know me, she thought.

I know more than you think.

His lips hadn't moved, but his smile faded as she heard these whispered words in her head, and his eyes were holding hers fast.

Darcy bit her bottom lip and watched as his eyes dropped to her lips. *I'm hearing voices. This is intense. Too intense.*

She took a deep breath and reached for her champagne glass, turning away from him slightly, finishing the rest of the glass in a single gulp.

"So…how have you been?" he asked, eschewing more hot glances for polite conversation.

"Fine. You?"

"Good."

"Twenty years," she said. "Since *The Music Man.*"

He nodded, his smile tentative and lopsided. "Best summer of my life."

"Really?"

"Surprised?"

"Very. You seemed…um, brooding, like you were angry for most of that summer."

He smiled at her more confidently then, and she noted the white shininess of his teeth. They were much whiter and shinier than most of the forty-year-olds she knew. *He must take good care of himself.*

He winked at her. "Probably just hormones."

"Huh." She looked away. Everything he said was throwing her off. She didn't know how to respond.

"So, is it still Darcy *Turner?*"

She had a strange feeling he already knew the answer to this question, the way he said it.

"Yep." She poured herself another half glass of wine and held up her left hand, naked of any rings.

"Never took the plunge, huh?"

"Maybe someday," she said, peeking at him over the rim of her champagne flute.

Don't do that. You hate that.

This time she sat up straighter, starting to feel really uncomfortable. His lips hadn't moved, but she had definitely heard his voice in her head that time. Her heart started racing, beating faster and faster against her ribs, almost painfully.

Now, going inside was one thing. She'd been going inside for years, for most of her life, in fact. But, hearing voices? In her head? In the middle of the day? Maybe Willow's idea was a good one. She'd ask Willow to set up that MRI as soon as possible, she'd—

"Sun's bright today." He said this loudly, gesturing to her head.

"Mmm. Oh!" She forgot that she had sunglasses on her head, and pulled them down. Immediately she felt her heart start to slow down until it returned to normal. Her cheeks cooled, and she filled her diaphragm with air. Since when did sunglasses work faster than Xanax? She didn't care. It was relieving.

He topped off her champagne glass and turned over an empty one, filling it for himself. Righting the bottle, he looked at the label. "This is decent stuff. We should toast."

"To Honoria and Bob?"

Jack smirked.

"To…" She held up her glass.

He lifted his and she heard the pleasant *cling* of glass barely touching.

"To Darcy and Jack," he said.

She didn't put the glass to her lips and he paused, his glass resting against the pillow of his lower lip.

"There is no Darcy and Jack," she said, unable to keep the slightest bit of bitterness out of her tone.

He stared at her for a moment, motionless except for the embers which crackled and leapt savagely in his eyes. Then he tilted the glass back and swallowed it in a single gulp, never taking his eyes off her.

WILLOW RETURNED WITH AMORY SHORTLY after to find Darcy and Jack sitting in stone silence, facing away from one another.

"Well, this is quite the happy little reunion."

Darcy raised her eyebrows. "Jack Beauloup, this is Willow Broussard. Willow, Jack."

Willow put out her hand, shaking Jack's before taking the seat between them. "Good to meet you. Amory's at the bar."

"Guess I'll join him there." Jack stood up gracefully, leaving the women alone.

Darcy pushed her sunglasses back up on her head. She watched Jack move away from her toward the bar and felt a queer pulling in her heart, like she wanted to jump up and run after him. Stay as close to him as possible. Not let him out of her sight now that he was returned to her.

Willow missed none of this high emotion. "After all these years, it's still like that, huh?"

"What is?" Darcy turned to her friend.

Willow raised her eyebrows at Darcy. "Darcy and Jack."

"I wish people would stop saying that," she mumbled.

Darcy looked beyond Willow to the edge of the church clearing and Proctor Woods beyond. She could smell the pine on the breeze, and Darcy wished she could leave the wedding behind and clear her head with a walk in the woods.

"How long before the cake, do you think?"

Willow shrugged. "They'll probably let everyone get good and liquored up. Then dancing, then food, then dancing again, then cake. A few hours. You've got time. What happens at the cake?"

Darcy made a sour face. "Pictures."

"And you, the very picture of a happy bridesmaid."

"I have to clear my head."

Willow nodded. Anyone who knew Darcy knew there was no place as soothing to her as the woods. "Do you have shoes?"

"In my car. I'm gonna grab them. If anyone asks, I'll be back soon."

"No one will." She looked at Darcy thoughtfully. "You want to talk about it?"

Darcy shook her head, standing up. "I wouldn't even know where to start."

Willow nodded, running three shiny black fingernails through her close-cropped black hair. "Wind's whipping up a little. Be careful, kid. Don't make me come looking for you."

FOR YEARS DARCY HAD FANTASIZED about seeing Jack again. In the very beginning, she jumped every time the phone rang, racing to answer it, sure it would be Jack's sultry voice on the other end of the line, calling from far away, unable to live another day without connecting with her. It never was Jack, but Darcy's hopes were undaunted.

He's busy! she reasoned. *He's settling into a new school, working, studying, meeting new people.* The idea that he could meet and fall for a college girl occurred to Darcy, even edged in on her chipper attitude at times, but mostly she was sure that they had shared something special. Something perfect. That kiss, she reasoned, had to have meant as much to him as it did to her. She had seen his face and she knew it hadn't been meaningless, which somehow assured her that she'd hear from him again.

Weeks turned into months and she held on to waning hope as her daydreams modified. She prayed she'd catch a glimpse of him when he came home from college for Thanksgiving break. She'd run an errand for her mom to the store, and there he'd be, ordering a cup of coffee at the Dunkin' Donuts kiosk, tan from sunny days studying outdoors. He'd apologize instantly, explaining that his feelings for her were so strong he didn't want to risk being distracted by her at school by calling or writing. But, now that he was home, could they spend his whole break together? She'd be mad at first, but forgive him quickly, and they'd spend the long weekend going to the movies and out to dinner and for walks in the frosty woods holding hands, and she would touch his face whenever she wanted to, and, and, and…

Her fantasy came crashing down around her a week before Thanksgiving. It was Willow who told her.

"Hey, it was Jack Beauloup who kissed you last summer, right? In the play?"

At the mention of his name Darcy's face flushed with happiness and she beamed at her friend. "Yep."

Willow had cringed before continuing. "Okay. Brace yourself, kid. I just heard through the grapevine from one of his sister's friends…the family moved back to Canada."

It was like Willow had smacked her face with maximum force, making her bite down with the force of the blow. Willow hadn't touched her, of course, but Darcy tasted the warm, metallic ooze of her bleeding tongue. "Moved?"

Willow nodded sympathetically, her eyes searching Darcy's face, wincing as she realized the full weight of this news for her friend. "So, I guess he won't be back…"

Darcy's eyes had filled with burning tears, and the purse on her shoulder slid to the ground with a final thud by her feet.

Willow snatched up the bag, grabbed Darcy's arm, and pulled her into the girls' room with a curt "Get out!" to the freshman girls primping in the only mirror. They scrambled out the door as she pulled Darcy against her and Darcy's tears had fallen freely on Willow's shoulder.

If there had been any ambiguity about the intensity of her feelings, everything was clear in an instant, and Darcy knew just how deep and real her feelings for Jack were. Because Willow's news wasn't a *That's too bad* sort of situation for sixteen-year-old Darcy. It felt devastating. It felt like glass shattering into a million pieces that could never, ever be put back together. It felt like a death.

She sobbed on Willow's shoulder, barely able to process the pain of her broken dreams, the embarrassing strength of her unreturned feelings. After months of daydreaming, she was finally forced to admit that a kiss that meant everything to one person could very well mean nothing to another.

Standing there in the girls' bathroom that smelled of disinfectant and coconut lip gloss, she wept, clenching her eyes shut against the agony she felt. The final thought in her mind before it happened was as solid as granite: *I don't belong to you, after all, and you don't belong to me.*

A split second later was the first time she ever went inside.

GRATEFUL THAT SHE WAS THE kind of girl who never went any-where without a set of decent hiking boots, and totally apathetic about the fact that she was headed for a walk in the woods in a Sunset Dream bridesmaid dress, Darcy shut the trunk of her Land Rover and leaned against the back bumper, bending down to lace up the sturdy boots. They were caked with mud from forages made during the winter thaw, but she wasn't the sort of person who let a little mud get in her way.

"You're getting your dress dirty."

She looked up and saw Jack gesturing to the dried mud that virtually covered the lower half of her car where she leaned to put on her shoes.

"Guess I'll have to stand in the back for the photos."

"Headed somewhere?"

She nodded, still pulling the laces tightly on the second boot.

"Woods, by any chance?"

She looked up at him and huffed, "What's with the third degree?"

He shrugged. "I like a walk in the woods."

"Then you should take one sometime." She stood up straight and put her hands on her hips. She knew full and well how ridiculous she must look: strawberry-blonde flyaway hair falling precariously from its tenuous up-do, melon-colored cardigan lumpy from the taffeta bodice under-neath, not to mention the Technicolor skirt, tan pantyhose (Honoria insisted), thick wool socks, and mud-caked, beat-up leather hiking boots.

But, she reminded herself, *this isn't someone who cared about you, Darcy.*

This isn't someone you have to impress.

He was staring at her face, not her ludicrous ensemble. Her face.

I did care. I do.

You left!

I had to.

She stared back at him, one question needing to be answered before anything else. *Am I going crazy or are we in each other's heads?*

"I had to," he repeated in a whisper, his eyes crackling with urgency.

She sucked in her breath, holding it, then stumbled back from him, almost immediately hitting the bumper of her car with the dress bustle, trapped between Jack and the car, unable to look away from him.

IMPOSSIBLE. This is impossible.

It should be, but it isn't.

How?

I don't know.

HOW?

"I. don't. know," he repeated aloud in a calm, even voice.

He wasn't shocked. He didn't even seem that surprised, she decided, as she searched his eyes. They ignited with a *whoosh* under her scrutiny, like a gas valve being twisted to turn on a BBQ grill. In a moment, they were blazing copper. He looked down, away from her, and spoke softly, as she would speak to a frightened child. "Let me walk with you."

Oh, my God, what is going on? Darcy had long come to terms with her occasional daydreaming, chalking it up to an overactive imagination when she heard Jack's voice or smelled pine needles in her head. This was different. This was interactive. *Jack Beauloup is back. Jack Beauloup is back and he can read my mind, and I can read his.*

"Just let me walk with you." He put out his hand, palm side up, still looking down, submissive, imploring.

"I, um—" She swallowed, her brain a jumble as she tried not to think of anything inappropriate. "I must have had too much champagne or, or—"

"It's okay," he said gently, softly, not looking at her, not moving.

"It's definitely *not* okay," she answered. Her eyes burned from keeping them open so wide. She blinked them quickly and felt them water. To her embarrassment, she realized she was about to cry.

"Hey, Darcy Turner," he breathed.

His voice was deep and soft, and she had a sudden flashback to him singing "It's You." *That boy and this man are the same person*, she thought, trying to re-establish some facts actually grounded in reality.

"I promise it'll be okay," he said in a soothing tone. "Let's just walk a little."

Darcy needed to understand what the hell was going on, and without the benefit of an MRI machine at the ready to confirm that she had officially lost her mind, Jack might be her only option for answers.

"Okay," she whispered, but she didn't place her hand in his. She scooted to the side, moving around him, shivering as she headed toward Proctor Woods with Jack Beauloup trudging beside her. "Be warned. I have some questions for you."

"Thought you might," he answered. Then, "I have a jacket in my car if you're cold."

She snapped her head to the side to look at him. "I didn't think that!"

"I-I know you didn't." He was still looking down, but she could tell he was smiling. "You shivered."

"Oh. Well, I'll be fine once we start moving."

He kept pace beside her, easily matching her quick stride as they walked through the parking lot, around the old white clapboard church. They followed the path through the parish rose garden which would bloom pink and red in another couple of months. Darcy's boots squished in the muddy ground.

"And don't *try* anything. I mean it."

That made him look up. "Like what?"

"I don't know. I barely know you. You show up in Carlisle after twenty years, attending my cousin's wedding with my little brother, somehow conveniently seated at my table, and for some reason, I can hear your thoughts and you can hear mine. Want me to use my imagination? Just don't touch me."

"Stop walking."

"What? Why?" She kept walking.

He spoke from behind her. "Stop walking."

She turned around to face him.

"I'd have grabbed your arm to make you stop, but you said not to touch you."

She nodded curtly as he caught her eyes and held them.

I would never hurt you. Never.

She swallowed.

I mean it, Darcy. It's a sacred pledge. I would never hurt you.

She put her hands on her hips. *And why exactly should I believe you, Jack? Because.*

He looked down, and when he looked up again, his eyes were on fire. *Because you belong to me. And I belong to you.*

Chapter 4

DARCY'S ENTIRE BODY FROZE EXCEPT for her heart, which did somersaults like she was fifteen again.

He started walking, taking the lead, and after a moment Darcy trailed behind him. They continued past the last of the grassy park to the right of the church where no one at the wedding in the back meadow could see them, and headed into the woods.

Proctor Woods had always held a special place in Darcy's heart. When she was a child, her father would take her and Amory for long hikes in the woods, showing them how various weather patterns affected the world around them.

Darcy knew every inch of the thirty-acre woods: the trails, the three ponds, meadows, falls, and the lake in the middle. She thoroughly credited summers spent in the rambles with her current profession—adjunct professor of botany at Dartmouth University. For most of her life, Proctor Woods had served as a place of study, reflection, and comfort for Darcy, although at present there was very little in the woods to capture her attention.

From her vantage point traipsing behind him, she could check out the man that Jack had grown into. He had been a muscular teenager, but his body radiated fully matured strength now, muscles flexing and relaxing in his back like a machine with every step he took. Her eyes drifted lower to his waist, and before she knew it, they had walked at least a tenth of a mile with her eyes trained on his backside, which, she determined with a grudging sigh, was a thing of extreme perfection. She swallowed nervously, wondering if he could hear what she was thinking. If he could, he didn't let on.

Nor did he look back at her as they walked in silence and Darcy tried not to think about his words, but the harder she tried not to, the more they danced in her mind, taunting her, teasing her, reminding her of the desperate, terrible longing she felt when she had disavowed them in the girls' bathroom.

Because you belong to me. And I belong to you.

How could it be true? What did it mean? And hmmm…how come he wasn't answering her?

"Can't you hear me?" she finally asked.

"I'm not looking at you."

"You're not—Ahhh…," she murmured. "The sunglasses."

He nodded his head in front of her, but didn't look back.

"So, you *did* know about this telepathy."

"I didn't know," he insisted, "for sure."

Her emotions were all over the place. Darcy was a scientist. She didn't believe in things like telepathy, and yet she'd just used the word to describe the strange, intimate communication between them.

"You're angry with me," he muttered.

She didn't respond. They had entered a clearing and Beaver Pond, surrounded by pine trees, lay before them, sparkling in the sunlight. Off to the right Darcy looked at the low peak of Magalloway Mountain, still white on top, and gestured to the small weather-beaten bench sitting in a clump of weeds a few feet from the pond. Jack dusted it off with his hand before she sat down, which made her lips twitch with a slight smile.

"Thanks," she said.

"You didn't answer me."

"You didn't ask me a question."

"You're an exasperating woman."

"Says the man who appears in my life out of nowhere after twenty years, following me around my cousin's wedding!"

"Darcy. Are. You. Angry. With. Me?"

She shifted her body to look at him. He stared straight ahead at the water and she realized he was probably fighting the urge to catch her eyes and take a look inside her head. She admired him for it. It made her smile. Again.

"I'm incredibly confused," she admitted. "And I'm a little nervous I'm going crazy."

He breathed in deeply and she saw him smile down at his clasped hands. "You're not going crazy."

"How do you know? *This* isn't normal."

"Let's play a game of *quid pro quo*," he said, glancing at her.

"How?"

"You ask a question and I'll answer the best I can. Then it's my turn."

"Okay." *Anything to get some answers.*

She leaned her head on the back of the bench and unbuttoned the top two buttons of her sweater, closing her eyes and basking in the warmth of the midday sun.

"Can you button back up?"

She opened her eyes slowly, squinting at him through the sunlight. He tore his eyes away from her breasts, but not before Darcy got a look at his face, which had flushed with full-blooded interest. Watching his profile, she saw him clench his jaw once as he stared at the pond.

"Sure." She buttoned up and turned to him, smiling merrily. "My turn."

"Wait a minute…"

"That was a question and I answered it. I didn't make the rules. I'm just following them. My turn."

His nostrils flared in frustration, but he nodded.

"Did that kiss mean anything to you?"

He turned to her, his eyes soft and naked. *Tenderness.*

"Everything. You have no idea. It changed my entire life."

Tears sprang unbidden into her eyes—leftover tears from the depths of her soul where the tiniest sliver of hope had rested its battered self, hidden and silent for all of these years. He raised his hand gently toward her head, reaching to sweep an errant strand of blonde hair out of her face. "Darcy, *please* let me touch you."

She shook her head no, sniffling and swiping at her eyes as he lowered his hand without touching her. "Then why didn't you—"

He leaned his elbow on the back of the bench and interrupted her softly. "My turn. Why didn't you ever get married?"

She used the sleeve of her sweater to swipe at the last of her tears and took a deep, shaky breath.

"It's not that I haven't dated. I mean, I have. Of course I have. I was very serious with one man while I was in grad school. Phillip…Proctor. We dated for several years, but in the end, we wanted different things from life." She shivered lightly, thinking about Phillip's heavy drinking and mysterious departure. He'd left Boston one day and never came back. She'd learned of his relocation via a scrawled postcard hastily left in her mailbox which had clued her in to the total of her worth to him.

She didn't want to think about Phillip, but with the exception of a few professors at Dartmouth, she really hadn't dated very much, and no one had ever felt "right."

"Are these *Phillip's* woods?" Jack's voice interrupted her thoughts, dripping with disdain.

"Proctor's an old Carlisle name. Can't throw a pebble down Main Street without hitting a Proctor."

"Continue."

"About Phillip? Nothing much to tell. He was a few years older than me in high school, but we both grew up here—my folks've known his family forever. We started dating in Boston while I was in grad school and he was working at a bank in Cambridge." She took a breath, banishing painful old memories. "Didn't work out."

"Why not?"

"My turn. How do you know Amory?"

"He's been helping me renovate my house. My folks signed over some land to me. Had a building on it, but it needed a lot of work. When I went looking for a builder around Carlisle last fall, I recognized the name Turner. I didn't remember Amory from my short time here, but I e-mailed him and he agreed to do some work for me. Helped refurbish the main building and built a new garage from my plans."

"Oh! *You're* the big project he's been working on. Did you say house? From what I've heard it's more a great-lodge. On the north border of the woods."

"That's right." Jack furrowed his brow, watching her. "You haven't— you haven't seen it, have you?"

"No," she answered. "Amory's been cagey about it."

"I appreciate my privacy. Don't need any Proctors coming around snooping."

"So, you've been here for a while. Why have you—"

"My turn, Darcy, but I'll give it to you if you let me hold your hand."

She couldn't help cracking a small smile at his wiliness. "You think you're clever."

"Oh, I'm *very* clever."

"And very modest."

He chuckled then looked at her, cocking his head to the side. The sunlight made the greys in his hair and beard sparkle like silver. It gave him an otherworldly glow, like something mythic and impossible.

Not yet.

Okay. He looked away.

"How come I can hear your thoughts and you can hear mine?" she asked.

She looked at his bowed head and saw him clench his jaw again, saw it flex under his cheek as Jack took a deep breath through his nose, then rubbed his chin with his thumb and forefinger.

"I'm not totally sure——"

"Come on! That's not fair. You were nowhere near as surprised as I was. You have to answer, Jack."

He looked at her, capturing her eyes.

Stop yelling at me and I'll answer you. I'm not *totally sure. But, some of the… um…married couples in my family can do this. It's a weird family thing that we don't talk about that much.*

We're not married, Jack.

I know that, Darcy.

"That's why I'm not sure," he finished.

"Sounds like a half-truth to me. I think you know more than you're saying."

"It'd never happened to me until an hour ago when I looked at you. I don't have all the answers. I promise."

She searched his eyes, but couldn't shake the feeling that he was holding back something significant. She felt like she was looking at the tip of a very large iceberg.

He smiled at her.

"Stop listening!"

His eyes danced merrily. "Are we on the *Titanic?*"

"Seriously. Quit it." Then something occurred to her, and she clapped her hands triumphantly. "No! We are not on the *Titanic*. My turn!"

He stood up. "I think I should quit while I'm behind."

"One more question. If you answer it, you can touch me."

He turned and faced her, hands on his hips, eyes narrowed—because he had just faced the sun or because he was suspicious, she couldn't tell. He wet his lips with his tongue and nodded curtly.

Darcy stood up before him. He was taller than she was, and she stared straight ahead at his throat for a moment, adjusting to his nearness, almost undone by the warmth of his body on the skin of her cheeks. She waited a moment before looking up at his face, seizing his eyes as mercilessly as he once had hers.

"Why did it take you twenty years to come back?" she breathed.

His eyes burned for her. She could see the copper joined by molten gold, churning and fierce. *Darcy, Darcy, Darcy.* She heard her name over and over again in his head like a litany. Was he blocking her from hearing his thoughts by repeating her name?

She looked away.

"You don't have an answer," she whispered, wincing at the disappointment she heard in her own voice.

"I do."

She captured his eyes again.

Then why?

He looked down.

"Do you remember what I said? When you told me not to touch you?"

"You said you wouldn't hurt me. That it was a sacred pledge."

He nodded.

"But, I had to learn some things. Before I could come back."

He hadn't stepped away from her and she stepped forward. One step. Close enough to him that the front of her sweater grazed his shirt. She felt her nipples harden into pebbles under her sweater and heard his breathing change—almost imperceptibly, like she shouldn't have been able to hear it, but she could. It caught for just a second then picked up cadence again. Faster. Louder.

"What things?" she asked.

"Control." He growled the word deliberately, his voice thick and low.

Her eyes fluttered closed, listening to the sound of his breathing. *In… and out…In…and out.* She realized that as she stood before him, her breathing had changed to mirror his, so that every time they took a breath, the tips of her sensitive nipples grazed his chest through taffeta and cotton. *In…and out…In…and out.* They touched like magnets, and she could feel the force field between them, pulling her toward him with every breath, making it almost impossible to retreat. She felt languorous and dizzy, almost hypnotized, until she thought she might faint. *In…and out…In…and out…*

"Darcy…" he whispered.

"No!"

Her eyes flew open and she stepped back from him, taking a deep breath that filled her diaphragm. She held it to break the rhythm between them. She turned her back to him, pressing her palms against her flaming cheeks.

He reached for her. "But you said—"

"No." She took another step away. "You didn't really answer me. More half-truths, I think, Jack."

"Walk with me a little more."

"Why?"

"Because I want to get to know you."

She turned to look at him again, biting the skin inside her lower lip and blinking back tears.

This is too intense for me. All of it.

Just walk with me.

"Fine," she conceded, taking off at a brisk pace. "We can take a walk over to the Powhatan Falls, and then loop back."

She didn't check to see if he was following behind her. She knew he was.

"Powhatan."

"It's an old Algonquin word," she explained. "It means *waterfalls*."

"It actually means *at the waterfalls*."

She looked at him over her shoulder. "That's right. How do you know that? You lived here for what? Half an hour?"

"Senior class had to map out Proctor Woods."

Darcy chuckled suddenly, nodding in remembrance. "Yes. That's right. The cartography class. I wonder if they do that anymore."

"It was a smart exercise. I know everyone uses GPS now, but no kid from Carlisle ever got lost in these woods. Plus, mapping's a good skill. I've certainly used it since."

She slowed down and turned to him as they entered Dooley Meadow, which was bathed in sunshine. She ran the palms of her hands over the tips of the tall spring grasses that came up to her thighs and tickled her pantyhose-clad legs.

"How much do you remember?" she asked, facing him until he caught up and walked beside her.

"Of what?" he asked.

"That night."

"Everything."

"That summer."

"Everything."

"Why did you act like it hurt you to look at me?"

"Because it did."

"*Why?*"

"Darcy, if I promise I will tell you—"

He stopped moving beside her, so Darcy pivoted to face him. She could still see Beaver Pond in the distance behind them, but she had no more answers than she had sitting on the bench playing *quid pro quo*.

Damn it, she was getting sick of this...she wasn't playing any more games with him. She wanted answers. She—

She furrowed her brows, focusing on his face. His eyes were wide and his chin was raised while looking over her shoulder, focused on the dark woods that led to Powhatan Falls. He closed his eyes and inhaled slowly and deliberately through his nose, then tilted his head, listening to something, *for* something.

His body was still, on high alert, taut and flexed as they stood at the edge of the meadow. He looked down suddenly, catching her eyes. *Don't move.*

"Why? What—"

Shhh!

What? What's going on?

He put out his hand to her, palm up. She looked at it and then back up at his eyes.

We had a deal and you didn't answer my question, so you can't just—

She heard the crack of a branch behind her before she heard the low, guttural roar, and watched as Jack's eyes changed color from brown to gold, widening in fear at what he saw directly behind her.

She swallowed as panic set in. She heard a snort and felt a bit of wet spray on her legs. Six feet away? Maybe less.

Darcy knew what it was. It was springtime in the northern New Hampshire woods. Hibernating bears were stirring. She was fairly sure that, right now, there was nothing between her and a riled black bear.

Chapter 5

JACK MET HER EYES—

I won't let it hurt you, do you understand? I'll die before I let it hurt you.

—then he looked back at the animal behind her.

Darcy's body trembled as her blood turned icy cold in her veins. She blinked her eyes rapidly, trying to remember what you were supposed to do when you encounter a bear, but her mind was blank. Her heart was beating so fast, she was afraid she might go into tachycardia and faint. She swallowed again, bowing her neck, wide-eyed with terror. If she moved any more than that, the bear might charge.

She heard grunting and a pushing noise, and raised her gaze to look at Jack from under lowered lashes. She watched as his eyes trailed slowly upward. A low, angry growl came from behind her, but it was positioned higher than before and Darcy knew the bear was standing on its hind legs now.

Jack's eyes flicked to hers—

Slowly. Get behind me, Darcy.

—then back to the bear's face.

She wanted Jack to look at her again so that she could tell him she was frozen. She could barely breathe and her legs had locked in place. She couldn't move.

He flicked his glance to her again, seizing her eyes.

GET. BEHIND. ME. NOW.

NOW, DARCY! NOW!

Jack's voice was amplified like a scream in her head and provided the shock she needed to pivot quickly behind him, gasping as she covered her ears and peeked at the bear over Jack's shoulder.

The black bear stood over seven feet high on its hind legs and stared down at Jack, who was motionless in front of her. It growled, agitated, throwing its head around and pawing the air with its claws extended in extreme frustration or fury, bellowing as it swiped at the air between it and Jack.

Jack took a deep breath, then spoke low and soft, throwing his words over his shoulder. "Darcy. Walk back to the pond. Slowly."

"What about you?"

"I'll be there soon."

"I can't just leave you, Jack!"

"It'll be okay. Go now."

"Jack," she whispered, tears and fear for him making her voice jagged.

"GO. NOW," he snarled over his shoulder, angry and insistent.

She turned and started back to the lake, walking slowly, rigidly, fear still making her body feel stiff and unfamiliar as tears coursed down her cheeks. After about twenty paces, she turned back. The bear lumbered back and forth in front of Jack, growling and grunting, as if an invisible wall separated him from Jack, who stood with his arms crossed over his chest.

It didn't make any sense. Why wasn't the bear charging?

Suddenly the bear stopped pacing. It stood on four legs directly in front of Jack, staring up at him. From where she stood, Darcy heard Jack hiss something that sounded like "Ship awaaaaaaaay...."

The bear stared at Jack as he repeated the hissed words once more. She watched, frozen and fascinated as the bear took a step back, then another, until it whimpered and turned, racing into the woods away from Jack, back muscles rippling at the force and speed of its gait...its...*escape.*

Jack stood still, watching its retreat, before turning to follow her. Darcy gasped. As he faced her, she noticed his eyes, glowing like embers, like golden lightbulbs in his head, alien or otherworldly. He stopped in his tracks when he realized she was watching him, and after several blinks, his eyes returned to normal.

That was it for Darcy. She'd had enough.

She turned and ran around the pond, arms crossed protectively over her chest, hurrying back toward the church. Her brain assaulted her with questions.

What just happened? Had Jack actually scared the bear into retreating? What was it he said? What did that mean and why did it make the bear run away, whimpering in fear? Why were his eyes glowing?

I am losing my mind. This is what it feels like to go crazy.

Without looking back, she ran past the bench at the pond, practically sprinting the rest of the way to the meadow at the edge of Proctor Woods. To the relative safety of Honoria's reception.

She'd spent about an hour with Jack, but instead of answers, she had more questions. Why had he kissed her so many years ago if it hurt him to look at her? Why did he leave? Why in the world was he back now? How had he kept that bear at bay? Men didn't scare bears away, and people's eyes didn't glow like molten lava.

She'd had enough confused feelings and unanswered questions for one afternoon. A walk in the woods hadn't provided the usual balm; it had only served to upset her. She was more turned around than ever and wanted to talk to Willow.

If she hadn't finally looked over her shoulder to see if Jack was following her, she would have seen—and definitely avoided—Vale. Instead, she slammed into his back at full force.

"Damn it to hell!"

Vale Proctor turned to her and Darcy realized that her clumsiness had caused him to spill a glass of champagne down the front of his crisp white dress shirt. He lifted his silver head, and Darcy met his narrowed his eyes as his nostrils flared in an indelicate sneer.

"Why, Darcy Turner," he purred, taking in her ensemble with one slow, lecherous, humiliating scan, "what a singularly unpleasant surprise."

"**V**ALE," SHE PUFFED, CATCHING HER breath. "M—Mr. Proctor. Sorry!"

"Who you running from, gal? Another unlucky suitor?"

Darcy put her hands on her hips and tried to catch her breath. She glanced up at his saturated shirt, his ribbed t-shirt materializing underneath as the wet stain spread.

"C-Can I get you a towel?" she asked. She scanned the woods behind Vale's head. No sign of Jack. Her shoulders drooped—in relief, but also in disappointment.

"What for? I've already been marinated in spirits." Her cardigan had unbuttoned during her escape and Vale gestured to her chest. "Showing off your…*charms?*"

Darcy looked down and noticed the tan skin of her right areole peeking out from the border of her awful dress. She tugged it up and re-buttoned her sweater.

"Now, Darcy dear, wherever were you coming from?" he asked again, beady eyes sweeping slowly from her breasts to her face. "What unlucky man was just left heartbroken in the woods?"

"This one."

Darcy whipped her neck to the side and saw a composed Jack standing beside her, offering his hand to Vale.

"Jack Beauloup."

Vale's thin, waxy lips tilted up in a smile that didn't quite reach his eyes. "Vale. Proctor."

He took Jack's hand, but released it quickly, as if it offended him to have to shake it in the first place.

Jack grinned, but Darcy saw his eyes flash. With what? Anger? Good Lord, were they going to do that weird glowing thing again?

He hooked a thumb over his shoulder. "Your woods, Mr. Proctor?"

"Once upon a time, Mr. Beauloup." Vale cocked his head to the side. "Unusual name. Beauloup."

"Canadian."

"*French* Canadian, I'd say." His eyes narrowed, looking at Jack appraisingly. "Maybe even a half-breed snowfrog from Queeb."

Darcy gasped. "You're drunk, Vale."

Jack's smile faded and even though they weren't touching, Darcy perceived his body stiffen up beside her.

"Ain't drunk, gal." His eyes flashed at her, furious.

"Some folks I know might take offense to that *colorful* description," Jack replied smoothly. His voice was lazy and deliberate, but his eyes had narrowed. Darcy looked closer and she could see the copper flecks darting and jumping under thick black lashes. She flicked her eyes to Vale. Couldn't he see it too? If he could, he didn't let on.

"Don't mean no offense, son. I'm an old-timer. Bitter from life's…misfortunes." Vale flicked an insulting glance to Darcy, raking his eyes up and down her body. "Good luck with this one."

Darcy dropped her gaze in embarrassment, but was distracted by Jack's corded hand curling into a fist. *Oh, no. No. Did he mean to hit Vale? No, Jack!*

She looked back up at Jack's face, trying to catch his eyes, needing to tell him Vale wasn't worth it, but Jack's glare was trained on Vale. She had to distract him before he did something stupid. If he wouldn't look at her, she had only one other option. She reached her hand out tentatively and gently covered his fist with hers, touching him voluntarily for the first time in twenty years.

She shuddered briefly at the feel of his hot, taut skin under her cool fingertips, but was almost immediately distracted by his reaction. He gasped softly and she felt the tightly coiled muscles in his fingers relax as he turned his head slowly to look at her. Surprise and disbelief crossed over his features before his eyes narrowed and she saw sparks quietly bank into burning embers as his fingers unfurled. She looked down to see him twist his hand until their palms were facing, then laced his fingers through hers.

Her breathing sped up and she felt a flush of warmth start at her palm and travel past her wrist, up her arm until the heat of his skin had touched the tip of every toe, every finger, the soft skin of her neck, the vulnerable smooth skin of her lips, which parted in surprise. And her poor, overtaxed, befuddled brain could only wonder: if touching palms feels this good, what in the world would it feel like to—

"Oh, ho! So, it's like that, eh?" Darcy turned to see Vale's black, rat eyes dart back and forth between her and Jack. He inclined his head to Jack. "My sympathies."

Jack whipped his glance from Darcy to Vale. "I'm sorry?"

"Yes. Yes, you will be. Take care, Mr. Beauloup." Vale's eyes narrowed at Darcy before smirking at her with delicate snort. "She's a...*heartbreaker*."

Darcy had no idea the word *heartbreaker* could sound so *dirty*.

"Don't go disappearing now," he said meaningfully to Jack. Then he dumped the rest of his champagne on the ground by their feet and sauntered back to the party.

As soon as he was a safe distance away, Darcy tried to disentangle her hand from Jack's. He wasn't having it. He tightened his grip until Darcy had no choice but to hold his hand or make a scene grabbing hers away. Since she'd had enough scenes for today, she relaxed and didn't fight him.

Darcy looked down at their joined hands. The last time her fingers had been laced through Jack Beauloup's, she'd been fifteen years old. His hand had trembled as it had reached for hers in the darkness of the backstage curtains. Adult Jack didn't quake or tremble when he touched her. Adult Jack burned her with the heat of his body, with the unmitigated desire pulsing in his fiery eyes. She still hadn't caught her breath since he'd laced his fingers through hers. It wasn't fair that other than a slight gasp, he was utterly composed.

"Can you let go of my hand?"

"No chance." Jack watched until Vale sat down at a table with several older ladies, who tittered worshipfully at something he said. "Proctor. He's an arrogant bastard."

"He's not my favorite," Darcy sighed.

Jack turned to her. "Sure doesn't like you."

"No. He doesn't."

"Why's that?"

"Remember Phillip Proctor? I mentioned him before?"

"The one that didn't work out."

"Yes. Vale is Phillip's father."

"Ahhh," said Jack.

He strolled back to their table, and Darcy, whose hand was still firmly clasped in his, had no choice but to follow. She noticed that the longer they held hands, the more she accustomed herself to the white hotness of his skin on hers.

"Why does he hate you?"

"Phillip and I dated for a while, before we had a—a falling out." She couldn't keep the uneasiness from tracking across her face.

"What else?"

"He relocated to Canada somewhere. Never came home again."

"Proctor blames you?"

Darcy nodded.

"I was the last one to see him," she answered, sitting back down at their table.

Darcy had expected to see Willow here. She wished she and Willow could go home, change into sweats, make a fire and curl up on their living room window seat with hot tea. Darcy needed to talk to someone, and as electric as she felt around Jack Beauloup, she was also feeling exhausted by the emotional roller coaster of their reunion.

"I get the feeling you don't want to talk about him."

"Not all of my memories of him are good," she answered simply, looking away. She was relieved to see Amory approaching them.

"Mom's been looking all over for you, Darce!" Amory pressed his lips to her cheek as Jack discreetly dropped her hand. "Honoria wants to do pictures before cake."

Thank God for small favors.

"I'll go find her. You seen Willow?"

"The elusive Doctor Broussard," Amory said, his eyes clouding over.

"She went home."

"Already?"

"Yeah, already. Reception's been going on for three hours, Darce. We had a pretty awkward lunch by ourselves, so thanks for that."

"What are you talking about?" Darcy laughed. She thought he was kidding until she looked at her watch and felt her brows knit together as she realized it was ten to three. But, the wedding had only ended about an hour ago! She dug her phone out of the purse she had left at the table. 2:51 pm. Impossible. She hadn't been in the woods for more than an hour. Tops.

Her stomach turned uneasily as she realized that the napkins and place settings that had been set on every table when she sat down for champagne after the ceremony were now gone. She looked down at the tablecloth and saw crumbs and a brown smudge. Evidence of lunch having been eaten.

"Time flies when you're having fun, eh, sis?"

Darcy turned to look at her brother, and he winked at her. "Don't forget about the pictures. Jack, I'll be over tomorrow to work on the garage if that's okay. I'm outta here."

"I don't understand," Darcy whispered more to herself than Jack, who sat beside her in silence. "It *can't* be three o'clock. It's only—"

Darcy's heart was racing, pounding so loud she heard the thumping in her ears. She swallowed, wishing she could calm down, turning her eyes to Jack, who looked at her, waiting, worried.

"Jack. What the hell is going on?"

Calm down. It's going to be okay.

"Get out of my head," she hissed, trying to take a deep breath, but starting to feel dizzy.

Nothing was making sense. Jack's sudden reappearance, hearing his thoughts, his glowing eyes, losing time. It was too much to try to understand. She felt like she was going crazy and Jack was the common thread that ran through everything.

He reached out to take her hand again and she flinched away from him, sitting ramrod straight in her chair, staring at him.

"Darcy," he started, slowly, softly.

"No. I don't want to talk to you anymore."

"That's fine. Let me take you home."

"No. *You're* not taking me anywhere."

"Darcy, we need to talk. There are things you need—"

"What I need is an MRI…and I probably had too much champagne. And *you*—" She stared at his brown eyes. She watched as a pool of copper lava surrounded his black pupils, growing brighter. She could hear him repeating her name over and over again in a loop. *Darcy Turner, Darcy Turner, Darcy Turner.* "—you need to stay away from me, Jack Beauloup."

Darcy stood up abruptly and grabbed her purse, intending to leave. As Jack rose from his chair, she looked up at his face, into his eyes, without thinking. She gasped at the deep regret she saw there.

I'm sorry, Darcy. I'm so damn sorry. But I can't do that.

She clenched her eyes shut as hard as she could.

When she opened them, he was gone.

D ARCY HELD HERSELF TOGETHER THROUGHOUT the photos, standing in back of her cousins to hide the rips on her dress, made polite good-byes to family and friends, and drove home. But once the front door clicked shut behind her, the floodgates opened. Willow found her sitting cross-legged on the floor in front of the door, head bowed and tears flowing. She helped Darcy up without a word, ushered her up the stairs and into her bedroom where she told her to change into comfy clothes and then come back downstairs. A few minutes later Darcy heard the whistle of the kettle through the old hardwood floors.

"Chamomile or Earl Grey?" called Willow from the foot of the stairs.

"Earl Grey. Thanks, Will."

As she headed downstairs, Darcy pulled her sleeve over her hand and brushed away the remainder of the tears. She settled in her favorite corner of the large, plush, chintz-covered window seat in the front room of the Victorian house she shared with Willow. Hugging her fleece-covered legs closer to her chest, she rested her cheek on her arm, looking out the picture window at Magalloway in the distance.

Willow marched into the living room with two big, brightly colored mugs, each with a tea string hanging over the edge and steam rising over the rims. She handed Darcy a cup that read "I climbed Mount Washington and all I got was this crummy cup." Darcy held the warm ceramic in her hands and gave her friend a grateful smile.

"So? Spill the beans. And I mean every detail, kid."

"I don't even know where to begin," sighed Darcy as Willow sat across from her, cross-legged in black yoga pants and a grey t-shirt.

"Well…you went inside during the wedding. We sat down at the table and Honoria came to say hello. And then Amory showed up with Jack. Start there."

"He can hear my thoughts."

Willow's brows creased momentarily before she neutralized her face.

"And I can hear his."

Willow nodded slowly.

"It didn't necessarily seem to surprise him and he said that it's a weird thing that married people in his family can do sometimes."

"Two things," said Willow crisply. "One, people can't hear each other's thoughts. And two, you're not married to Jack."

"Uh. I know. I mentioned that."

"And he said…"

"He didn't have an answer. He kept saying that. He kept saying he didn't have all of the answers and while I definitely get the feeling he knows more than I do, I believe him. On some level." She thought of his voice when he said *I don't have all the answers, I promise.* She was pretty sure he'd been telling the truth.

"What else?" Willow prompted, averting her eyes, sipping her tea.

"Umm. Besides the fact that he was my first kiss and he's shown up here out of the blue after twenty years? Besides the fact that he can hear my thoughts and I can hear his? Hmm. Well, let's see. He said he would never hurt me, that it's a sacred pledge or something."

"Uh-huh. What else? Why was he gone so long?"

"He said he had to go away to learn things." *Control.* "And there was this encounter with a bear…"

"A *bear* bear?"

"We came across a black bear while we were walking. Jack put himself between me and the bear, then told me to run. I didn't want to, but he insisted. I looked back after about four or five yards, and he and the bear were in a showdown, almost. The bear was mad, but not charging, and Jack wasn't moving. Then he hissed something and the bear took off into the woods like a shot."

"What did he say to it?"

"I don't know. It sounded like 'Ship away' but I probably heard it wrong."

"Ship away?" Willow looked up, eyes alert. "Are you sure?"

"Yeah, I think so. Who knows? I was freaked out. And his eyes were glowing."

Willow shook her head quickly back and forth. "G-Glowing, Darce?"

"It looked like it. But, it was so sunny and we were in Dooley Meadow."

"Could have been the sun?"

"Could've been, I guess."

Darcy took a deep breath, sipping her tea. It could've been the sun in his eyes. And heck, people who work in the circus or the zoo learn ways to soothe predatory animals. She wanted so badly to explain everything—to give it context and common sense and not be crazy. But she couldn't explain her way out of hearing his thoughts or losing over an hour of her life, could she?

"Is that it?"

Darcy looked up and saw the worry Willow was trying to hide.

"No." She swallowed another gulp of tea and took a deep breath. "I think I lost time."

"You went inside? Again? After the time in the church?"

"No. I can't explain it, but time went too fast. It went much faster than it should have."

"I'm not following you, kid."

"Okay. There was the wedding. Then we went outside and had champagne. Then Jack and Amory came over. Then I decided to take a walk in the woods. We walked to the pond where we stopped and talked, and through the meadow. Then I ran back to the reception and bumped into Vale."

"Ugh." Willow looked disgusted.

"Yeah, that was fun. He called Jack a half-breed snowfrog from Queeb."

Willow's eyes widened in fury. Willow, who was a quarter Métis, French-Canadian on her father's side, and born in Quebec, shook her head. "Bigot! I *hate* the Proctors!"

"You and Jack have that in common."

"Back up to 'losing time.'"

"All of the activity I am describing to you should have taken about an hour. Maybe an hour and a half tops. But, the reception started at twelve o'clock and it was almost three o'clock when I got back to the table. Why? How?"

"How many glasses of champagne did you have?"

Darcy thought back. "Three or four."

Willow gave her a look. "Alcohol can impair our sense of time, kid. Three or four glasses is quite a bit."

"I wasn't drunk, Will. I didn't feel drunk at all."

Willow sipped her tea. Darcy knew the wheels in her head were turning, but she wasn't prepared for the worry in her friend's eyes when she looked up again. Willow sighed heavily. "I don't like it, Darce. You know me. I'm smart enough to know that not everything can be explained. But…hearing voices? Losing time? Seeing things?"

"I want an MRI."

Willow nodded. "I agree. It's time."

"How soon can you book it?"

"Monday in North Conway. I'll pull strings if I have to. We have to see what's going on up in there." She pointed to Darcy's head, giving her friend a brave smile.

Darcy's shoulders fell and tears filled her eyes.

"Hey, kid," said Willow, reaching out her hand to rub Darcy's arm. "It's going to be okay. We'll figure it out."

Darcy nodded, biting her lip.

"What else?" asked Willow softly.

"Jack," she breathed, looking up at her friend with watery eyes. "Just… Jack."

"It must be hard to get your head around it. I guess you still have feelings…"

"Twenty years, Will. I don't think I'd ever stopped hoping that I'd see him again."

"Yeah. I could see it on your face."

"But, now he's back and…I'm so…"

Willow patted Darcy's arm and slid off the window seat, taking a blanket off the back of the couch and handing it to Darcy.

"Take a rest, kid. It's been a long day. We'll get that test on Monday."

Darcy watched her friend walk into the kitchen, then spread the blanket over her body, leaning back on the plush pillows and closing her eyes. She remembered the way her body shuddered as she covered his fist with hers. How hot and liquid and alive she'd felt touching him. Suddenly she felt the swirling inside and placed her mug on the windowsill just in time.

She went inside.

WHEN SHE OPENED HER EYES, the first thing she saw was snow. Snowflakes drifted from the white sky, falling into her hair, onto her eyelashes, landing softly on her cheeks. But they weren't cold and they didn't melt. She breathed deeply, recognizing the sweet, delicate scent of crab apple blossoms. It wasn't snow, after all. Tiny white petals floated softly down from a newly flowered tree overhead, covering her in a blanket of soft white.

She was lying down, her head and the top half of her body resting languorously on something warm and padded. As the seconds ticked by, she realized that her head rose and fell softly, as it would if she were lying on someone's chest. She raised her hands over her head and her fingers curled into a bristly coat, which she would have examined had she not been distracted by the sound of low cooing.

She looked up to see a mourning dove, fat and brownish-grey on a branch over her head.

Ooo-oo-ah-oo. Ooo-oo-ah-oo. The black wolf is back-ah-oo.

Darcy turned her head slowly, and saw the black fur next to her shoulder. Before she could rouse herself any further, she heard the whispered words,

I can't do that.

low and urgent in her head.

Her eyes flew open and she was initially surprised that the brightness was gone. She was curled up on her window seat at home, twilight infringing. She touched a finger to her teacup, finding it cool. As she stretched her arms over her head, she furrowed her brows. Something immediate was bothering her.

And then it occurred to her.

After twenty years of hearing the whispered words *It's you* at the end of her soul flight, the words inside had changed. *It's you* were no longer the last words Jack Beauloup had uttered to Darcy Turner. The last words were now "I can't do that," after Darcy had asked him to stay away from her. Darcy took a deep breath, sitting up and folding the blanket on her lap.

I'm sorry, Darcy. I'm so damn sorry. But, I can't do that.

As much as she hoped the MRI could calm her concerns, she knew deep in her heart it was almost certainly Jack, and Jack alone, who held the key to what was happening.

Chapter 6

"I AM DELIGHTED TO TELL YOU that your frontal, temporal, occipital, and parietal lobes, in addition to your cerebellum and cortex are—and don't take this the wrong way, kid—unremarkable." Willow smiled at Darcy from behind the desk in her medical office located on Main Street in Carlisle.

It had taken four days to get the results back, but Darcy had mostly come to the conclusion that Willow wasn't going to find anything significant on the scan. She'd gone inside twice more over the last three days, a record in terms of frequency, and both times she'd been lounging against the body of a black wolf, and both times the episode had ended with the words *I can't do that.*

It was as if he was communicating with her—reaching out to her in the only manner at his disposal and forcing her to keep him at the forefront of her mind. As if she could think of anything else but beckoning, beautiful Jack Beauloup. She didn't know how he was doing it, but she was getting fed up.

"Hey! You don't seem pleased."

Darcy forced a smile.

"No! I am! That's great, Will. Should have done it years ago."

"So, I'm thinking too much champagne on Saturday, right? Explains the loss of time…even hearing and seeing things. Anyone who's ever been to a college frat party knows you can black out and lose hours if you overdrink."

I wasn't drunk. I know that. This has nothing to do with champagne.

"I'm sure you're right," Darcy answered.

Willow tilted her head, tenting her hands under her chin. "No, you're not. I know you, Darcy. You're still thinking this has something to do with Jack Beauloup?"

"I've gone inside three times in four days, Will. Since *he* arrived in Carlisle." She swallowed, looking down, wishing she could explain her certainty to Willow. "It has something to do with him. I'm sure of it."

"Remember the first time you told me about going inside and we did all that Métis research?"

"Yeah. Over that Christmas break."

"And you know I dabble."

Darcy glanced pointedly at the red door in Willow's office and nodded. It looked like a coat closet, but Darcy was one of very few people who knew it led to a small room where Willow dried herbs and practiced non-invasive Métis shaman techniques. Willow believed strongly that Western medicine wasn't the only answer to solving medical mysteries, and she often consulted Métis texts and traditions for unusual problems.

"That word you said Jack used. With the bear."

"Ship away?"

Willow nodded. "*Shipawaytay* in Michif means 'leave.'"

"You don't speak Michif."

"Right. But I know that word. My *Nohkom* used to say that. When I was underfoot. She'd be trying to bake something in the kitchen and I'd keep grabbing for the mixing bowl or bothering her for the spoon, and she'd say '*Shipawaytay, Nidanis.*' And it meant, 'Leave it be, grandchild.' Do you think that's what Jack was saying? To the bear? Leave it be? Leave *you* be?"

"Could be, I guess. You think Jack's Métis?"

Willow shrugged. "No idea. But his last name is French. The family moved back north to Quebec after the year they spent here, right? I mean, you've got to start somewhere."

Willow stood up and turned to the bookcases behind her desk. She took out a book titled *The Métis People* and handed it to Darcy.

Darcy flipped through it before tucking it in her purse and standing up to leave. "Thanks, Will."

"Hey, with all these distractions, I haven't asked you lately. How's the book coming?"

"I've barely written a word. I'll work on it today and tomorrow. Had to cancel one of my classes this week, but they understood. Miss Kendrick e-mailed me this morning—she's been babying my samples."

Darcy spent at least three days a week at Dartmouth, where she was a professor in the natural sciences department, and had a standing fellow-ship as research associate in the Life Sciences Greenhouse. Because it was a two-hour drive from Carlisle, Darcy generally left for Dartmouth on Monday morning and came back on Wednesday evening. She spent Thursdays and Fridays finishing her thesis in the small studio over the detached garage at home.

"How anyone can devote a lifetime of study to…"

"Bryology, Will."

"Bryology," scoffed Willow. "That's just a fancy word for the study of… moss."

"And lichen. And liverworts. Why does everyone always forget the liverworts?"

"You're a lost cause, kid." She handed Darcy an envelope with her MRI images. "Glad you're not crazy. Don't let the door hit you in the ass on your way out."

Darcy winked at Willow and turned to leave.

"Darce?"

She turned to look back at her friend, who was half turned away from Darcy, looking out the window between the bookcases behind her desk.

"If you're ready to talk to Jack Beauloup," she pointed to the window without looking back at Darcy, "I think he's ready too."

DARCY WALKED OUT OF WILLOW'S office, turning right to walk by Willow's small white, picket-fenced herb garden, then stopped abruptly. She'd known he was waiting there, but she still wasn't prepared for the impact of seeing him so close to her.

Jack Beauloup stood at the edge of the garden, one elbow leaning lazily against the corner fencepost. He was impossibly handsome standing in the mid-morning sun, the light picking up the silver strands in his hair and close-cropped beard. The scruff made her fingers tingle by her sides as she approached him, longing to reach out and run her fingers over the prickly texture. He wore a heather grey, long-sleeved Henley t-shirt pushed up to his elbows that showed off his tan, corded arms and hugged the insane contours of his muscular chest. Her eyes drifted lower, lingering on his waist as her heart thumped like crazy, and finally dropping to muddy hiking boots.

If she could call the Almighty and ask him to deliver the most perfect, delicious, mind-bogglingly beautiful man to the corner of Main
and Chilton, even He in all His power couldn't have improved upon the
person who stood waiting for her.

Jack had noticed her frank perusal and a teasing smile tilted the corners
of his mouth up as his eyes sparkled with delight. *Shoot.* Where were her
sunglasses when she needed them anyway? She took a deep breath, steeling herself for another possible brush with crazy.

"Darcy Turner. Imagine running into you."

She gave him an exasperated look and started walking again. He fell
into step beside her.

"You stalking me, Jack Beauloup?"

"Pretty crappy stalker if that's my game. Haven't seen you since Saturday."

"Well, Saturday was just about enough for me."

"So, are you crazy?"

"Not officially."

"Told you it would be okay."

She turned to face him, locking her eyes with his.

Please leave me alone?

I can't.

She started walking again. "What do you mean, you *can't?*"

"I have to talk to you. I came back to Carlisle for—"

For me? Her head whipped to face him and she missed an uneven seam
in the sidewalk. She would have fallen if Jack hadn't snaked his arm light-
ning quick around her waist, hauling her up against his chest. She heard
his breath hitch as she relaxed in his arms. His other arm moved around
her waist, pulling her flush against his body as she raised her eyes to his.

Darcy.

Jack.

She saw the familiar expression in his eyes as he stared at her—the pain
she used to see on his face when they were teenagers and she'd discover
him watching her from across the library or auditorium. But, it dawned
on her, with the experience and wisdom that comes with age and adult-
hood, that what she had translated as pain when she was young was
nuanced with age, and—in fact—it wasn't pain at all. It was longing. All
these years she'd thought he'd found something objectionable or unlike-
able when he looked at her, but that wasn't it at all. It hurt to look at her
because he *wanted* her, and—for whatever reason—he must have believed

she was off limits to him.

She felt her face soften with tenderness as she stared at him and he closed his eyes, leaning forward to rest his forehead against hers. She closed her eyes too, but her thoughts kept circling back to one specific place. She wanted to kiss him. She wanted to feel his lips on hers again after so long. His breath on her skin was hot and ragged as he pressed his lips on the tissue-thin shades of each eyelid in turn. She moved her hands up the hard contours of his chest to his neck, her fingers lightly tickling the hairs on the back of his neck as she pulled him—

"Darcy." He spoke aloud, his lips a breath away from hers. She could feel the force of his breathing, the hot puffs of exhaled breath on the sensitive skin of her lips. His voice was hoarse and raspy as he cleared his throat, taking a big gulp of air. "Not here. Not on Main Street."

Her eyes flew open and her face flushed hot with embarrassment as her neck snapped back to look at him. "You're shutting this down?"

She dropped her hands from his neck, palms splayed on his chest to push him away.

He tightened his arms around her. "No! No, I'm not shutting anything. I just—"

"You just don't want to kiss me." She looked away from him, trying to back out of his arms. "Let go of me." He didn't.

"Can you please let go of me, Jack?"

"No," he murmured. "Look at me."

She shook her head, looking down.

"I'm not letting you go until you look at me, Darcy."

She lifted her head up to face him, eyes narrowed, grinding her jaw in frustration. The message in his eyes made her knees weak.

I want you so much, I'm in agony, Darcy.

As if to prove his point, he lowered his hands to her hips and pulled her closer so she could feel the unmistakable evidence of his erection against her belly. Her eyes widened, but remained fixed on his. His voice in her head was ragged and gruff.

But we're on Main Street in the middle of broad daylight, and once we start, I don't know if I can stop.

His nostrils flared with the force of his breathing and his eyes were churning with fire. Darcy's legs turned to jelly, but Jack's muscular arms held her tightly against him.

She licked her dry lips and his eyes dropped to her mouth, staring, transfixed. She knew he was telling the truth. He wanted her as much as she wanted him.

"I'm okay now," she breathed, planting her feet firmly and pulling away from him. She felt his arms reluctantly loosen and she took a step back from him, smoothing her cardigan. "Thanks for not letting me fall. I owe you one."

He traded her lips for her eyes.

Do you mean that? You owe me one?

What'd you have in mind?

Dinner at my place. Tomorrow night.

Darcy took a deep breath then nodded. She hitched her bag up on her shoulder and ran a hand through her long strawberry-blonde hair before turning to go.

"Fair warning," she said, turning back to him as she walked toward the parking area where her car waited. "I have a lot of questions."

"Fair warning," he answered, his eyes sweeping up and down her body slowly before meeting hers. *We won't be on Main Street anymore.*

And then he turned and walked away from her, leaving her staring at his perfect backside in retreat with her mouth hanging open.

SINCE DARCY'S FATHER PASSED AWAY ten years ago, her mother, Cassie, hosted a family dinner every Thursday evening and expected all of her "ducklings" to attend. This tradition included Darcy, Amory, and Willow, who had been—more or less—adopted by the Turners decades ago.

Willow's parents separated the week after her eighth birthday and her family, once happily situated in Carlisle, had imploded. Her father had relocated to his hometown of Montréal, while her mother returned to New York. But while Joanna Faulk Broussard longed for the bright lights of the big city, she wanted her daughter, Willow, to have an all-American childhood safely ensconced in her own hometown, Carlisle. So Willow had grown up under the less-than-watchful eyes of her aging maternal grandparents, with only occasional visits from her very busy, profoundly un-maternal mother. And every summer was spent with her paternal grandmother, her *Nohkom*, in Quebec City where she avoided her father's awkward attempts to connect with her, eschewing his casual interest in her life, and choosing to immerse herself in her grandmother's

Métis culture instead.

This arrangement left Willow somewhat lacking in stable family life, which the Turners were more than happy to provide as much as possible. And after the passing of Willow's elderly grandparents, leaving Willow the house that she shared with Darcy, Cassie Turner welcomed her—even expected her—every Thursday evening for family dinner.

Darcy and Willow arrived first and were chatting with Cassie about Amory's surprise guest.

"So, what do we know about her?" asked Darcy from her perch beside Willow on the kitchen counter.

"Not much, duckling," answered her mother. "He didn't bring her to Honoria's affair on Saturday, but when he asked if he could bring her tonight, I said yes. That's all I know."

Darcy turned to Willow. "You spent some time with Amory at the wedding. Did he mention he was dating someone new?"

Willow shook her head no, but Darcy noticed that she flinched and seemed to brace herself when they heard the front door open a second later. Anyone else would have missed it, but Darcy knew Willow. She watched as Willow's lips tightened to a thin white line, her arms crossing over her chest after she hopped off the counter.

Suddenly Amory was taking up the entirety of the doorway between the kitchen and the front room with his huge contractor's body, tousled ginger-colored hair and goofy grin. Darcy watched as he found Willow's eyes first.

"Hey, Will," he said softly, acknowledging her with a nod.

"Hey, brat," she mumbled in a tight voice, keeping her eyes down, wiping her hands on her jeans.

Amory pursed his lips at her, turning to his sister and mother with a forced smile. "Hey, Darce. Evening, Mom."

"Amory." Cassie opened her thick arms for a hug and Amory stooped down to press his cheek against hers. "How's that big project you're working on?

"Almost done. Had to get one last coat of finish on it before sundown today. You know him, Mom? Jack Beauloup? Apparently Darcy knew him in high school."

At the mention of Jack's name, Darcy's heart skipped a beat, remembering the way he held her this morning and instantly reminded of her plans to have dinner with him tomorrow night. Darcy's eyes flicked to her brother's face, wide and annoyed. Just about everyone in Carlisle knew

Cassie Turner was a mother who wanted to see her unmarried daughter happily settled. Amory was baiting the hook with Darcy and grinning as she wriggled.

"Is that right, duckling?" Cassie asked, turning to Darcy with a hopeful smile and one eyebrow raised. "Is he nice?"

"I barely know him. We were in *The Music Man* together, Mom. That's all."

Cassie gave Darcy a hard look before turning back to Amory. Darcy knew she hadn't heard the last of Jack Beauloup from her mother.

Darcy turned to Amory. "Didn't you bring a guest tonight?"

As if he had forgotten something important, Amory looked around sharply to his right, then left, where he found the object of his search standing in the living room just short of the kitchen doorway. Looking around Amory, Darcy caught the bright blue eyes of a petite young woman holding a wrapped bottle, looking cheerful, if forgotten. She had short blonde hair cropped in a Mia Farrow-style pixie cut and her nose was covered with a sprinkling of freckles.

Yep, cute as a button.

Not to mention…a blonde-haired facsimile of Willow Broussard.

Blonde, blue-eyed and a good ten years younger.

Amory took her free hand and drew her closer until he could put his arm around her shoulders and draw her close to him with a tug.

"This is Faith!"

Darcy's eyes nervously flicked to Willow.

Willow's eyes narrowed, watching as the interloper offered her hand to Cassie.

"I've heard so much about you, Mrs. Turner."

"Oh, it's *Cassie*! Please, dear," said Darcy's mother warmly. "I hope you like lasagna."

"I love it," said Faith. "In fact, I've brought some red wine to go with it…"

Cassie took the bottle with a squeal of delight and out of the corner of her eye, Darcy caught Willow's icy stare.

"I'm Darcy," she said, offering her hand to Faith and running interference. Faith smiled at her, and Darcy watched the freckles dance across the bridge of her nose. "And this is Willow."

Faith turned to Willow and if she noticed Willow's cool demeanor, she didn't let on. She dropped Darcy's hand and offered hers to Willow. "Hey, there. I'm Faith."

"Mmm," breathed Willow, running a hand through her close-cropped black hair, her almost-black eyes capturing Faith's blue ones. "Yes."

Turning away without shaking hands, Willow grabbed the salad bowl from the kitchen counter and headed for the dining room without a word.

"She's the town doc," said Cassie, watching Willow go. "Always so much on her mind."

Faith smiled politely at Cassie, who drew Faith's attention to the bottle of wine she was opening, asking if it was a favorite of Faith's. Darcy looked at Amory, who had his eyes trained on the dining room doorway, and sighed. *Oh, Amory. What a mess you're making.*

At twenty-six, Amory was eight years younger than Willow, and despite some half-hearted attempts at flirting with her as the years went on, Willow had always maintained Amory's status of her "surrogate little brother." That Amory had been deeply and irrevocably in love with Willow throughout his adolescence was no big secret, but as far as Darcy knew, nothing had ever happened between them. Only recently Darcy had noticed the way Willow delighted in baiting Amory in conversation and how Amory seemed to show up more regularly to family events that included Willow. He seemed to seek her out, showing up with amusing anecdotes to share with her. Not to mention, he'd become especially clumsy over the past year: it seemed like he injured himself on the job at least once a week—a dropped hammer here, a minor laceration there— necessitating visits to Willow's office.

Darcy wondered if something had finally happened—or *not* happened— at Honoria's wedding, because Faith seemed like less of a girlfriend and more of a statement, somehow. The timing felt funny.

Darcy picked up the pitcher of water on the kitchen counter and followed Willow into the dining room where she found her friend seated at the table, checking messages on her phone.

"Everything okay?" Darcy asked.

"Sure," answered Willow without looking up. "So...what's the deal with Faith? You heard about her before now?"

Darcy set the pitcher down carefully. "What do you mean?"

"Just that I didn't know he was dating someone. Did you?"

"Nope." Darcy shrugged noncommittally. "But, you know Amory..."

Willow's eyes shot up and cut to Darcy's as she continued.

"...he's sort of a serial dater. Sort of an 'If you can't have the one you love, love the one you're with' dater. Just have to hope one of the ones-he's-with doesn't eventually *stick* while the one-he-loves takes her sweet time getting off her ass to give him a chance."

"*Huit années*," muttered Willow in French, giving Darcy a sour look before looking back down at her phone.

Eight years.

Darcy sat down next to her and nudged her friend's arm, ignoring the familiar refrain. "Did something happen? At the wedding?"

"No, kid," sighed Willow, finally looking up, a good swath of bitterness in her tone. "Nothing happened."

"*Should* something have happened?"

Willow met Darcy's eyes, and Darcy was surprised by the emotion she saw there from generally cool Willow. Was it…regret? Yes, regret. Darcy furrowed her brows. How come Willow hadn't said anything? Had Darcy been so wrapped up with Jack and her own life that she hadn't noticed something going on between Willow and Amory?

"What happened, Will?"

Willow opened her mouth to respond when Cassie entered, carrying a tray of lasagna, trailed by Amory and Faith. "Are we ready to get started?"

Darcy gave Willow a look as if to say, *This isn't over yet.*

Willow rolled her eyes back at Darcy, signifying that it was.

A MORY AND FAITH LEFT PROMPTLY after dinner and Willow soon followed them, insisting she had some files to finish up at her office. Darcy suspected that Willow just wanted some time alone. She had kept her head down at dinner, barely saying a word, but coolly assessing Faith from under dark lashes more than once. These glowers were carefully timed to be missed by Faith, but Amory, who sat across from Willow, appeared keenly aware of her irritation, and Darcy watched his expressions range from satisfied to worried as dinner progressed. While he may have enjoyed the attention at first, Darcy wondered if he had overplayed his hand by bringing Faith. Time would tell.

Darcy kissed her mother good-bye and started her walk home, surprised by the balminess of the evening. Late April in northern New Hampshire was unpredictable, as prone to snow as sun, and just about every weather pattern in between. Darcy guessed it to be about fifty-five degrees and she breathed in deeply, enjoying the serenade of the spring peepers and the brightness of the young, waxing gibbous moon rising. Five more days until the full moon lit the night sky.

Darcy's father, a renowned meteorological researcher who had spent more than half of his life atop Mount Washington observing extreme weather patterns at the famous observatory, had originally regarded astronomy as a hobby. Darcy remembered many evenings with her father on the high school football field, telescope pointed at the sky. But, over time, Steckler Turner—better known as Doc Turner by the scientific community—had come to believe, in the manner of the Native Americans, that lunar cycles had a direct effect on weather patterns.

At first, his hypothesis was ridiculed as "superstitious hocus-pocus" and Darcy remembered once—following a lecture by her father at UNH—a young heckler had asked her father if he also had "a great aunt Betty who predicted snowfall via her rheumatism?" Her father had colored red with embarrassment as the auditorium tittered with the muffled chuckles of his peers. But Doc Turner wasn't one to be waylaid by doubters, and what sweet vindication when it turned out that a decade of collected data supported his claims. In an article published in *Scientific American* the last year of his life, Doc Turner's hypothesis was finally proven true: Rain and snow increased a few days prior to a quarter moon, which was roughly halfway between the full and new moons.

Darcy smiled sadly, remembering her father's passion. It may not have been a well-read article in the non-science community, but everyone in Carlisle had tried their best to read and understand it. And practically speaking, their pride had paid off in one important way: no one in Carlisle ever planned a wedding, picnic, or BBQ anymore without consulting the almanac to check on the moon phases. And not one big event had been rained out in a decade.

Strolling through town, Darcy noted the small crowds at Mitzi's Coffee Cup, Murphy's Tavern, and at the Live Free or Die Diner. Most of the other businesses in Carlisle kept strict nine-to-five hours, and most stayed closed on Sunday too, except for Young's Grocery, which opened from one to four in the afternoon at a respectful distance from Sunday morning services. If you were in a bind on a Sunday morning, you could always head down to Berlin where they had a Wal-Mart, or North Conway, where they had just about every factory outlet store you could imagine.

Why would Jack Beauloup return to sleepy Carlisle where he had no family, no business, no ties?

It was a question that had rolled around in her head since Saturday afternoon, and although she couldn't escape the feeling that she was somehow part of his decision to return, she couldn't figure out how. They had barely gotten to know one another that summer so long ago and except for that one scorching moment backstage, they really hadn't even interacted with each other. They hadn't communicated for twenty long years. How in the world could she have anything to do with his return?

And yet…she felt more and more certain that Jack was somehow connected to her soul flight. For most of her life she had assumed that Jack's voice saying *It's you* was a vestige of her obsession with him, words her own mind had kept fresh because she couldn't bear to let go of them. But after seeing Jack again, the words had suddenly changed and Darcy had to consider the possibility that going inside wasn't something her brain had created to deal with the teenage heartbreak of losing Jack. Was it possible that Jack was somehow part of her soul flight, or even responsible for it? Was it possible that she and Jack were somehow connected on some otherworldly level?

And going inside wasn't even the half of it…it was impossible that she should be able to read his mind, yet she could. It was impossible that in a standoff between a man and a riled bear, the bear would flee. It was impossible that she should lose over an hour of her life for no good reason at all.

For a woman of science, the fact that the impossible kept *happening* was extremely discomfiting, but with the benefit of knowing her brain wasn't damaged and creating hallucinations, she had to start considering why and how the impossible seemed to be repeatedly possible for her and Jack. For the first time in Darcy's well-ordered, grounded life, she had an idea of her father's struggle to prove a theory that his community had regarded as quackery. She desperately hoped that seeing Jack tomorrow night might afford her some answers.

Darcy walked up the steps of her veranda and plopped down in the restored porch swing only to notice a cellophane wrapped bouquet of yellow tulips set lovingly against the swing cushion, tied with a voluptuous yellow bow. Picking up the bouquet gingerly, she gently pulled the card from the ribbon and opened it.

Tomorrow.

-JB

Darcy's heart hammered as she raised the flowers to her nose. Surely Jack wouldn't have known the meaning behind yellow tulips; he would only have bought them for their cheerful color, or because they were in season. Only a florist or a botanist, like Darcy, would take quiet pleasure in their hidden meaning.

Hopelessly in love.

Cradling the flowers in her arms, she pushed off with one foot, then leaned back in the swing, searching for Jack's seventeen-year-old face in her mind—his dark handsomeness and fiery eyes, his fingertips on her throat, his lips brushing against hers, the anguish in his eyes.

It can't be…It's you.

She winced and the image faded like watercolor as the face of thirty-seven-year-old Jack came into focus and she heard the whispered words in her head, as soft as velvet:

I belong to you.

And you belong to me.

Chapter 7

AMORY STOPPED BY DARCY'S STUDIO on Friday morning to give her directions to Jack's place, with a handwritten note, inviting her to join him for dinner at six o'clock.

"You and Jack, huh?" Amory teased, handing her the cream-colored note onto which Jack had scrawled the invitation, directions, and his phone number.

"You really want to go there, Am? After that stunt you pulled with, um, Faith?"

"I like Faith."

"Yeah. But you love Willow."

"Willow doesn't want me, Darcy. I have to move on."

"How do you know she doesn't?"

"Because if woman wants a man, eventually she's going to have to let him know."

"You don't see her eyes watching you?"

"It's not enough. I've tried, and she just…Believe me, Darce. She doesn't see me like that. I'm just your little brother."

Amory's eyes had looked so sad and heavy, Darcy didn't push him any further, and she changed the subject, asking about Faith instead. Amory invited his sister to join them for drinks sometime and Darcy had smiled and nodded. If Faith was going to stay in the picture for a while, Darcy may as well get to know her a little.

For the rest of the day, when she wasn't completely distracted thinking about her impending dinner with Jack or frustrated by Amory and Willow's inability to see their compatibility, she worked on her thesis. She had set a difficult objective for herself: to find an unknown element of moss or lichen that could be synthesized into a useful herbal or medical remedy.

She made some good headway sorting her notes, and even made an interesting discovery. The olivetol she'd found in a certain form of lichen she'd discovered in New Hampshire was a cousin element of the olive-tolic acid found in cannabis. She'd chuckled at that, wondering how many college kids would run out to the woods to harvest, dry, and smoke lichen if she made her discoveries known. She'd have to talk to Willow about it, and see if the Métis had already discovered the useful properties of olivetol hundreds of years before. Perhaps it could be combined with some other element of substance to boost its effect. *Hmm…*

She caught her watch face out of the corner of her eye and glanced at the time, gasping. Five o'clock! She only had an hour! She shut down her laptop and hurried back to the house to get ready.

Looking at her reflection in her bedroom mirror as she fastened small silver hoops into her pierced ears, she smiled at herself. *Not bad for a quick change.*

Her strawberry-blonde hair was parted to one side, and she had French-braided a small portion of the wider side to sweep it off her face. She had used nude powder to blend the freckles that settled across the pale skin of her high cheekbones, and some dark brown mascara to make her green eyes pop. She opened a tube of the melon-colored lip gloss she had started wearing at grad school in Boston and swiped the foam wand back and forth across her lips, liking the sensation of the slick, thick gloss.

She chose fitted, dark blue, skinny-fit jeans and a forest green cashmere scooped-neck sweater. Turning slightly, she surveyed her ass, wishing she was still a size eight, but she had gained a few pounds in the past few years, and the size ten jeans simply fit more comfortably now. Darcy didn't much care about that sort of stuff anyway. She hiked often, ate well, and got enough sleep. She didn't need to look like a supermodel.

She looked down at the offerings in her meager jewelry box. A simple silver necklace settled in the back of the second row caught her eye, and she gasped softly. *Where have* you *been?* The necklace had been a present from Willow one summer after she returned from her *Nohkom's* house: a silver chain with a sideways figure eight at the bottom. Willow had explained that the charm was also known as an infinity symbol and could be found on the national flag of the Métis people. Darcy had worn the necklace almost constantly for the rest of high school, but lost it in college soon after Phillip had left her. And yet, here it was again. Returned to her.

She smiled at it like an old friend then clasped it around her neck, grabbed her car keys, and turned off her bedroom light behind her.

AS DARCY NEARED JACK'S HOUSE, she was grateful for her Land Rover's V8 engine and four-wheel drive. She was further grateful that Jack didn't appear to be an ax murderer because, Lord, his house was way back in the woods. Darcy, who prided herself on knowing every inch of Proctor Woods and most other wild rambles in and around Carlisle, followed Jack's directions and was surprised to find an easy-to-miss access road partially hidden by dense overgrowth in the north part of town.

The dirt road she traveled was rough and windy and she wondered, fleetingly, how in the world she was ever going to find her way home without overhead lights. Luckily, her SUV had brights, but still, she'd have to take her time to ensure she was staying on the "road" and not trail-blazing her own dangerous path back to downtown Carlisle. She enjoyed the woods around her and appreciated that very few trees had been cut down to make the road—instead the road weaved in and around the trees, messy but inoffensive.

As Darcy cleared a small ridge and rounded a bend, she found the most beautifully situated house she had ever seen. She gasped, braking, as she took in the sight before her.

Enchanting. It was simply enchanting.

A babbling river, acting almost as a moat, maybe six or seven feet across, lay between Darcy and the house, and a rustic-looking bridge offered the only conveyance between the woods from where she'd come and the modest semicircle driveway which presently held one Jeep Grand Cherokee.

Behind the driveway, there was a large lodge, the size of a small hotel, built of ancient logs covered in lichen and vines; it almost appeared imbedded into the woods, as though it had been there forever. There were mature trees within inches of the house footprint, signifying its age, which Darcy guessed at 150 years old or more. The lodge itself appeared to be one story, but Darcy noted four half-sized gables, roughly hewn, creating peaks in the roofline and implying a second floor, perhaps with eave bedrooms. The windows were ablaze with soft gold and yellow light that shined through gleaming windows, and the front of the house had been prettily landscaped with flowering bushes and a modest lawn in the middle of the semicircle driveway. A sprawling porch that spanned the entire north side of the lodge had several rocking chairs and a split-rail fence to keep people from toppling into the river below. Ivy climbed around the front door and smoke rose warmly from one of three stone chimneys.

Darcy put her car back in drive and crossed over the bridge, pulling up behind the Jeep she assumed was Jack's. Off to the left, and a little behind the house, she noticed the log-cabin-style barn/garage that Amory had been working on. He'd done a nice job incorporating it into the style of the house although there was no mistaking its newness. But the lighter wood wasn't visible before a visitor crossed the bridge, maintaining the illusion that the lodge had existed in its place forever as the woods grew up around it.

Amory had mentioned that Jack's place was grand. Darcy just hadn't expected it to be so entirely charming—so much a place that she would choose for herself, down to the last detail, had she the means and the need. It was almost unnerving to come face to face with your dream house, with an enchanted lodge buried deep in the north woods.

Darcy took a deep breath, checking her reflection in her rearview mirror and wishing that her pounding heart would calm down. She grabbed her bag and opened her door, only to be greeted by Jack, who offered her his hand and a beaming smile. She hadn't noticed him approach her car.

"Where'd you come from?" she asked. He wore a white button-down shirt untucked, the first two buttons undone, and worn-in jeans with bare feet. She looked at the wiry hairs peppering the tanned skin pulled taut over the well-defined bones beneath. She loved that his feet were bare and suddenly wished hers were too. Even his stupid feet made her heart beat faster. Geez!

She lifted her head to find him staring at her with raised eyebrows and an amused grin. "The house."

"Some *house!*" Darcy exclaimed.

He looked back at his offered hand, remembering the way her insides had turned to lava when he had unfurled his fist and laced his fingers through hers at Honoria's wedding. *Keep your head on straight, Darcy. No feet, no hands. You need discussion, not distraction.*

"Thanks, I've got it."

His eyes narrowed as he withdrew his hand, stepping back so she could stand up. She turned around slowly, taking in the bridge and woods from where she'd come, the river, more woods and Amory's barn-style garage, a flagstone pathway between the two buildings, then the corner of the lodge. The façade of the house was built of large, boulder-like stones, mismatched and misfit into a grand entry, which had a proper front door flanked by windows, and a gabled roof with a copper weathervane that had a crescent moon in place of the usual rooster. At the northwest corner of the house, the porch started and curved around the side of the lodge, following the same path as the river. Finally, Darcy's eyes returned to the bridge again. This wasn't so much a house as a compound.

Darcy breathed in deeply, comforted by the familiar earthy smells… pine, dampness, and rotted wood, accompanied by the warm smell of smoke from his fireplace. Leaves rustled gently in the early evening breeze and she heard squirrels chittering as they scrounged for their dinners. A tapping in the distance bespoke a woodpecker hard at work, and the river gurgled musically, moss-covered slippery rocks detouring its path, rewriting its journey.

"Jack," she finally murmured. "This is beautiful."

He had been watching her intently and she shivered under his scrutiny. He seemed so *aware* of her. His eyes swept down, lightly resting on her chest before returning to her face.

You're beautiful.

She smiled at him, shaking her head gently, feeling a blush warm her cheeks.

"You like it?" he asked. "My house?"

She nodded and he beamed at her as though her approval meant more to him than anything else in the world. She had never seen his eyes so unguarded—his face was so open and pleased, she was sure she saw shades of the little boy he must have been once, a long time ago. Her heart suddenly felt full with tenderness for the strange, captivating man before her, and she reached her hand up to touch his face, about to caress his cheek when she caught herself. She swallowed against the lump in her throat then lowered her hand quickly, taking a breath and looking away from Jack at the lodge.

"What's not to like? It's out of a dream. It's the most amazing place I've ever seen."

"I wanted you to like it."

"Why?" she asked, smiling at him.

"Just did." He shrugged, and she thought she saw a little awkwardness in his wobbly grin. "Want to see the rest?"

"Absolutely!" He started toward the main lodge, but Darcy gestured to Amory's garage. "Maybe start with my brother's work? He's sure to ask me what I think."

She wasn't sure because it was so brief, but she thought she saw a mild wariness cross over Jack's face before he gave her a tight smile. "The garage?"

"If that's okay?"

He swallowed, bowing his head. "Of course."

Darcy followed him over the pebbled driveway to the two-storied, two-car garage made of logs varnished to a medium brown. One bay was open, so Darcy stepped onto the new cement, smiling at her brother's handiwork.

"It's nice."

"He's talented."

"Can I go upstairs?"

"Sure," said Jack, standing at the foot of the stairs.

She brushed by him, and as her elbow grazed the hardness of his chest, her stomach ignited with heat like striking a match. She paused on the first step, adjusting to his nearness behind her. If she turned, they'd be face to face, eye to eye, her lips a breath away from his. She took a deep breath, running her hand up and down the smooth banister to her left.

"Is everything okay?" he asked softly, his voice low directly behind her.

"Th-this banister is unique," she blurted out, cringing, wishing she could recapture her composure.

"It's from a tree that used to be on the property." He leaned forward and she could feel his breath on her neck. "I cut it down. Sanded it. Shined it. I like working with my fingers."

Was it just her imagination or did she feel those fingers touch down lightly on her hips? Her eyes shuttered closed and she took a deep, ragged breath, trying to steady herself. All she had to do was turn around and the hot, soft miracle of his lips would be waiting for her.

A small whimper sounded with the force of her breath escaping and she swallowed, opening her eyes, steeling herself.

Don't get distracted, Darcy! Answers first.

Her feet were like lead, but she forced herself to move them up the stairs, not looking back at him, placing distance between them. After three steps, she heard him moving up behind her.

Her fingers skimmed lightly over the banister and her heart pounded with the thought that his hands had touched every inch of the hard, satin wood lovingly, working it, molding it, smoothing it. She imagined his hands on her body, touching every inch of her skin, working it with his muscled fingers, molding her flesh, smoothing it, soothing it with his long, long awaited touch.

When she reached the top of the stairs she sighed, grateful to be distracted by the most comfortable, welcoming studio she'd ever seen. The walls were paneled in bright white bead board, and the floor had been painted a light gray. Dying light poured in through windows to her right and a skylight overhead.

She sighed, stepping into the cheerful room and turning to Jack with a smile. "What a lovely room! Do you use it much?"

"No," he answered. "But, I thought…at some point…"

His words trailed off and he shrugged lightly from his position at the top of the stairs where his hand rested lightly on a newel post, watching her with a slight smile and dark, warm eyes.

"This is just like mine," she said, moving to stand beside the desk, feeling hot and self-conscious under his gaze. She looked away from him, peeking out the windows, which looked out at the front drive, bridge, and river.

She gestured to the desk chair. "May I?"

"Of course," he said softly, still watching her with the same steady, hungry stare.

It made her shiver as she sat down and swiveled in the chair, straightening her back to look out the window again. Anywhere else but at the intensity of his face.

"It's a beautiful view," she murmured. "I'd barely be able to work. I'd daydream all day."

He stepped closer to her, resting one hand on the desk and using the other to turn the chair to face him. He squatted down before her.

"What would you dream about?" he asked.

She was incredibly aware of him so close to her, his bent knee grazing hers, his face just slightly lower than hers, but no more than a few inches away.

Jack, I don't—

He looked down at the hands on her lap, releasing her eyes. He reached out and touched one of her hands, tracing her index finger with his, a feather touch, a breath, a whisper.

"What would you dream?" he asked again, his hand gently covering hers, his thumb massaging the soft, sensitive skin of her palm.

"I'd dream...I'd..." Her heart was slamming into her chest and she was suddenly aware of how very alone they were in this little light-filled studio that smelled of fresh paint and timber and Jack. She swallowed, wanting nothing more than for him to raise his eyes to hers and see how desperately she wanted him. *You. I'd dream of you. Like I always do. Like I always have.*

But he didn't. He released her hand and stood up. She heard him take a deep breath as he turned toward the stairs, his back to her.

She stood up on shaky legs, noticing the bathroom in the corner. "Do you mind if I—"

She gestured to the bathroom and he turned his head just enough to nod at her slightly.

Once inside the little room, she sat down on the closed toilet and tried to catch her breath, calm the wild hammering of her heart. Trying to get rid of the butterflies in her stomach would be impossible, so she ignored them.

What was this insane attraction she had to him? She had never, ever felt this sort of heat with any other man in her life. She stood up, running the cold water and soaking her hands.

She looked at herself in the mirror.

You're here for answers. How can he read your mind? How is he associated with your soul flight? Did you lose time on Saturday? Stop acting like a hormonal adolescent, Darcy Turner. Get your head on straight.

She nodded curtly to her reflection, turning off the water and wiping her fingers on a plush, mint green hand towel that looked brand new. Pep talk initiated and accepted, she turned to leave when a frame on the wall caught her attention. She flicked on the light to get a better look. It was a shadow box and contained pinned samples of lichen in various colors and textures beautifully mounted and labeled.

"Crustose...foliose...fruticose," she murmured, lightly touching the glass with her fingers. *What an unusual choice of decoration for a powder room.* She heard Jack clear his throat as she stepped out of the little bathroom, flicking the light off behind her.

"Interesting...*art*," she said, unable to shake the feeling that between the desk and chair—that were identical to hers—and samples, the small studio was somehow created just for...*her.*

He nodded once and looked away, awkwardly gesturing with one hand. "Sort of goes with the whole woodsy theme."

Of course! Her rational mind chided her immediately: it was absurd and completely self-important to think for a moment that a virtual stranger—an acquaintance from high school, at best—would custom decorate a room for her, and she cringed internally at her ridiculous presumptions, feeling her face flush with heat. He had probably found the shadow box at some gallery and purchased it. It had nothing to do with her.

"They're nice samples," she said, unable to keep the note of sheepishness out of her tone. "Did you know I study mosses and lichen?"

"Is that right?" Jack said absently as he headed back down the stairs.

Had he seen her face color? Oh, she was acting like an idiot! *Get your head in the game, Darcy! Ask him about the telepathy.* Darcy took one last look at the room before following him.

But when she got to the foot of the stairs, her thoughts were distracted by a formidable metal door at the back of the garage which she hadn't noticed before. It had an imposing handle and a complex-looking security keypad beside the door.

Jack was standing by the mouth of the garage, ready to continue the tour at the main house, but she couldn't resist asking, "Where does that go?"

"Oh, um…that's um…"

"What?" She walked between the hood of the parked sports car and the wall to take a better look at the door. "What's in here?"

"Wine cellar," he responded.

She reached out to touch the cold metal of the door, taking in the keypad. It had a standard keypad of numbers, but also additional buttons and a scanner pad the size of a man's thumb. She placed her thumb on the scanner and a light turned red and beeped angrily at her.

"Protective of your wine, huh?"

"I'm protective of anything that belongs to me," he rumbled, closer to her ear than she expected him to be. "*Anyone* who belongs to me."

The taut possession in his voice made her heart burst, and she felt her body responding to him. Her insides churned hot and demanding, making her fingers tremble and her eyes close as she gasped to fill her lungs. She could feel the heat of his body directly behind her, smell his soap and sweat. The fresh, masculine scent made her breath catch. If she turned around, she knew her breasts would brush up against his chest and she'd be face to face with him.

After a lifetime of waiting to feel his lips on hers again, this was the moment. Her defenses were stripped and the wait was over. No matter what else happened tonight, no matter what else they needed to discuss or say to each other, what she needed right now—*right this moment*—was for Jack to touch her. She took a tiny step backward, her heart pounding with want as her back stopped flush against his chest.

"Darcy," he whispered, and she could hear the ragged emotion in his voice. The low tautness from before was replaced with heat, with intensity, with a hunger that rivaled hers.

His fingers gently pushed her hair to the side, exposing the skin of her neck. Her eyes closed as she felt his warm breath behind her ear and she bent her neck languorously to the side, offering up the smooth plane of her throat to him. A small sound of pleasure escaped her throat as she felt his lips, soft and hot, press lightly against the pulse point under her jaw.

It was the same spot he had touched with his fingers so long ago and it filled her with longing for this man whom she had loved so desperately as a boy. Whatever vestige of self-control she held onto collapsed in a heap at their feet and she turned slowly to face him.

His eyes were like lava, copper flames dancing and leaping in the brown pools that spoke of hunger and need and want and long separations finally at an end.

"Jack," she murmured, dropping her eyes to his full, soft, waiting lips, remembering the feel of them like he had only kissed her yesterday. "Kiss me again."

His lips lowered to touch hers and she felt his breathing change as he moved his hands to hold her cheeks, tilting her face so that his lips fit full and flush across hers. She raised the hands hanging limply by her sides until they covered his and he parted his fingers so hers could lace through his. He caught her lower lip gently, slowly, pulling lightly before sealing his lips over hers again. Her breathing was shallow and hot and she could feel how much he was holding himself back, easing into their intimacy, careful not to startle or frighten her. But the same kiss that had rocked her fifteen-year-old world in high school wasn't enough now. A wild dart of pleasure shot through Darcy's body as she boldly broke the seam of their lips with her tongue.

It was as though she'd touched him with fire. A strangled sound rose from his throat, and he dropped his hands from her face, urgently lifting her up onto the hood of the car beside them. Darcy raised her hands to his face frantically, palming his cheeks, threading long fingers through his thick, black hair, her body flooding with wet heat under the erotic sensation of his tongue swirling around hers.

She wanted to make up for twenty years apart; she wanted everything he had to give, and more. She had never felt such an all-consuming burn for anyone or anything in the entirety of her life. It was like being under a spell, like a fever or an obsession, meeting his tongue stroke for stroke, desperate sounds of passion muffled between them as he kissed her. She felt his hands move slowly from under her arms, down her sides until they rested on either side of her breasts, the foot of his palms pressed up against the softness there.

"Darcy." He leaned back to see her, panting. "My God, I've waited so long…"

She pulled his head back down to hers roughly, finding his mouth and demanding its heat again. He growled as she raised her legs, wrapping them around his waist. He moved his hands to her hips, shoving her up against the enormous, rock-hard bulge in his jeans, grinding into her softness with increasing passion. His hands, his hot, gentle hands, slid under her sweater, his fingers skimming the aroused skin of her waist and belly until they cupped her breasts through the lacy material of her bra, his thumbs massaging her nipples into hard peaks as he kissed her relentlessly.

She arched toward him, moaning into his mouth, locking her feet around his waist, trying to get closer, only she couldn't. She couldn't get closer through the layers of clothes between them and her frustration made her bite his lip lightly. He bucked against her, grinding into her and pinching her nipple, his low, surprised growl of pain and passion swallowed by her mouth. He moved his lips to her cheek, to her neck, to her throat, slowly kissing a trail from her mouth to her chest.

She was starting to feel hot and faint and she couldn't catch her breath. She opened her eyes and saw his were closed, but they glowed under his eyelids just as they had after his encounter with the bear. It was just strange and startling enough to jolt her out of the dream.

"Jack!" She leaned back, panting, her chest rising and falling dramatically with the force of her breathing. "Your eyes!"

His eyes flashed open, fiery and bright until he blinked twice quickly, which returned them to their normal brown.

Darcy stared at him, aroused, frightened, confused. His hands relaxed on her breasts, but he didn't release them. He stared at her in surprise, as if coming out of a fog of desire and want.

"Your eyes were…glowing."

He shook his head lightly, taking a deep breath and blinking again.

"Okay. Yeah," he panted. "They do that. Sometimes."

He leaned forward to rest his forehead on hers. She felt his breath, hot against her cheek.

"Why?" she asked softly. "Eyes don't do that."

He lowered his hands from her breasts slowly, letting them lightly caress the aroused skin of her belly before resting them on the skin of her waist, under her sweater. She lowered her legs from his hips until the backs of her feet touched the front tire of the car.

Like hers, his chest rose and fell dramatically with ragged breaths, brushing her chest as he inhaled and exhaled. He licked his lips as she unlaced her hands from his neck and raised them to his face, running her fingers lightly over his prickly beard, and vaguely thinking it had seemed softer when he was kissing her.

"Why do your eyes do that?" she asked again.

"I don't know," he answered. "It's a family thing…"

"Another family thing?" she asked weakly, thinking she'd have to talk to Willow about retinal anomalies when she had a moment.

"I'm sorry," he whispered, his low baritone raspy as he found her hands and grasped them, lifting the knuckles to his lips. "I lost control. I just want—"

"—you," she finished for him. "Me too."

He nodded, leaning forward to kiss the bridge of her nose. "It's hard to stop. Being with you…God, it's like a fever. Like nothing I've *ever* felt before."

"Me neither, Jack. It's like a spell."

His fingers laced through hers and she felt him take a deep, shaky breath before leaning back from her just enough to see her eyes.

There's a reason for that.

What do you mean?

She could see the worry in his eyes, besieging hers, as he bit his lower lip. He swallowed, looking down, before meeting her eyes again.

"That kiss, Darcy. That night in high school. It was…" He tried to look away and Darcy wiggled her hands away from his, placing them gently on his face, forcing him to look at her.

"What? It was what?" *Besides the most amazing moment of my life until five minutes ago.*

"Binding," he breathed, his fingers curling into fists in her lap. *It was binding.*

"B-binding?"

He nodded once, his face a mixture of worry and remorse as he courageously held her eyes.

"What does that mean?" she asked, desperate to understand, searching his eyes for answers. "I don't know what that means."

It means what it meant from the beginning.

"It means that I belong to you...," he whispered.

"...and I belong to you," she murmured.

The vow came easily, but Darcy still wasn't sure what he meant. She knew what the word "binding" meant in terms of contracts, but it was nonsensical that a kiss between two teenagers could mean anything that serious. And yet...

Without realizing it, she had dropped her hands from his face and was surprised to feel the cool metal of the car under her fingertips.

"Binding," she murmured again.

He nodded at her again, taking a deep breath and watching her intently, as though worried she might scream or faint or try to run away. Suddenly nothing felt as important as reassuring him. She met his eyes, finding his hands in her lap and clutching onto them, feeling her face soften with the strength of her feelings for him.

I'm not going anywhere, Jack...

"...but I don't understand."

He brought her knuckles to his lips again and kissed them tenderly.

"Let's have dinner. We'll talk. I don't have all the answers, but I'll try to explain more."

She nodded, lacing her fingers through his as he led her out of the garage her brother built and into the lodge of her dreams.

Chapter 8

H IS HOUSE WAS BEAUTIFUL.
Decorated in earthy tones, with soft, ambient light in every room,
the home couldn't have been more perfect if Darcy had decorated it herself. They entered the house by the front door, and she found herself in a
small coatroom with a slate floor and brass hooks for hanging coats to her
right and a small bench for taking off muddy or snowy shoes. To the left
of the door was a room housing a veritable mountain of chopped wood.

"Did you chop all that?" she asked, eyebrows raised.

He smiled at her and winked. "Keeps me in shape."

He pulled her into the living room, which was more of a great room
with high ceilings, exposed beams and skylights. A massive flagstone fireplace dominated the wall to the right with full bookcases on either side. A
sofa faced the fireplace with reading chairs and lamps to the left and right.
A stuffed elk head with fifteen points was mounted over the fireplace.

"You?" she asked.

He nodded. "Do you like to hunt?"

"No," she answered. "I wouldn't know how to kill anything. My
brother...Amory, he hunts. Sort of the state pastime, I guess."

"But not for you?" he asked, watching her intently.

She shook her head and shrugged. "Not for me."

He took her hand and led her to the kitchen, which was relatively small
for such a large house, but the deck that ran the length of the living room
and kitchen made both rooms feel larger. Two sets of French doors in the
living room and huge picture windows made the outside feel like part of
the rooms.

"I love how you've decorated, Jack," she said approvingly, squeezing his hand.

"I had a decorator come up from Boston to make recommendations," he said, running a free hand over the rustic table in the kitchen.

"From Boston?" she asked, trying not to sound impressed.

He shrugged. "I worked in Boston for years."

"I went to school there," said Darcy. "Harvard. Botany."

"I remember." He gave her a tight smile. "Um, *hearing* that. I remember hearing that you studied there."

"What did you do there?" she asked, anxious to learn more about him.

"Security. Private security."

"Like a bodyguard?"

He seemed surprised and chuckled a little, facing her. "Sort of. I had more duties than that, but it was part of the job, yes."

"You're certainly big enough," she said, feeling her cheeks get hot and probably color red as she realized what she'd said.

"Is that right?" he asked, his thumb lightly stroking hers, doing crazy things to her stomach.

"I—I just mean…you're in good shape."

He raised his eyebrows, giving her an amused grin. She knew she was crimson now. She wasn't making things any better.

"What's through there?" she asked, gesturing to an old-fashioned swinging door.

"Dining room," he said, pulling her back into the living room toward the stairs. "But you'll see it at dinner. Want to see the upstairs too?"

She loved his house and was dying to check out every inch, but looked down instead, their smoking hot kiss in the garage and her recent observations about his body making her wonder if seeing the bedrooms in his house was such a good idea when she had so many questions that still needed answers.

He dropped her hand, sensing her shyness. "I won't touch you. Promise."

She looked up at him and grinned, hands on her hips.

What if I want you to? she teased.

Do you?

What if?

Your wish is my command.

He grinned back at her wickedly, grabbing her waist, and pulling her up against his body. His teasing eyes went dark and intense as he captured hers.

Is this what you want? he asked.

She shook her head. *No. This is what I want.*

She reached up around his neck and pulled his head down to her, pressing her lips against his, all traces of teasing vanishing as the warm velvet of his lips captured hers. He wound his hand through her hair, bunching it at the back of her head, holding her head back so that his mouth could pillage hers. She leaned into him and his hands released her hair, skimming down her back to grab her hips and pull her tighter into his embrace.

She gasped as she felt the thickening of his erection against her pelvis, growing inside his jeans, evidence that he wanted her as much as she wanted him. She suddenly had the insane urge to drop her hands from his neck and touch him there, press her trembling fingers against the taut, hard flesh that she ached to feel inside her body.

Wait! Her mind screamed a warning, trying desperately to block out the knee-weakening sensations of his lips and tongue loving hers. *You're thinking about sex and that's exactly where this is leading.*

And she had a sudden though that sex was exactly where she wanted the night to go. She wanted him to pick her up and carry her up the stairs to his bedroom. She wanted him to undress her in the firelight and press his lips to every inch of her hot, panting body. She wanted that hot thickness to thrust inside of her and she'd scream out his name, making up for all of the years she longed for him to return to her. To return to her. God, how she wanted him.

She unlaced her fingers, digging them into his thick hair and moaning into his mouth as his hands slipped under her sweater, thumbs and forefingers massaging the skin of her waist insistently, moving closer to the button of her jeans.

No! Her mind broke through the haze of white-hot desire she felt for Jack Beauloup. *You don't want this! Not yet. You came here for a reason!*

She tore her mouth away from his, trying to catch her breath, swiping the back of her hand across her lips as much to protect herself as to prevent herself from seeking his lips again.

His chest heaved up and down. "Darcy, you're like…an addiction to me."

She swallowed, resting her forehead against his. She skimmed her hands down to her hips and removed his fingers from her waist gently, lacing their hands together by their sides. She didn't know what to say. Her body longed to feel his, flush and naked, beside her. But, their intense, explosive chemistry aside, she needed to understand the strange bond that seemed to pull them together.

He leaned back, capturing her eyes with a smile. She was grateful he didn't look disappointed in her for breaking off their kiss.

"Want me to make a fire?" he asked, glancing toward the fireplace.

"I think we just made one," she whispered, still feeling limp against him. Something occurred to her. "Didn't I see smoke as I drove up?"

"I had one in my bedroom before you got here," he answered, dropping a sweet kiss to her lips before pulling back. "I'm sure I can stoke it back up if you want to—"

"Oh! Um…"

YES! Screamed her body. *Let's go up to his room and—*

NO! You're here for answers, insisted her head.

"Darcy?

She looked up to see Jack's amused eyes and teasing grin. Her internal battle must have been playing out on her face.

"What?"

"I'm just kidding."

She exhaled shakily, sitting down on the edge of the couch, and watched as he knelt before the fireplace with his back to her, rolling up newspaper and laying kindling under larger logs that looked newly chopped.

"Jack."

"Mmmm?"

"I have to understand what's going on."

He kept his back to her, reaching for matches on top of the mantel then squatting down again.

"Ask me anything."

"How come we can read each other's minds?"

"We can't do that. We can only hear each other's thoughts when we're looking at each other. It's called Eyespeaking. It has to do with the binding."

Eyespeaking. Huh. So, he did know more about it, as she had suspected. She decided to let it go for now. "Okay. The binding. Tell me about that."

He grabbed a poker and moved the logs around to better catch the heat then replaced it, turning to her. She had never seen him more beautiful than he was tonight, his face watching her, lit by the growing flames of the fire behind him.

He approached her, sitting on the leather trunk in front of her that doubled as a coffee table. His knees touched hers and he reached out to take one of her hands, stroking her fingers gently as he started speaking again.

"There's a legend in my family. It says that a man will find his, um… his woman the summer before his eighteenth birthday. If he believes he's met the one to whom he should be bound, he kisses her, and…well, it says that for them it will feel as though the world disappears, and is born again around them." He looked up from their hands, his voice a whisper. "Ever felt like that, Darcy Turner?"

She nodded. "Once."

"It was you."

He said this so tenderly, the timbre of his voice almost made her cry. She squeezed his hand lightly and he raised her fingers to his lips, bowing his head, resting his lips on the back of her hand.

When he looked up, his eyes had darkened.

"But it shouldn't have been you. It should have been one of the girls I grew up with. If I'd known"—he shrugged, his eyes shuddering with seeming regret—"I never would have kissed you. I just liked you so much, and I…"

Darcy put her hand on his cheek and he leaned into it, closing his eyes and exhaling low and soft. "Hey. Hey, come on, now. It's just a legend. It's just a story."

He swallowed, opening his eyes and turning his lips into her palm for a moment before answering. "I never got over you. It's been twenty years. I never forgot. I never found anyone else I wanted to be with more than you."

She smiled at him gently, sorry to break the romance of the moment with what she was about to say. "Jack, we barely know each other."

His eyes burned into hers, copper flecks churning into fire.

"Okay. Then how do you explain the Eyespeak between us?"

"I can't explain it. But there are mysteries the human body hasn't revealed to us. I guess it isn't impossible that we're…evolving."

"Okay." He nodded slowly. "Then answer me this: Do you *really* feel like you barely know me?"

She looked away. She'd be lying if she said yes. She felt like she'd known Jack her entire life. She felt like she knew him better than any other person on the face of the earth. Oh, she might not know his favorite color or what kind of toothpaste he used, but she felt intimately connected to his mind, to his body, to his heart, to his very soul. Since she couldn't explain this logically, she didn't answer.

Finally he squeezed her hand and returned it to her lap. "I have to check on dinner. Do you want a glass of wine?"

"Please."

"Red okay?"

"Oh—" she started. Red gave her hives.

"Sorry. That's right," he said, walking away from her. "I have white out in the cellar. I'll grab a bottle then check on dinner."

She heard the front door slam behind him and it took her a minute to realize that she hadn't actually said that red gave her hives, nor had she been looking at him when she thought it. Maybe she'd mentioned it at the wedding while they were drinking champagne. There was no other way he'd know.

Left alone in his living room, Darcy turned her attention to the bookcases that flanked the rustic stone fireplace and walked over to look at the titles, running her fingers over the leather- and paper-bound spines. She wasn't surprised, but strangely relieved, to find several about the Métis people: *The Métis People, Contours of People: The History of the Métis, Métis Lore and Legends, Children of the Fur Trade.* Knowing what she did of the Métis people, both from Willow and from her own research, Darcy was quickly settling into the idea that Jack was of Métis origin, complete with superstitions and some unexplained mysticism.

She kicked off her ballet flats and curled up on the comfortable leather couch across from the fire, watching the flames leap higher, trying to understand what was happening between her and Jack Beauloup.

He seemed convinced that they somehow bound themselves to one another as teenagers with one scorching kiss, and while she loved the romantic intentions behind such a story, the scientist inside of her was skeptical. Despite her own personal experiences with Jack Beauloup, she wasn't disposed to believe in such unsubstantial fairytales. She felt more comfortable believing that two kids who shared a passionate moment couldn't quite shake each other over the years, drawn to one another by the sheer force of their attraction. Still, she'd have to look up this Métis legend of eighteen-year-old men confirming their soulmate in the space of a single, perfect kiss, because it was such a beautiful love story. But as far as Darcy was concerned, Jack was a boy with whom she'd shared a glorious teenage moment, with whom she still had a strong connection. Now that he was back, they'd have to get to know each other better to figure out the rest.

"I like your necklace," said Jack, returning with two glasses of white wine and scattering her thoughts. "I meant to say so before."

"Thanks, I thought you might."

"Did you?" He sat back down on the leather trunk across from her and smiled, but his eyes narrowed. "Why's that?"

No more beating around the bush.

"I figured out what you are."

She saw the copper start leaping around his surprised eyes before he looked away sharply. His nostrils flared and his jaw clenched tightly.

"What am I?" he half whispered, half growled.

Damn Vale Proctor and every other bigot who make the Métis and other Native Americans feel inferior! She was desperate to let him know she bore no such prejudice against his people.

She leaned toward him. "When you—you know, on Saturday? With the bear? You used a word. *Shipawaytay*, right?"

He looked up and nodded, his face still guarded, but slightly more curious now.

"It's Michif. Willow recognized it." She smiled at him, taking his hand. "You're Métis, Jack, aren't you?"

He looked down at his wine, swirling it around in his wineglass with his free hand. "What do *you* think?"

"It makes a lot of sense. It explains a lot. The beautiful legend you just shared with me." She let go of his hand and reached up to run her fingers through his thick, black hair. He put his wineglass on the coffee table and leaned into her hand, closing his eyes. "Your last name sounds French-Canadian and I know your family went back to Canada after high school. Your dark hair and brown eyes. Your way with the bear on Saturday. I know the Métis have a…a *mystifying* relationship with nature."

"What else?" he breathed, turning his head to press his lips against her palm.

"The um…" She swallowed. He was distracting her with nibbling kisses on her palm and the occasional hot lick with his tongue. "The mystical traditions fit…like um, soul flight and—"

"Wait. What did you say?" He drew back, looking up at her, his face surprised yet tender.

"Umm, soul flight?"

"Soul," he said so softly, she almost couldn't make out the sound.

"I—I also call it 'going inside.'"

"Going inside?"

"Inside my head. It's like daydreaming. It started, um, in high school. After you left."

"You call it soul flight," he said softly, reverently, nodding slowly, taking her hand from his face and massaging it with warm fingers. "How often does it happen?"

He knew what she was talking about. He *was* connected to it, as she had guessed.

"Every few weeks. Lately more. It's no big deal."

Jack pressed her hand to his trembling lips, closing his eyes.

"How does it feel?" he murmured. "Does it feel okay?"

"Like a daydream. Familiar. Safe. I don't know. Don't you—"

"Yes, I've experienced it," he whispered, opening his eyes.

She was struck by the depth of tenderness she saw there. And pity. And sorrow.

"It's Métis, right?"

He stared at her for a while, as if collecting his thoughts. She tried to hear his thoughts but only heard the word "soul" in a soft, ceaseless loop.

"Yes," he finally answered, giving her a sad smile. "It is."

He let go of her hand, looking away for a minute, then asked, "How many times this week?"

"Three."

"Yes." He nodded slowly, still averting his eyes from hers. "Three."

"Jack…is everything okay? This is all so…"

He looked at her, tilting his head to the side and biting his lower lip again.

"I cause it," he finally admitted. "I make it happen. I've always made it happen, from the very first time when you screamed that you didn't belong to me."

She gasped, remembering the day in the girl's bathroom with Willow when she'd gone inside the first time. The thing is, she remembered that day very well, and she hadn't uttered a word aloud. Jack was referring to her *thoughts*.

She felt like a broken record as her shoulders sagged and she heard the all-too-familiar words escape her mouth in a defeated sob:

"I don't understand."

"Then listen to me. I want to help you understand. I know this is a lot to absorb at once and you probably want to believe that we're random coincidence. Two kids who met in high school and kissed. And hey, I show up here twenty years later and we have that short, sweet history. But, there's a lot more than that between us, and it's not random and it's not coincidence."

She took a big gulp of wine, feeling her heart speed up and her face flush hot and red. Tears pricked the back of her eyes because she knew he was right and it frustrated her that it wasn't logical, that it defied explanation.

"So, what? What are you saying? That we kissed once in high school and we're now somehow cosmically bound to each other for life? That's crazy. Seriously, Jack? That's totally insane."

"I know it *sounds* crazy. But it's not." He stared into her eyes. "Darcy... did you ever forget me? Did you ever find happiness with someone else? Find completeness with someone else? Does anything feel as good as being with me? No, no, no, and no. I know the answers, because mine are the same."

This doesn't make any sense.

You're right.

It troubles me.

I know. I'm sorry.

Hold me, Jack?

In a flash he was sitting beside her. He put his arm around her, drawing her up against the solid warmth of his chest. As she rested her cheek on his chest under his chin, his other arm encircled her and she closed her eyes against the comfort he offered.

"We're complicated," he said quietly against her hair.

There had to be better answers than the ones he was offering. She was determined to track down every book on Métis legends and pore over them to try to understand what was happening between them and make sense out of it. But she'd had enough of it all for now.

"I came here wanting answers, but I don't think I can handle any more tonight." She leaned her head back, tilting her chin up. "Do you think we could do something?"

"What'd you have in mind?"

"Could we—could we *pretend* that we're just a couple of people who haven't seen each other in years and we're having a first date? I mean, could we shelve the Métis legends and the soul flight and the binding and all the rest of it? Just for a little while? Just have dinner, and talk, and get to know each other? Could we do that?"

He brushed his lips against hers. "Yes."

"Yes?"

"Absolutely."

She smiled at him. "Okay."

He sighed and twisted his wrist to check his watch. "Dinner's ready. I set the table in the dining room, but I could just scoop it into two bowls and we could—" He gestured to the fire.

"I'd love that." She leaned forward, dropping her feet to the floor. "I'll help."

He handed her a blanket from the back of the couch. "Make yourself useful, Turner. Why don't you spread this out in front of the fire? I'll get the *coq au vin*."

"*Coq au vin*! Wow, Jack!"

"Crockpot," he tossed over his shoulder as he sauntered to the kitchen. "Don't be too impressed."

She watched him go, admiring the way the top of his jeans hugged his hips and fit over his firm backside. The way his untucked, white button-down shirt moved with him, showing the contours of his back as he walked away from her. He looked a lot younger than thirty-seven years old. He was perfectly built. Insanely male. A shiver went down her back with the force of her attraction to him and she felt the blanket slipping from her slack hands. She shook her head and quickly gathered it together, spreading it in front of the fire just as he returned with two steaming bowls of French chicken stew.

She reached for her wine and sat down on one side of the blanket, cross-legged, accepting the bowl he handed to her. He took one of two silver spoons from his mouth, handing it to her with a sexy grin.

"Sorry. I only have two hands."

She raised her eyebrows at him and put the spoon in her own mouth, holding his eyes with hers as she sucked on it.

He stared at her, cocky smile fading, and she watched his eyes ignite in an instant, his expression changing from playful to hungry, and not for *coq au vin*.

"Better quit it."

"Or what?" she asked, popping the spoon out of her mouth and tonguing it slowly.

"Or all that hard-won control I have is going out the window."

"Ahhh," she breathed. "That's right. *Control*."

She picked up her bowl and dipped her spoon to fill it.

"Couldn't come back without it."

"Took you long enough," she muttered before blowing on her spoon.

"Can you quit it with that?"

She looked up at him and grinned. She wet her lips slowly, then took a deep breath and pursed her lips, letting her breath come out in a slow and steady stream over the spoon as she held his eyes.

What? This?

I'm going to throw you on your back and—

Jack!

I mean it. Cut it out. It's hard enough.

About to think the words *What is?* she lowered her gaze quickly and shoved her spoon in her mouth, at once surprised and distracted by the delicate flavor.

"Mmm. This is delicious."

"Yeah?"

Darcy nodded. "Willow makes a good *coq au vin*, but not this good."

He took a spoonful. "Tell me about Willow."

"We've been friends since fourth grade. She's more like a sister than a friend. We live together in one of the old Victorians off Main Street, which Carlisle doesn't like at all."

"Why's that?"

"Because we're not actually sisters. There's gossip."

"People think you're—"

"Yes, but we're *not*. Like I said…sisters." Darcy giggled. "I have the utmost respect for homosexual people, but I'm not—I mean, Willow and I aren't—"

"Don't need to convince me, Darce."

"Anyway. She's Métis, like you. But only a quarter. She's a regular doctor, but she also practices some shaman wisdom and remedies, you know, for those folks who're interested. She's…" Darcy's voice trailed off, thinking about Willow and Amory.

"She's what?"

"She's in love with my brother," Darcy murmured more to herself than Jack.

Jack finished off his stew and put his bowl on the leather trunk, lying down on his side, his head propped up on his hand. "Tell me about *that*."

"It's been a long time coming."

"Lot of that going around, huh?"

She smiled at him, taking another bite of the succulent stew before putting her bowl beside his on the trunk and lying down across from him, one hand propping up her head and the other holding her wineglass.

"Amory is eight years younger than Willow. I mean, when they met, she was in fourth grade and he was in diapers. When she was a sophomore in high school, he was in second grade. When she was starting college, he was finishing grade school. Age gap. Big one. She actually—still, to this day—calls him 'Brat.'" She thought of Amory's face last night, the way he seemed drawn to Willow like a magnet when he first entered the kitchen. "But he adores her. Always has. Right from the start."

Jack swirled his wine, taking a sip. "And…"

"You know, Amory was in fifth grade when Willow was a high school senior and he gave her the most amazing Valentine. All it said was '*Attends-moi.*'" Darcy paused, remembering the red construction paper valentine trimmed with one of their mother's pilfered doilies.

"Wait for me," whispered Jack.

Darcy nodded.

"But, I don't know," she continued. "Willow's—well, she's um, she's cagey. Her parents didn't stay together, and she has some trust issues, and…Anyway, it doesn't matter. She *didn't* wait for him. She dated half of Boston when she was at Harvard. She got married and quickly divorced. Dated the other half of Boston. Her grandmother passed away and she ended up back here."

Jack finished his wine and set the glass beside his bowl. "I don't get it, though. What about now? He's a grown up, she's a grown up. Why not now?"

"Eight-year spread." Darcy sighed. "She's never given him a chance, which, I believe, has made him a serial dater. He's got this new girl. Faith. And Willow? I don't even know what it would take to tie her down." She shrugged and smiled sadly at him. "I sort of love seeing them together in my head, you know? Like, fantasizing that Willow could really *be* my sister one day. But I can't imagine how it would ever happen. I know them both. It's impossible."

Jack took her empty glass, placing it beside his, then lay down next to her on his back, his head pointed toward the fire. He folded his hands on his chest, glancing at her. "That's a little too final, don't you think? I think—I *believe*—that some things are meant to be."

He started that assessment lightly but Darcy felt an edge in his tone as he finished speaking.

"I think you're a romantic." She put her arm flat on the blanket and laid her head on it, staring at Jack's lightly bearded cheek, wanting to touch him, telling herself not to.

He propped himself back up on his side, looking just a little bit embarrassed. "Maybe. I mean, I don't read chick lit, or run out to every romantic movie that comes along. But, sure. I like happy endings. Don't you? Don't you want a happy ending?"

With you. I only want one with you.

His eyes widened and she realized she hadn't looked away in time. She didn't even know where the thought had come from and he'd heard it. Her cheeks flushed with heat and she quickly rolled onto her back as a tear of embarrassed frustration snaked its way out of the corner of her eye.

"Darcy."

She wouldn't look at him. She felt him stand up without another word, and after a moment she heard soft acoustic guitar music start playing. When she looked up, he was leaning down, taking her hands in his.

"Dance with me?"

She let him pull her into a standing position and fell gratefully into his arms, resting her cheek on his shoulder, loving the feeling of his arms around her, resting on her lower back.

"What is this?"

"'My My Love.' Josh Radin. You know it?"

"No. But, I love it."

She had her hands lightly on his shoulders, but now she moved them to his neck, needing to feel the heat of his skin under her fingers.

"Sometimes I've wondered if that night was a dream."

"It wasn't."

"I know." She leaned back to gaze at him. "Why'd you do it? Kiss me?"

"Don't you know?"

She shook her head no.

"Darcy, I was crazy about you that summer. Every second. Every—"

"No," she murmured in disbelief, shaking her head. "You barely—"

"Yes." A whisper. Absolute.

"I didn't think you saw me."

"I didn't see anyone but you. That night was my last chance. To let you know—To try to let you know…"

"Jack, you were my first kiss."

She felt a jolt go through him at her admission. She leaned back in his arms, taking in the surprise on his face; the gold flecks burned like liquid copper in his eyes, flashing with need and hunger. He licked his lips and swallowed. That was her undoing.

I don't care if you can hear me. I don't care if we're complicated. I don't care if it doesn't make sense right this minute. I want you.

She placed her hands on either side of his face, tilted her head and pressed her lips to his.

He growled, animal-like, desperate, slamming his body against hers, his hands clutching her backside and pushing her roughly up against him. She gasped in surprise then sighed, her fingers curling until she held his face with her fists, barely able to stand, trying not to faint.

As if he sensed this, he suddenly lifted her off her feet. He carried her to the couch and placed her on her back, moving with her to rest on top of her, never breaking contact with her lips. He plunged deeper and deeper, taking over her mouth and Darcy gasped and twisted beneath him, feeling a stirring in her belly she had never felt before. She drew her legs up to his waist and locked her ankles behind his back, cradling him, and felt him gasp with pleasure, his hands holding her face firmly, forcing her to keep meeting the hungry demands of his mouth. She moved her hands to his back, pushing his shirt up over his smooth, blistering-hot skin.

He broke their kiss and leaned back to help her finish the job, throwing his white shirt on the floor beside the couch. Darcy looked up at his chest, sitting up, pushing him back into a kneeling position. "Oh, Jack…"

She knew he was going to be well built, but she hadn't quite expected this. This was the body of a god or a movie star, perfectly toned, strong and beautiful…and covered in scars. He heaved in and out, panting, trying to catch his breath.

"What happened to you?" she murmured, her heart hurting for what he'd endured, the crisscrosses of scar tissue covering the expanse of muscle.

"I'll tell you someday." He took her hand, flattening it over his chest to reassure her. "None of it hurts anymore. All of it was needed to become who I am today."

He let go of her hand and she started touching him with tentative, then confident fingers, splaying them out as if to measure him. "How do you keep this up?"

He looked at her face, which must have been kiss-bruised and heavy-lidded. He flinched as she ran her fingers through the black hair on his chest. His ragged voice held a note of humor. "Darcy, I don't date, I work…I work for…ohhh…"

His voice trailed off as she leaned forward, pressing her lips against one angry slash of white under his left nipple. He lay back slowly, drawing her with him until she was lying across his chest, peppering his torso with kisses and licks. Finally she straddled his lap and bent her head, finding his lips and kissing him gently, tenderly, like she would if she loved him, if she had always loved him.

He moved his hands down to the bottom of her sweater and tugged it up over her head then reached up to cup her breasts. Darcy shuddered with pleasure as her nipples tightened instantly into pert peaks under his palm. He pushed the thin lace aside and leaned up, taking one in his mouth to suckle strongly, making her writhe against him, moaning in pleasure-pain. He moved to the other nipple to do the same, and Darcy couldn't help gasping at the sharpness of the pressure, the heat of his lips on her sensitive skin. She ran her hands through his black hair, holding him against her breasts as he licked and circled. She grabbed handfuls of his hair, eyes closed, heart beating out of her chest.

He finally eased her down onto her back and knelt on the floor beside her, leaning over her, kissing a path from her breasts down over her belly to the waist of her jeans. He unbuttoned and unzipped them, slipping his hand under the waistband, under her panties, flattening his palm over the soft, springy hairs there. She breathed in sharply and Jack looked quickly at her face.

Please let me, Darcy. Please let me touch you there.

How could she possibly say no? She had never felt anything as exciting, as hot, in her entire life. It was like she'd die if he didn't move his fingers lower, if he didn't touch the secret parts of her. She closed her eyes in acquiescence and he moved his hand lower, one finger searching for the little button of pleasure hidden in the sensitive folds. When he found it, she bucked against his hand lightly, feeling her insides slicken in pleasure as a whimper escaped her throat. He rubbed lightly in hypnotic circles and then up and down, the occasional friction of his fingernail on her clit making her almost see stars.

His thumb took over his ministrations and she felt one of his fingers move slower, stopping briefly at the opening of her sex before entering her body, sliding in slowly, the hot, wet walls of muscle clinging to the welcome intrusion. He moved the finger all the way in then withdrew it slowly, his thumb still circling the hardening nub with increasing pressure. The world started swirling and Darcy opened her eyes.

Please, Jack. Help me.

A second finger joined the first, hooking forward, and pressing against the wall of her sex as his thumb rubbed the sensitive folds right above his moving fingers. Darcy threw her arm over her eyes, moaning as pleasure and urgency increased to such a climax that her body exploded and she bucked hard against his hand, moaning his name, stars bursting behind her eyes.

At the same time, it was as though her heart exploded too, and she felt the full, unbridled, unfettered force of her feelings for Jack Beauloup—feelings that hadn't lessened over the long years away from him, but had amplified to such a pitch that they crashed over her like sound, like waves, like certainty in a coupling fraught with ambiguity. She had argued with him about the binding, but she knew in that moment, as her heart contracted with the rest of her body—she was bound to Jack. She belonged to him just as she always had.

He moved from the floor to sit on the couch, gently lifting her limp head onto his lap then coaxing her into his arms, cradling her face against his chest.

"Oh, my God," she whispered, curling up against him and finally opening her eyes. She tried to catch her breath as shudder after shudder still racked her body.

"Easy, baby," he said softly, stroking her hair and rubbing her back lightly. He pushed her hair gently off her forehead and kissed her tenderly.

She leaned back from his chest to catch his eyes.

That was the first time I ever…

I know.

He smiled and kissed her lips gently, nudging her head back to his chest. Darcy could hear the racing of his heart. The evidence of his arousal was still rampant in his lap and he was probably aching. She leaned back to catch his eyes again, her starched New England sensibilities deeply relieved that she didn't have to articulate her thoughts aloud in order for him to hear them.

But what about you? Are you…okay?

I'm fine, Darcy. Better than fine. I got to watch you…

But you—

I can wait.

With infinite tenderness it dawned on her that he had stopped when she had climaxed, and hadn't pushed her to satisfy him in turn. She wondered what kind of strength it took to take care of her and deny himself. Phillip had never been overly concerned about her pleasure when they'd been intimate, but even including several college flings and a one-night stand with a visiting professor from England, Darcy hadn't known what she was missing. She was thirty-five years old, and tonight she'd had her first orgasm.

Darcy reached down for her sweater and pulled it over her head, adjusting her bra back over her nipples, catching his frank assessment of her breasts before they slipped out of view.

He exhaled loudly and grinned at her.

"That was…" She was at a loss for words and suddenly a little self-conscious.

"Yeah, it was."

She smiled back shyly. "I should get going."

"Wow. Just like that?" He reached out and took her hand, his face tired but happy. "Stay with me."

She ran her other hand through her messy hair then put her palm gently on his cheek. "I shouldn't."

"Please stay." He reached up to cover her hand, leaning into it, closing his eyes.

She looked at his impossibly perfect chest and messy hair, the gentle way he held her hand against his face. *Couldn't she stay? Couldn't he carry her up to his room and couldn't she stay all night? Couldn't he make love to her over and over again on his big bed—?*

No. Not yet. Her body wanted every inch of him, but her head still had to adjust to his return, his strangeness, the sheer force of their connection.

"Jack. I'm not ready yet." She shook her head, giving him a small smile. "*Attends-moi?*"

"Thief. Stealing your brother's line."

"What he doesn't know won't hurt him."

"Come back tomorrow? Come for a walk in the woods."

She beamed at him, chuckling softly. "You know my weak spot."

"I'm counting on it," he whispered.

"What time?"

"I'll pick you up at sunrise."

"Sunrise," she agreed, before kissing him softly and saying good-night.

Chapter 9

J OY COMETH WITH THE DAWN.
Darcy woke up to the lavender early morning light filtering in
through the voluminous, white cottage curtains on either side of the
windows in her bedroom. She stretched her arms straight back over her
head until her knuckles found the headboard and curled, then she snug-
gled back under the thick down comforter and sighed.

Jack.

She smiled drowsily and turned to hug her pillow, her body hot and
sensitive and tingling. Her dreams of him had been relentless.

Oh, Jack.

She stretched again then placed her hand on her thigh, sweeping it
slowly along the outside of her hips, to her waist, grazing the side of her
breast, over the bunched fabric of her nightgown to her neck, where her
fingers found the pulse point he had touched so long ago. The same place
to which he had pressed his lips in the garage last night. She kept her
fingers there for a moment, as if in communion with him.

She thought of him squatting in front of the fire, firm thighs straining
against the confining denim of his jeans. She knew if she had knelt beside
him and touched him there, he would have been hard and warm. She
remembered him blowing on his hot stew, lips pursed but still soft, just
how they were when she kissed him. She moved her fingers to her lips
and closed her eyes, searching for the physical imprint of his lips brushing
hers all those years ago. For the briefest moment, a thrill shot through
her, as she remembered: *really* remembered. His fingers pressing lightly
on her throat. Phantom lips brushing hers in the dark. A trembling hand
reaching for hers.

Then Darcy moaned softly, memories of last night closing the gap of so many years, flooding her mind, and she closed her eyes, watching the scenes as if from a movie. It was one thing to know that theoretically, your body was capable of bucking and shuddering in climax…it was something else entirely to experience it for the first time.

She swung her legs out of bed and headed into her bathroom to shower and brush her teeth. As the hot water pounded against her sensitive skin, she thought about his theory on their first kiss—that it somehow bound them to each other. Darcy knew firsthand how much the Métis culture influenced Willow on a very real level and Willow was only one-quarter Métis. If Darcy truly cared for Jack, she would try to make space in her heart—and more importantly, in her head—for his family's traditions, and stop labeling them as superstition.

Anyway, she considered, as she pulled on some soft, broken-in jeans, a white t-shirt, a navy and white plaid flannel shirt and a heavy, navy blue wool sweater, there could be worse things than a sweltering hot man with a gorgeous house being bound to you.

Darcy braided her hair into a single French plait that trailed down past her shoulders and pulled on some cotton hiking socks. Not to mention their chemistry. She always thought it was cheesy when authors wrote about characters setting off sparks between them, but for the first time in her life, she understood what that meant. She remembered the bonfires they'd light in her backyard at the end of summer…the way the sparks would crackle and snap, tiny particles of fire dancing, floating up into the air toward the sky to mingle with the stars. That's how it felt to be with Jack. That's how it had always felt to be anywhere near him.

A week. It had only been a week since she looked out the windows of the Second Congregational Church and saw Jack standing at the edge of Proctor Woods. And yet it felt like so much longer. Darcy looked at herself in the mirror.

"It's because you waited for him for so long," she murmured to herself.

And while she was still trying to figure out some of the mysteries that accompanied Jack's reemergence in her life, Darcy found she cared less and less about the intricate web of whys in their relationship and more about the feelings she had for him—the whole and complete way he made her feel—for the first time in her life.

She walked downstairs quietly and scribbled a note for Willow, whom she hadn't seen since dinner on Thursday night.

With Jack. Back tonight.

She grabbed her sunglasses and a banana then ran back to the kitchen counter and added a saucy:

Maybe.

She grinned at the note then went to sit on her porch steps until Jack picked her up.

"SO, YOU LIVED THERE? WHEN you went to high school here?" Jack had picked her up and driven her right back to his house, suggesting they climb the small peak on his land before returning to the lodge for lunch. She followed behind him as he led the way and she couldn't have wished for a better view, frequently sighing as he maneuvered over a fallen tree or boulder, offering his hand to her far more often than she actually needed it. The wonders of nature, aside from Jack's incredibly toned ass, were completely lost on her.

He was dressed similarly to Darcy in two or three layers, the outermost of which was a brown leather field jacket with a black corduroy collar. The way the coat picked up the color of his eyes made her heart smile with pleasure. But presently, it was the back of his light blue, worn jeans—and the way they molded to the muscles of his legs—that was capturing her attention.

"Yep. This land's been in my family for a long, long time. Since before Proctor Woods was…Proctor Woods."

"What was it before?"

"*Bois Loup Garou,*" he said matter-of-factly, navigating another fallen tree trunk.

Darcy tilted her head to the side, watching the muscles in his thigh flex as he made his way over. She sighed. Again.

"Huh. I had no idea. Other than the Abenaki Indians, I thought the Proctors and Turners were the first people here."

"Do you know what Abenaki means, Darcy?"

"Nope." She pushed a branch out of her path, and worked to keep up with him.

"*Wabum* means light and *a'ki* means earth. Light of the earth. Abenaki. But the French called them *Natio Luporem*, the nation of wolves."

"Huh," said Darcy, pausing to catch her breath. "The Métis are half Abenaki and half French, right?"

"That's right." He had walked several paces farther than Darcy but stopped and turned around, smiling at her from a slightly higher elevation. "How'd you get so smart?"

"You haven't heard? I'm *very* smart. I'll have you know I'm a doctor."

He swung the backpack off his pack and rooted around for a water bottle, handing it to her. "Can you keep going, Doc Turner? I want to make the summit before the sun gets too high."

Darcy took a swig and wiped her mouth with the back of her hand. "Don't call me Doc Turner. That was my Dad's handle."

"His…handle?"

"He worked up on Mt. Washington. In the observatory. MWOBS. When we radioed up the mountain, that's what they called him."

"I don't remember him being at the wedding on Saturday."

"He wasn't. He passed away a few years ago." She was quiet for a moment, thinking about his prematurely weathered face and twinkling blue eyes. "He spent more time at MWOBS than any other single place on the planet."

"I'm sorry," he said softly, taking her hand again. "Must have loved it up there."

"Yeah. He was more interested in stormy weather than spending time with his family." She dropped his hand. "That's unfair, I guess. He loved what he did. He was good at it."

"You must have admired him on some level," said Jack, pushing a stray strand of light hair behind her ear tenderly. "You're a scientist. Like him. Maybe you didn't love everything about him, but you still loved him?"

She didn't want to talk about her complicated relationship with her father anymore. She took his hand and pulled him so they'd start walking again.

"What about your parents, Jack? I don't ever remember meeting them."

"They live north of Quebec."

"Sisters and brothers?"

"They're all up there," Jack answered without elaborating. Darcy decided not to push him.

"Your parents gave you this land?"

"Not technically. I told them I wanted to move back and they said that the old lodge hadn't been touched in two decades. When I got here, the garage was in a heap. My guess was too many heavy snows. The lodge wasn't in such bad shape. Lots of overgrowth and the squirrels and raccoons had gotten in there. But Amory is a fast worker."

"He has a good crew too," Darcy agreed, pride in her voice. Amory had eschewed traditional education in favor of starting his own contracting business. Her parents had been skeptical at first, but they had to admit that Amory was a hard worker and he'd chosen a field in which he could excel. He was one of the most popular contractors in Carlisle and the Colebrook area and on his way to building a solid, reputable business.

"So, did I understand you right when you said that the French were here before Proctors?"

"Carlisle wasn't settled by migrating Bostonians until the late 1700s. The French and Métis settlers were here as early as the 1600s."

"Whew! And your family somehow held onto this land?"

"Something like that," he grumbled.

"Beauloup…Like *Bois Loup Garou*? Wait. *Beau* means beautiful, right? Beautiful what?"

"Wolf. Beautiful wolf." He turned and faced her, biting his lower lip, his face tense. He chuckled, but it sounded tinny and didn't match his expression. "Try having that surname at grade school in Quebec. Endless hours of amusement for your schoolmates."

"I think it fits," she said gently, smiling at him encouragingly. "I love the Métis names, the way they honor the natural world."

She could have sworn she saw him wince before turning around quickly and making his way around a boulder.

"Jack?" she called. She didn't see him up ahead on the other side of the boulder. "Jack?"

She hurried toward him, yelping as his arm snaked out from his hiding place behind the boulder and pulled her up against him. It took her a second to catch her breath, and she leaned back in his arms, grinning, still panting from exertion and surprise.

He smiled at her. "You make me happy."

She tilted her head to the side, looking at his dark hair and brown eyes under thick black lashes. She reached up to touch the lightly bearded skin of his cheek. "I love that you're Métis, and you have pride in who you are. I love…it."

He stared at her, furrowing his brows in confusion or remorse, but all she could hear was *Darcy, Darcy, Darcy*. He didn't want her to know what he was thinking, so she looked down. One of his arms released her and she felt his finger under her chin, tilting her face back up to his.

His eyes closed as he swooped down to close his lips over hers, his tongue parting the soft seam to make love to hers. Touching, stroking, his hand caressed her jaw as he kept her face at the perfect angle for him to kiss her. Darcy's hands were trapped between them, but she flattened them against his chest and felt the heat of his skin through the layers of his two shirts and jacket, and she swore she could feel the pounding of his heart.

Abandoning her mouth, he kissed her jaw, pressing his lips against her neck until his teeth found the soft skin of her earlobe. He tugged on it gently, his breath warm and soft in her ear, and a shiver of pleasure made her back arch, pushing her breasts against him.

She heard him chuckle softly and his teeth let go.

"You *like* that."

Darcy leaned back, opening her eyes.

"I guess so," she sighed.

He chuckled again and let go of her, taking her hand.

"What exactly did you and Phillip *do*? Play tiddlywinks?" His tone when he said Phillip's name wasn't lost on her. Darcy understood. The thought of Jack with another woman was enough to make her sick.

"Yes, Jack. You guessed it. We played lots of tiddlywinks. That was our favorite."

"Okay, Sass Mouth."

"*Sass Mouth?*" she asked, grinning up at him.

He stopped walking and his grip on her hand got suddenly tighter.

"Jack?"

"Shhhh."

She looked up at his face. He closed his eyes and breathed through his nose as he had done before their encounter with the bear. He dropped her hand and put his arm around her waist, hauling her up against his side.

"What is it?" she whispered. "I don't hear anything."

"Quiet," he murmured.

"*Awena kéya?*" he growled low and slow. "*Tánde kéya? Shipawaytay.*"

Darcy could feel her pulse in her ears, as she scanned the forest before them, feeling a measure of safety with her back up against Jack's side. She could feel how wide her eyes were, burning from staying open, but clearly Jack felt there was a threat to them.

"*AWENA KÉYA?*" he repeated, and his arm tightened around her like a vise.

It would take Darcy a while to put together what exactly happened next, but she heard the roaring growl of the wolf at almost the same time her body hit the ground. One minute, she was safely pressed against

Jack's body. The next, she tasted the dirt on her lips, felt the pine needles beneath her hands and under her knees.

When she looked up, she saw Jack hunched over, locked in a face to face standoff with a gray wolf, and the only thing between her and the bared teeth of the angry, snarling beast. She watched in horror as the wolf charged Jack, but with an almost unbelievable strength and grace, he caught the wolf by its neck, hauling it up and over his head like a puppy and turning once before throwing the entire one-hundred-pound animal into the trunk of a nearby tree. Darcy heard the vague whimper of the injured wolf before she felt Jack's hands under her arms, raising her to a standing position.

"Quick. I think it's a cast-off beta, but I don't know for sure. We have to go."

"Wolves don't come this f-far south," she murmured, taking his hand and being pulled behind him. She could barely catch her breath. "D-did you th-throw that wolf into a tr-tree?"

"I did what I had to do."

"You picked it up and th-threw it."

"Darcy, come on. We have to move faster."

He kept up a fast pace, just short of a run, and didn't ease up until they'd been walking fast for at least twenty minutes. Finally Darcy yanked her hand back. "Gimme a…b-break!"

He turned to look at her, fishing the water bottle back out of his pack and handing it to her, then looking behind her, into the woods.

"We're not having very good luck with big game."

"I'm in the w-woods all the time and I n-never see bears or wolves!" She took another long sip and a deep breath then handed back the bottle and rested her hands on her knees, panting. "What did you say to it? Before it lunged?"

"I asked where it was. I asked who it was. I told it to leave."

"How'd that work out for you?"

"Very funny." He was looking at the woods in back of her. "I don't think it's following us. I think we're okay."

"Following us? You threw it into a tree. It's probably dead."

"Better it than you."

"Thanks."

"I'll never let anything hurt you, Darcy. It's a—"

"—sacred pledge. I know. You're stronger than I would have guessed."

His brows furrowed briefly as he dropped her eyes, putting the bottle away and securing the pack on his back.

Darcy was distracted by a drop of water on her arm. One drop…two. Three drops. Soon, her arm was covered with drops, and she could hear the pitter-patter of rainfall throughout the woods around them.

"Well, that's *great,*" he sighed, putting out his hand to her.

"How far are we from your house?" she asked, squinting through the increasingly fat raindrops that were coming down harder and faster.

"Another ten or fifteen minutes? If we're fast?" he guessed.

"There's pretty good tree cover," she said, trying to look on the bright side. His mood was clouding over as fast as the sky.

"We're going to get soaked," he said, looking up at the sky with a sour expression. He shook his head and she was sprayed by more raindrops. "Come on."

They walked in silence the rest of the way back to the lodge and Jack was right—they were completely soaked by the time they reached his house. Darcy could hear the river rushing by the lodge as they got closer, and it was one of her favorite sounds, but she was suddenly very tired and nothing sounded as nice as curling up in some dry clothes.

Huh. Dry clothes. *Well, that would be nice.* If she had some.

Jack unlocked the front door, holding it open so she could precede him inside. In the foyer, she took off her drenched wool sweater, hanging it on a wooden peg and watching the drops of water fall to the floor in rivulets. She shrugged out of her flannel shirt, which was similarly soaked and hung it up beside her sweater. She bent down to untie her shoes and took off her squishy socks, wringing them out over the flagstones and laying them flat across her boots.

She looked up at Jack, hugging herself and shivering.

"You're cold," he said, standing to face her in soaked jeans and a damp grey t-shirt.

"I d-didn't think th-that," she teased, through chattering teeth.

"I know you didn't. You're shivering." He grinned at her. "I don't want you to get sick. How about a warm shower?"

She nodded her head gratefully, her tongue darting out to lick a raindrop off her lip as she looked up at him.

Want some company?

Her cheeks flushed crimson as she heard his voice in her head, and she looked away quickly.

"Darce?"

When she glanced at him, he smiled. "I was just kidding."

"Oh." She chuckled nervously and he took her hand, leading her up the stairs, and she felt just the littlest bit disappointed. "Stop teasing me."

"You can use the guest bathroom. There are towels in the cabinet. If you'll throw your clothes out into the hall, I'll put them in the dryer. You can borrow my bathrobe…if that's okay?"

"Thanks, Jack."

"No problem."

He showed her to the bathroom door, pushing it open for her, and she headed inside, flicking on the light. Without thinking, she poked her head back out and called to his retreating form.

"Jack!"

He turned to face her, but didn't make a move toward her.

"About the shower…"

"You *do* want company?" he asked.

"No." She smiled at him to soften her lie. "Well, sort of. But—"

"Just get warm." He winked at her, and disappeared into his bedroom.

Darcy closed the door behind her, sighing, as she looked at her wet-rat hair in the mirror. Damp wisps were pasted onto her face and flattened on her head.

You should have just said yes! Idiot!

She shucked off her cold, clingy jeans and pulled her shirt over her head, throwing both into the hall. She added her bra and panties to the pile, relieved she'd worn fresh, new underwear.

It suddenly occurred to her that he'd know she was naked under his bathrobe.

That should certainly make for a charged afternoon.

Afternoon. She looked at her watch. Sure enough, it was noon. She counted back. He had picked her up at six o'clock. After the drive and the walk, it shouldn't be any later than ten o'clock, which she felt was generous. Noon made no sense. Time was going too fast. Again.

Darcy unbraided her hair, turned on the water, and stepped into the steamy shower, letting the water course down her cold, weary body. She had long accepted soul flight as part of her life and she was even coming to terms with binding kisses, Eyespeak, and Jack's strange rapport with wild animals. But losing time still bothered her. Very much. Plus, it seemed to be increasing incrementally. On Saturday, she lost about an hour. Last night, about an hour and a half. Today she'd already lost two hours. It made no sense, Métis or otherwise, and she intended to get to the bottom of it.

When she finished with her shower, she found a soft, navy blue flannel bathrobe waiting for her, draped across the bed. She toweled off with a big, fluffy towel, then ran her fingers over the robe, imagining the times it had pressed up against Jack's hard, naked body. She pressed the fabric to her face and inhaled deeply, smelling the essence of Jack—his aftershave, laundry soap, and fresh air all mixed together. It made her knees go weak.

She wrapped herself in the too-big bathrobe and tied it securely with the cord. She found a pair of thick, gray wool socks underneath and smiled at his thoughtfulness as she pulled the warm socks over her feet. There was a comb in the bathroom and she combed out her long reddish-blond hair until it was slick and smooth, and then pushed it behind her ears.

She still looked a little bit like a drowned rat but at least she was a warm, clean drowned rat, wrapped in Jack Beauloup's bathrobe...and nothing else.

Chapter 10

H E WAS SITTING ON THE living room couch, and on the leather trunk was a tray with two steaming mugs. The rain was still falling in sheets outside, making it dim in the living room, except for the golden light of the fireplace. Jack's feet were bare, propped up next to the tray, and he wore a pair of warm, soft-looking jeans and a plaid flannel shirt, buttoned once or twice, leaving very little of his gorgeous chest to Darcy's imagination. He turned his head to watch her pad into the room and smiled, holding out a hand to her.

Damn, you look good in my bathrobe.

Is that right?

Never seen anything that looked as good as you right now.

She took his hand and he pulled her down next to him.

"You smell good too," he whispered, bending his head over her hand and kissing it, then leaning back to trace the blue veins that forked on the back of her hand. "Hot cocoa?"

"Sure." She took her hand back and leaned forward to take one of the two cups between her hands, then scooted back into the couch corner opposite him, putting her feet up on the trunk and crossing them. He watched as the bathrobe parted, baring her legs up to her thighs.

"You're way too far away, Darcy Turner."

"If I come any closer I doubt we'll end up talking much and I want to talk."

"Why do women always want to talk?"

"An observation based on your vast experience with women?"

"What makes you think I have vast experience with women?"

"I don't want to give you a big head."

His gaze dropped to her legs again then back to her eyes.

Too late.

That's not what I meant and you know it.

"Then what do you mean?"

"Well…" Her eyes swept his body, starting at his feet, following the muscled strength of his legs, lingering at the top of his legs where she saw a bulge that made her bite back a small grin before taking in the hard contours of the chest that peeked through his shirt to his neck to his face. She wet her lips as she met his eyes.

Jesus, Darcy!

"What?" she teased.

Do it again and see what happens. I dare you.

The look in his eyes sobered her. If she kept teasing him, he was going to jump on her and she knew it. Part of her wanted that, but she didn't want to get sidetracked again and miss an opportunity to understand him—to understand *them*—better. She looked away.

"I can't imagine it's hard for you to find female companionship, Jack. You're charming, you have means. You're fun and funny and…"

She smiled into his eyes.

…you make me feel safe and special and beautiful.

Maybe that's how I am with you. Only you. Maybe there weren't any others that mattered. Ever.

"Mathematics says it's unlikely."

He leaned forward and picked up his hot chocolate, blowing the steam away. "Screw mathematics. Not everything can be boiled down to neat formulas and explanations and proven theories, Darcy. There's more in this world that *doesn't* make sense than does. Sometimes you have to have faith."

She watched him, aware of the edge that had crept into his voice but unwilling to allow it to make her back down. "Okay. Well, then, you're not going to like my next observation…something else has been bothering me that *doesn't* make sense. I think the time we spend together goes faster than normal time."

He blew on his cocoa then took a long sip.

"Jack? Have you noticed that too?"

He nodded.

"So, it's actually happening."

He nodded again.

"Any idea why? Any theories? Proven or unproven?"

He looked up at her.

"We're different. It takes a lot of energy to keep us together. It has to come from somewhere."

Her heart twisted that he should feel so different from her just because he was Métis. She shifted closer to him until her hip nudged against his. He put his cup back down on the trunk, and then took hers and did the same.

"We're not that different, Jack. Please stop thinking that we're so different just because of our backgrounds. We're both *human beings*."

As soon as the words were out of her mouth, his eyes seized hers and she perceived the fathomless, intense, deeply conflicted emotion behind them as the copper flecks brightened before her, swirling and angry, turning his eyes from brown to gold. She tried to hear him, but either his mind was blank or he was blocking her from him, because all she could hear was a roaring—a growling, guttural roaring in her head.

"Jack?" she whispered, her breath quickening with worry at his expression, his eyes, the void of roaring instead of his soft, low voice.

He lunged toward her, his lips connecting directly with hers, with such force and passion that their teeth scraped together. Turned on by his urgency, she wound her arms around his neck, pulling him down on top of her, wanting to feel the hot weight of his body pressed against hers. He kept his hands on her face, and the gentleness with which he held her cheeks tempered the passion of his lips, which demanded and plundered greedily, sweeping her mouth with his tongue over and over again.

One of his hands slid languidly down the contours of her jaw, as he took his time to feel her, explore her, sliding to the pulse point on her neck where his fingers rested for a moment before sweeping lower and pushing the bathrobe aside to cup his hand over her bare breast. The sensation was so searing, hot, and exciting, Darcy arched up against him, moaning into his mouth, and his kiss intensified as he gently pinched her already-firm nipple between his thumb and forefinger and she cried out with the sweet sharpness of his attentions.

He abandoned her lips, kissing a trail of heat from her mouth to her jaw then down her neck. He leaned back, untying the cord at Darcy's waist and pushed the sides of his bathrobe away from her breasts.

She watched his eyes devour her breasts before he met her eyes with hunger and deep emotion.

Darcy. You're so beautiful, it hurts me to look at you. Just like it did then.

He was referring to himself in high school. And even though she had already figured it out, the sweetness of their connection, the long-unrequited thirst finally quenched in his company made tears fill her eyes and they fluttered closed as she reached up to thread her hands through his thick, black hair, drawing his head down to her breasts. She felt the heat of his mouth, the slick wet fire of his tongue on her nipple as his hand covered her other breast, and she threw her head back, small sounds of pleasure escaping her lips. He moved his lips to her other breast, but she was so surprised by the sudden, sharp tug of his teeth on her nipple that her knee reflexively shot up, accidentally connecting with his groin. Her eyes flew open as he cried out in pain, rolling off her and falling onto the floor.

Darcy sat up, disoriented at first, pulling the robe around her. She found him on his back, staring up at the ceiling with both hands covering his groin.

"Oh, my God! Oh, my God, Jack, I hurt you!"

Darcy scrambled off the couch to kneel beside his head, cringing at his red face and the tear that rolled from his eye into his hairline.

"Jack!" She used her thumb to gently swipe another tear away, cringing as she watched him try to take a deep breath and fail.

"Ooooo-uh," he groaned, swallowing deliberately. She watched his throat bob slowly, as his eyes closed and reopened in pain.

"Are you okay?" she asked in a small, embarrassed, deeply sorry voice.

"Gimme a sec, Darce. I wasn't expecting that."

"Do you—do you need ice? Or something?"

He moved his hands, bracing himself to sit up.

"How about massage?" he quipped.

"Would that...help?" she asked timidly to his back.

"I'm kidding." He leaned back on his arms, his legs spread out in front of him. His voice was low and still a little strangled and breathy. "No. I take that back. If you're offering, I'll take a rain check."

Darcy felt like such a complete and total idiot. Frustrated tears filled her eyes and she sat back on the edge of the couch, while he stayed seated on the floor. She didn't know what to do. She had hurt him, and more, she had ruined their beautiful moment together. Part of her felt like she should find his dryer, put on her clothes, and leave.

He struggled to his knees then shifted back to the edge of the couch, a couple of feet away from her.

She couldn't bear to look at him.

"Darcy?"

She knew if she spoke, the tears would fall.

"Darcy, I'll be fine in a few minutes. Wasn't even the worst shot I've ever taken to the nuts. Not by a long shot. Just…unexpected. Hey…what's going on?"

She swiped at her eyes. "I should go."

His hand shot out and grabbed her wrist. "No."

This only made her tears fall faster.

"Don't go. It was just an accident."

She slid next to him.

"I'm so sorry," she sobbed, all of the confusion and frustration and the intensity of her feelings for this man bursting and drizzling down her face in a wet, pathetic mess.

He groaned as he put his arms around her waist and sat back against the couch, pulling her up against his side and kissing the top of her head. "No, baby. Please don't cry."

She leaned her cheek on his shoulder and wept, as he rubbed her back gently, his other hand hovering protectively over his lap.

"That f-felt so good, and I kicked you in the b-balls, and r-ruined it," she sputtered through more tears. "I should just go h-home."

He leaned back and put his hands on her face, turning it up to see his, searching her watery eyes.

"Darcy. Listen to me. There is no scenario—*none*—in which I can imagine not wanting you beside me. Not right now. Not ever." He rubbed the tears away with the pad of his thumb.

She swallowed, her heart fluttering at the earnestness of his words, at once captivated and frightened by them, by the faith he seemed to have in them, the absoluteness of his regard for her. She rested her head on his chest and he resumed rubbing her back. Could she trust him? History proved otherwise.

"But, you *left* me," she argued quietly. "Where did you go when you left me?"

"I got in my car that night, as soon as the play was over, and I drove north. I went straight to the pack elders in our Bloodlands north of Quebec."

"Bloodlands?"

"It's what we call our native land, our homeland. I asked about the binding. How it was possible that I should be *bound* to you, when tradition states I should be bound to one of my own. I knew it had *happened*. But I didn't trust it. I didn't understand it. I'd never heard of one of us becoming bound to one of you. But—"

"Should I be offended?"

"Why?"

"You talk about 'us' like we're a whole other race or something."

"It just had never happened before…that I knew of. So—"

"No Métis ever married a—"

"Stop interrupting."

She furrowed her brows, snuggling closer to him.

"But to answer your question…sure, you can ignore the binding, but you can't choose for yourself and you can't change it once it happens. It's for life. And if you ignore it, you, um, you miss out on, um, some things."

"Like what?"

"Like Eyespeak and, um, you called it 'soul flight' and 'going inside.' Like the connection I have with you, Darcy. Like last night when you…"

Darcy jerked her head back to look at him, eyes wide.

…when you climaxed. You've never experienced that with anyone else before, have you?

No. Wait, Jack…Have you? Have you ever had an orgasm?

She cringed against the bald delivery of her rushed thoughts but held his eyes bravely.

Maybe on my own…but, no. Not with a woman.

Never?

He shook his head, his cheeks coloring pink under his thick, black stubble.

Can you…with me?

He glanced down at his abused lap and made an annoyed face before catching her eyes again. *I think so. But we'll have to wait just a little longer to find out.*

Darcy's heart pounded as she leaned her head back down on his chest and felt his hand stroking her back. His belief in this binding was so firmly founded that he didn't believe he could climax with another woman other than her? Again, she was simultaneously enchanted and terrified by the absoluteness of his beliefs, but if she hadn't had enough reasons to want him, now her body *ached* to fuse with his, to find out if she could give him something that no other woman had ever been able to. It was heady, this power she had over him, whether it was actual or in his head. It made her heart beat faster and her belly leap with excitement.

He continued, "Anyway, sure, I've heard of others marrying—or just sleeping with—someone they aren't bound to. But, I'd never heard of anyone being *bound* to someone different from us. Until you.

"The elders didn't like it. They acknowledged it, but they didn't like it. They encouraged me not to see you again and they felt sure that my infatuation with you would calm down. Even if it took a while, they were sure I'd eventually forget you.

"I tried. Oh, God, Darcy, I tried. I tried so hard to forget you. I practiced meditation and self-control, and sometimes I even felt like I was making some headway. But the binding's forever. In my heart, I always returned to you. I learned that early on. I…"

"What do you mean, *early on?*"

"It was a few months after we kissed. Right around Thanksgiving. Suddenly it felt like someone had reached into my chest and was trying to rip out my still-beating heart. I couldn't breathe and I was starting to lose consciousness when I concentrated on the memory of your face, and I…I don't know—yeah, I do. I can't totally explain it, but I smelled coconut. I smelled disinfectant and coconut. I know it sounds crazy. But, I smelled those things and I could *feel* you. I could feel your heartbeat somewhere in the world. I could feel how sad you were in that moment, and even though I felt sad too, I could breathe again. I could breathe because I could feel you."

"I know what you're talking about. I remember that day," Darcy murmured, as she remembered sobbing on Willow's shoulder in her high school bathroom. "It was the first time I went inside. I could feel you too."

"I tried to love other women. It was no good. I finally realized that if you weren't in my life, it was meaningless. And I didn't understand *how* we were bound to each other, but I decided to stop fighting it. So, I made a plan to come back to Carlisle. To find you. And it took twenty years, but here I am."

The rain still hadn't let up and the sun was lowering in the sky. It was late afternoon now. The fire, immune to the racing time around it, still crackled and snapped, burning with strength and power, casting the room in a warm, golden light. Darcy leaned back to look at him.

"You came back to Carlisle for me?"

"*Only* for you. I would never have returned if not for you. But I'm bound to you, Darcy Turner. I belong to you. Until I die."

Darcy's skin rippled—a physical manifestation from the pleasure of his words, and the last of her resolve melted away as her brain finally accepted what her heart had always known: the binding was real and true, and she belonged to Jack with the same force and depth that he belonged to her.

"Jack," she whispered, holding his eyes, "make love to me."

A dozen emotions shifted across his face: elation, anguish, hope, despair...*want*. His tongue darted out to wet his lips. *Want*. "Are you sure?"

She scooted away from him, lying back on the couch and pulling on the cord of the bathrobe until it opened loosely. She heard him take a ragged breath and she smiled at him, holding his gaze.

I'm sure.

His eyes smoldered from his seat on the opposite side of the couch, but he didn't move, as if frozen by the reality that what he wanted most in the world was now being offered to him. Darcy could see his hesitation, so she leaned up on her elbows, putting her foot on his lap, gently grazing the growing bulge in his jeans, as if their mishap before had never happened. As she leaned up, the bathrobe fell back from her shoulders, revealing her entire body, bathed in firelight, offered to him. Jack shifted to a kneeling position between her legs and picked up her foot, kissing it, nibbling along the edges, up past her ankle to her leg.

Darcy took a deep breath, tingling with anticipation and lay back, closing her eyes, trembling with her awareness of him, her need of him. His lips slid, hot and wet, up her leg, occasionally blowing on a kiss, making shivers dart up and down her leg. Past her knee to her thigh, he laid his cheek on her thigh for a moment, letting her get used to him moving toward her so intimately.

He kissed the skin high on the inside of her thigh and she bucked.

"Jack!" she gasped, bracing herself up on her elbows.

He looked up at her surprised expression and grinned.

"You've never? No one's ever—"

She shook her head, eyes wide. He leaned up, lowering his clothed body over the length of her naked one and kissed her lips, biting on the lower one, sucking on it, loving it, while she unbuttoned his shirt and pushed it down his arms, marveling at the thick, hard biceps she found underneath. He pulled the shirt off and threw it on the floor.

She arched up so that her breasts were flush against his chest and felt his breath hitch. "You're so soft, Darcy. So beautiful, so soft..."

He bent to take one pert nipple in his mouth, sucking on it until Darcy felt like she would scream with the pleasure-pain of the sensation, then moved to the other, sucking then blowing on it until a strong, throbbing tension started building in her belly. Her breathing was ragged and louder cries and moans of pleasure filled the space between them, her fingers threading and twisting through his hair.

Jack's lips moved lower until he knelt between her legs again.

"Let me do it, baby," he murmured in a thick, deeply aroused voice with his rough, bearded cheek against her belly. "Let me make you feel good."

He kissed her thigh again, trailing feather-light kisses into the apex of her legs, spreading her with his fingers, and finding her throbbing sex with his tongue. As he licked, sucked, and kissed, Darcy clenched her eyes shut, making mewling sounds in the back of her throat, one arm thrown over her eyes, and the other cupping her own breast. She moaned loudly, a strangled, keening sound, then threw her head back and arched her body toward him, pressing her clit into his face.

"Jaaaaaack…," she gasped, as her insides rushed hot and wet, and her muscles convulsed over and over again.

"Oh, my God…. Oh, my God…." She sucked in air and panted, inert, riding wave after wave of pleasure.

Jack's lips found hers as he slid back up her body, his chest lowering gently onto the sensitive tips of her breasts. He brushed his lips across hers once, twice. She wished she could move. She wished she could respond, but she felt like a ragdoll, like all of her muscles were temporarily unavailable.

"You okay, Darce?" he asked, brushing her hair away from her forehead.

"It just gets better…"

"Mmmm," he murmured.

She breathed in deeply and sighed, opening her eyes to look at him as her head finally started to clear. She gave him a lazy smile and leaned up to wiggle her arms out of the bathrobe and he watched her, nostrils flaring, breath audible.

She reached up to touch his face with her fingers, trailing them down his neck, over the hard muscles of his chest, leaning forward to suck on his nipples as he had sucked on hers. He gasped, plunging his hands into her hair and throwing his head back. She sucked and licked, gently using her teeth, until he put his hands under her arms and pushed her away. His eyes were melted gold when she looked at him.

Take off your pants.

He was up in a flash, unbuttoning his jeans and shucking them to the floor. He stood before her, completely naked, godlike in the firelight, evidence of his passion for her rampant and ready. She reached out her hand, grasping onto his sex, feeling the hot, satiny, muscled strength of him against her hand. He was big. He was so big that she worried for a moment until he distracted her with a sharp intake of breath and she wondered if her hands were too cold. "Cold?"

He opened his eyes and tried to smile, but failed and grimaced instead. "Hot, Darce."

"It's you, Jack." She took his hand and pulled him down on top of her. "I want you."

"You're everything to me, Darcy. Everything."

She lay back on the couch and he covered her naked body with his. Flesh to flesh, hot, and perfectly fitted, he nudged her legs apart as he held her face between his hands, pressing his lips to hers.

The weight of his naked body on hers was incredibly erotic. He was hard and toned every place she was soft and pliant. His hard, muscled chest pressed against her breasts, his strong thighs draped against hers, his rock-hard sex intimately kissing her inner thigh.

He touched his lips to her eyelids and her nose, and trailed kisses down her cheek to her ear. He bit the lobe and Darcy bucked up lightly against him, moving her hands slowly down his back. She wanted him to know she was ready, that there was nothing else she wanted in the world than to feel him inside of her. She raised her knees up to cradle him, locking her ankles behind his back.

He leaned back to look at her.

"You're sure, Darce?" he asked, panting. "Are you…I mean, do you use—"

I'm on the pill, she confirmed.

Her fingers kneaded his backside, pushing him forward.

"We've waited long enough. I want you. In my whole life, I have *only* wanted you."

He braced himself over her and she felt him start to enter her, more and more, inch by swollen inch, until his massive shaft was buried inside and then he paused. She gasped with the fullness of having him inside of her body, the heat and strength of him stretching her, filling her, the otherworldly swirling in her belly making her dizzy, making every nerve ending beg for release.

He groaned then stilled, putting his hands on either side of her face, making her look at him.

I love you, Darcy Turner. Forever.

Closing her eyes, she arched her back to meet him and felt his cock sink into her to the hilt. He found her lips in the near-darkness, moving rhythmically inside of her slowly, in and out, in and out. She closed her eyes and rose to meet him, lifting with every thrust to guide him deeper, to *feel* him deeper, to be one with him, bound to him.

Her eyes filled with tears from the intensity of her feelings, the perfection of being joined with him. She moaned into his mouth, the sweetness almost unbearable, the tension in her body building and building until she ached for its climax. She arched her back higher and higher and felt his hands under her backside, keeping her tightly, mercilessly, bound to him until something inside of her exploded, shattered into a million pieces that could never be put back together again.

She dragged her nails across his back, crying out "Jack!" as her muscles released like tightly compressed springs, spiraling up and away, to the moon and back, making her body buck and ripple with pleasure and abandon. She felt him pull back and her eyes fluttered open. He seized them with his, liquid, molten gold, and she heard him in her head:

You belong to me, and I belong to you.

Then he closed his eyes and plunged back into the depths of her body, thrusting against her womb one final time, and growling "Darcy!" as his body tensed then shuddered, the scorching heat of his come offered in tribute as Jack Beauloup climaxed with a partner for the first time in his entire life.

Chapter 11

THEY EVENTUALLY MADE THEIR WAY up to Jack's bedroom, making love twice more before falling into an exhausted slumber. When Darcy woke up the moon was high and bright. She pulled a blanket over her shoulders as she swung her legs over the side of his bed and went to the window.

She didn't hear him get up, but felt his arms close around her, pressing, laced, against her heart. She sighed with extreme contentment.

"Rain's stopped," she murmured, leaning her head back against his shoulder, feeling his lips press softly on her neck. She looked toward the moon. "It looks full, but it's not. It's waxing gibbous. It's not full until Tuesday."

"I'll be gone," he whispered, his lips moving against her neck.

She reached up to cover his hand and felt him hardening against her backside.

"Where?"

"Just business. I'll be gone from Monday to Wednesday."

Darcy couldn't help the way her heart dropped. She hadn't really thought any farther in her mind than tomorrow morning when she would wake up beside Jack on Sunday. And practically speaking, she had to put in some hours at Dartmouth on Monday and Tuesday. But knowing that he would be gone affected her. She didn't like it. It made her unaccountably sad to think she wouldn't be able to see him for three days.

As if sensing the dip in her mood, he turned her in his arms, pushing the blanket off her shoulders until she stood naked before him. He sucked in his breath, taking a leisurely look at her body before meeting her eyes and pulling her loosely into his arms. He didn't press himself against her even though she wanted him to.

"Come for dinner on Thursday." He kissed her forehead. "Bring work and stay the weekend. You can use the studio. Just…"

"Stay?" Placated, Darcy smiled and took a deep breath and exhaled slowly, feeling her breasts rise and rub against the skin of his chest then ease away as her lungs emptied. "Okay."

He surprised her by lifting her off her feet into his arms and carrying her the two or three steps to his bed. Placing her in the middle of the bed gently, he lay down behind her like a spoon.

She felt his thick, swollen sex against the back of her thighs and adjusted slightly, pushing back against him, and felt him slip, hard and smooth, into her waiting warmth.

"Ahhh," she breathed, as his arms encircled her, and his hands found her breasts, squeezing and kneading them to the rhythm of his thrusts behind her.

As the inevitable liquid swirling took over, she placed her hands on top of his, lacing her fingers through his, curling their fingers as they climaxed together, shuddering their release, their incomparable unity, their requited longing for one another.

"Darcy," Jack breathed, tightening his grip around her as tremors still shook his body.

"Jack, it's so—"

"—good," he finished nuzzling her neck and starting to pull out of her.

"No," she murmured, fighting against the heavy draw of sleep as the muscles inside of her body still contracted lightly around him. "Stay."

He pushed back into her body, tucking his knees back behind hers, and they fell asleep with their bodies bound together.

HE HAD BEEN RIGHT. SHE had never experienced anything in her life like sleeping with Jack Beauloup. Never.

Darcy had read the cheesy romance novels about climaxes that quaked the earth but she had yet in her own life to achieve anything close to the fulfillment she had read about…until last night, which felt wonderful and terrifying and frustrating all at once. Physically, she couldn't deny that being with Jack was mind-blowing on every possible level, which some-how gave credence to his theory about them being bound to each other.

Her heart, in cahoots with her body, was ready to believe the absolute truth of the sweet fairytale, but her mind wasn't ready to make the leap. It wanted to reject such a fantastic, unsubstantiated claim. Could she truly believe that she and Jack were in the grip of an old Métis spell that bound one person to another? It made no scientific sense. And yet…. How else could she explain the heartbreaking, staggering perfection of merging her body with his? How else could she explain the explosion of feelings she had for him—for someone she barely knew, whom she hadn't seen in years?

Last night, he had been deliberate about holding her eyes when he told her he loved her. That wasn't a misplaced thought he had in the heat of the moment that she happened to pick up on. No, he had looked at her. He wanted her to know.

On one hand, she knew that she should feel uncomfortable with Jack using the word "love." They hadn't spent more than a handful of hours together since their reunion last Saturday. How was it possible that he should love her? Yet maybe for Jack, who had spent the last twenty years of his life feeling bound to her, it was not only possible, but deeply, irrevocably true.

And the truth for Darcy was that she wasn't uncomfortable hearing him tell her that he loved her. Although she wasn't ready to reciprocate the words, it was only because some misguided propriety told her she should wait. The reality was that Darcy felt as deeply for Jack as he felt for her. She had never felt this sort of visceral, invasive, all-consuming love for anyone, ever, in her life, and all other previous relationships faded, gray and gauzy, against the vibrant totality of his hold on her heart.

She breathed deeply, rolling over onto her side, and had two immediate thoughts. The first was that she was alone. The second was that her body was on fire.

Darcy had taken a trip to Mexico with her family when she was a preteen and while her parents had been busy entertaining young Amory, they hadn't noticed that Darcy had fallen asleep in the sun. Two hours later, rousing her for a late lunch, her mother had gasped at the color of Darcy's skin. An angry, blazing, red had taken over her daughter's normally pale, freckled skin.

"I can't see your freckles!" he mother had almost screamed in a panic.

Darcy had opened her eyes to the extreme pain of her raw, blistering skin, and spent the remainder of the week in the hotel room either lounging in the cold bathtub or lying supine on the bed, covered in aloe vera and soothed by the cool breeze offered by a ceiling fan.

Her skin didn't precisely feel as bad this morning as it had in Mexico, but that Mexico was her only comparison wasn't a good sign.

Wincing, she carefully lowered her feet to the floor and stood up. Whoa. Pain. She looked down at her arms and saw the angry sunburned skin. Walking in the stilted steps of Frankenstein, she made her way to Jack's bathroom where she gasped. A good portion of her body was covered in pink and light red burns. She turned to look at her back and winced, noting it was similarly afflicted.

What happened? What is this?

Darcy tried to remember the last time she was in the sun. Certainly not yesterday when she was wearing layers of clothing on an overcast day.

A rash, Darcy. It could be a rash.

She considered the possibility. It made a lot more sense than sunburn. Darcy's skin was fair and more than once she'd needed to switch detergents when she realized she was overly sensitive to one with colors or fragrance.

She walked gingerly back to the bed and put her nose against his sheets. It wasn't a cloying smell, per se, but it did smell strongly of some synthetic floral scent. She started to sit back down on the bed, then stood up quickly.

Don't sit on the bed, idiot! You could make it worse.

She opted for a wooden rocking chair in the corner of the room instead. She sat down carefully, naked, then sighed with pleasure. The wood was smooth and cool, a balm to the back of her bare thighs. She sat rigidly, trying to adjust to the painful heat of her body, as she looked around Jack's bedroom. This was the first time she'd seen it in daylight.

It was an attractive room—exactly what Darcy would have chosen if Jack had asked for her help in decorating instead of his fancy designer from Boston. She loved the woodland tones in tans and creams, and the simple lines of his enormous cherry bed. Two large dormer windows had alcove window seats and built-in bookcases that made them snug reading nooks, and two traditional rocking chairs flanked the fireplace. It was a warm and inviting room, elegant in its simplicity, and Darcy felt completely at home.

The only thing that bothered her, she realized, was the absence of any personal photos. Not that it was obligatory that a grown man should have a picture of his family in his bedroom, but he'd been so closed about them when she had asked yesterday. It would have helped her to get an idea of his family dynamics if she could have seen one. She made a mental note to ask to see one.

She was so distracted by her reverie, she didn't hear Jack come back into the room, bare-chested, only dressed in his jeans from yesterday and a pair of shearling slippers. He was standing in the doorway of the room watching her, a concerned expression on his face.

"Hi," she murmured, smiling at his tousled black hair, his intense brown eyes.

"I love you," he whispered from across the room, gazing at her, not moving.

"You do."

"I do." He approached her slowly, wincing as he noticed her skin. "Are you okay?"

"I think I got a rash from your sheets." Darcy looked down at her arms and thighs. "Not so pretty, huh?"

Jack squatted in front of her. "Beautiful."

"You need glasses, Mr. Beauloup."

He shook his head lightly. "I don't need anything but you."

Darcy grinned. "Then you're all set."

He pressed his lips lightly to her kneecap and she sucked in a breath.

"You're in pain?" He didn't look at her. He leaned back to take a better look at the redness of her legs and she saw him grimace.

"A little."

"How can I help?"

"Do you have any antihistamines?"

He shook his head regretfully.

"Can I take a cold bath?" she asked.

"I'm on it." He leapt up and beelined for his bathroom and she heard the water running. "I'll umm...I'll get your clothes out of the dryer and bring them up."

"Hey you didn't use softener sheets in the dryer or anything, did you?" she called to him. "Whatever you're using, it doesn't agree with me."

"Nope. Just heat."

Darcy stood up and shuffled into the bathroom, finding him kneeling on the floor, hand in the bathwater. She stood naked behind him, plunged her fingers into his hair, pulled his face back and leaned down, her breasts grazing the back of his head as she gave him an inverted kiss. Then she stepped over him, gasping at the cold water on her skin as she stepped into the bath.

She sat down, easing herself back against the tub, and sighed.

Jack didn't move. His fingers still dangled in the water and his head was bowed.

"Last night was the best night of my life, Darcy."

Darcy closed her eyes, loving the feel of the cool water on her hot skin.

"Mine too," she sighed, finding his fingers beside her and clasping them. Minutes ticked by in silence as the water turned warmer, heated by her hot skin, and still their hands stayed laced together.

"I can't lose you now," he finally whispered, and his voice was ragged with emotion—with desperation and despair. He let go of her hand.

Darcy opened her eyes to look at him, to reassure him of her feelings for him, her love for him, but he was gone.

S HE DRESSED CAREFULLY IN HER jeans and t-shirt, skipping her bra and panties for fear that they would further irritate the rash. She could change into something light and breathable as soon as she got home. Maybe Willow could prescribe a strong antihistamine too. Sad though it made her feel, all signs pointed to her needing to head home.

She made her way downstairs and found Jack in the beautiful farm kitchen, watching the news in French.

"Wow!" she said. "Your French is that good?"

"It's my first language," he admitted, pouring her a cup of coffee. "I don't know how you take it."

"Light and sweet."

"Just like you." He grinned, kissing her gently as he handed her a coffee cup. He turned and opened the refrigerator, taking out a carton of milk and found a sugar packet in an overhead cabinet. He set both on the counter in front of her.

She stared at his chest, at the well-defined pectoral and abdominal muscles and the muscles on his lower trunk that started a perfect V on each side of his hips, the apex of which ended at his…

"Whew," she sighed, looking up at his face.

He beamed at her, then chuckled lightly, biting his lower lip. His face turned serious as he stared at her. "I want you again, Darce."

She looked down at her red arms and thought of the irritated skin of her chest and back. "I don't think it's a good idea. I have to go."

His face clouded over and he shook his head. "No…I thought, I mean, I hoped that you'd stay—"

"Jack, I haven't really been home since Friday afternoon. Willow will think you abducted me!"

He took his phone out of his back pocket and handed it to her. "So call her and let her know you're fine. Then stay for the rest of today."

She took a sip of her coffee, biting back a smile, and shook her head. "I have to go home."

"Fine. I'm not going to beg you," he muttered, shoving his phone back into his jeans. "I'll get dressed and drive you home."

He stalked out of the kitchen without a word, without looking at her, and she realized he was upset. She was sorry for that. Honestly, she didn't really want to leave him either, but felt like she should. She needed to shower and change, get control of this rash and check her messages. Her book had been ignored for days and who knows how many e-mails had piled up. If she was needed for teaching tomorrow or Tuesday, she'd need to get her notes in order. As much as she wanted to stay and pretend they were the only two people in the world, life intruded. She had to go.

She finished her coffee and headed to the front foyer to find her socks and shoes. She had finished pulling on her socks as Jack found her.

"Wow. All ready to go. That anxious to leave, huh?"

Darcy stood up slowly, recognizing the tone in his voice. Worry. He was worried. What was he worried about? *I can't lose you now.* She'd never gotten the chance to reassure him.

She put her hands on his face and tilted it to the side, leaning forward to press her lips against his. His mouth was hot and soft, but he didn't respond to her. He was pouting. He was telling her how much it bothered him that she wanted to go home. She laced her hands around his neck, pulling him down to her, rubbing her body against his, gently wiggling her tongue between his lips.

She heard his keys fall to the floor as his arms swooped around her, lifting her off the ground, into his arms, flush up against his body. He sighed into her mouth, his tongue stroking hers with the same rhythm he'd used to make love to her, and she felt her hunger for him pooling, throbbing and insistent, below her waist.

Sounds of passion escaped her throat as he grappled for the button of her jeans, urgently unzipped them, and then pushed them down. She unbuttoned and unzipped his pants as fast as she could, freeing his hard, ready sex. Without breaking contact with her lips, he put his hands under her arms and lifted her against the back of the front door, holding her hips with his hands and sinking without warning into her wet, waiting body, thrusting upward as she cried out his name.

She felt vulnerable and confined, at his mercy, which she found incredibly hot, and she wound her hands in his hair, throwing her head back against the door as he plunged deeper and deeper into the recesses of her body, his pelvic bone rubbing the nub of sensitive flesh over her entry. The sharp sweetness of their mating became more and more tightly coiled until—

"Jack…Jack…Jaaaaaaaaaaack!" Her head fell forward on his shoulder and her body convulsed around him as he thrust into her one final time, emitting a loud, roaring growl from his throat and howling her name— "Darcy!"—as they climaxed together.

H E WAS QUIET, BUT LESS petulant, on the drive home. "I'm going to be sore tomorrow."

Jack glanced at her. "Wish I could say I'm sorry about that."

"Don't worry. I'm not sorry either."

They rode in silence until Jack reached the edge of the woods and turned out onto the access road that led into town.

"Where are you headed?" she asked.

"Huh?"

"On business? Where are you going?"

"Oh. Umm…Quebec," he answered without looking at her, stopping at Carlisle's only stoplight.

Darcy scooted down in her seat in case anyone from church saw her driving around town with Jack Beauloup while skipping services, but when she looked over at the Second Congregational Church parking lot, it was empty. She checked her watch. 12:00 pm. They'd lost at least two hours this morning.

"I don't like this losing-time thing," she muttered.

He glanced over at her before the light changed to green. "We'll work on it."

"How?"

"I don't know. I'll think of something."

"I'll ask Willow too," Darcy suggested. "She knows just about everything about the Métis culture."

He glanced at her briefly and she saw his jaw flex, but he didn't respond.

All too soon, he pulled into her driveway. He put the Jeep in park and let the engine idle as he looked at her.

Je t'aime, Darcy. Attends-moi.

I'll be here when you get back.

I don't want to say good-bye.

Then don't. Say: See you on Thursday.

He took a deep breath and nodded, and Darcy saw the sadness on his face.

It's just three days.

He nodded and gave her a small smile, but it didn't reach his eyes. Then he leaned over and touched his lips to hers.

I belong to you.

He kissed her again then she turned and opened her door, feeling him watch her as she walked away.

S HE HEARD HIS CAR PULL away as she closed the front door and leaned back against it. Nonsensical tears gathered in her eyes as she processed with finality that she wouldn't see him for three and a half days. She'd been brave for him, but it was just as hard for her. She wished life could stop and they could hole up in his house together for a month…or in Jack and Darcy time, she thought ruefully, three weeks.

She brushed the tears from her eyes and looked up to see Willow coming down the stairs in her silky, Chinese embroidered robe.

"Kid!" Willow stopped in her tracks, looking nervously back up the stairs before hurrying down to Darcy. "Where've *you* been?"

"Jack's," she sighed.

"Does *Jack's* have a tanning bed, *DARCY?*" Willow practically yelled her name, pulling her by the elbow into the kitchen and flicking on the overhead light.

"What are you doing? Why are you pulling me into the kitchen? Why are you yelling?"

Willow took hold of Darcy's chin, twisting it back and forth.

"This is some burn, kid!"

"I think it's a rash. His sheets or something. Hoping you can give me an antihistamine."

"His *sheets*? Oh, boy, we need to talk…"

Willow took one of Darcy's arms, studying it. Darcy heard a bump overhead.

"Is someone here?"

"Damndest rash I've ever seen, Darce. It's too uniform, unless it all bled together. It looks like sunburn to me. I mean, we won't know unless it blisters—a rash won't blister—but I'd put my money on a burn."

Darcy heard light footsteps on the stairs.

"Who. Is. Here?"

"I am."

Darcy turned to see her brother in the kitchen doorway, holding his toolbox in one hand.

"Hey, Am."

"Hey. So, yeah, Will. Like you thought. You had a clogged…thing."

"A clogged *thing*?" Darcy raised an eyebrow.

"You know…drain."

Darcy looked back and forth between her best friend and her brother. She was about to make another comment when Amory took his coat off the back of a kitchen chair and struggled into it.

"Thanks, Brat," said Willow softly, looking down.

Amory stared at her for a second longer than necessary before saluting her awkwardly and heading out the back door.

"See ya, Darce."

The door slammed shut behind him.

"Let me write you a script," offered Willow quickly, opening the drawer where she kept an extra prescription pad.

Darcy looked back and forth between Willow, who was concentrating a little too deeply on writing out a generic script, and the back door where Amory had just departed. *Hmmm*. The air buzzed and crackled with left-over energy. Something had happened, or *almost* happened.

"You have lunch yet, Will?"

"Hmm?" Willow looked up. "Nope. Got up late. Tried to take a shower, but it backed up, so I called Amory…."

"I see."

Willow watched her intently, and Darcy sensed they were in the middle of a standoff. "Well, why don't we each grab a shower—assuming mine is working?—and go over to the Live Free or Die for a late lunch?"

Willow smiled, ripping off the prescription and shoving it into Darcy's hand before hurrying out of the kitchen. "Sounds good to me!"

WILLOW WASN'T OFFERING ANY DETAILS about Amory's sudden plumbing assistance, but she sure wanted every detail about Darcy's weekend with Jack.

"Five times? FIVE TIMES?" Willow stared at Darcy from across the table.

"You sound like the guy in *Ferris Bueller*," Darcy answered, feeling her face flush hot, not that anyone could tell under her no-sun-sunburn.

"That was nine." Willow's eyes were about to pop out of her head, they were so wide. "How did that *happen*?"

"It just…happened."

Darcy looked at the menu again. She looked at her watch. Time was crawling. It was only one o'clock and she missed him. How was she going to make it to Thursday?

"Somewhere you need to be?" Willow flicked her glance to Darcy's watch.

"No. I just…I miss him." She shrugged sheepishly.

"Oh, kid. You've got it bad."

Darcy leaned across the table suddenly and spoke in an urgent whisper. "Will, would it be crazy if I loved him?"

Willow had leaned forward when Darcy did, but now she leaned back, staring at her.

"You've known him, what? A week?"

"He thinks we're bound."

"He thinks you're what?"

"Bound. It's a Métis thing."

"Not that *I* know of."

The waitress came over to take their orders. Darcy ordered a cheeseburger and fries, and Willow, who was a loose vegetarian, ordered a grilled cheese with tomato.

"Well, he explained it to me. Apparently it started as a legend, but he definitely believes in it. A man will find the woman he's supposed to be with the summer before his eighteenth birthday. If he's supposed to be bound to her, he'll kiss her and that'll tell him."

"Tell him what?"

"If she's the one. But, he wasn't supposed to be bound to me. He should have been bound to a Métis woman. Not me. He said that there was no precedent for being bound to me. He, like, presented it to the pack elders or something."

"Pack? Do you mean tribal?"

"Yeah. Yeah, he said 'tribal.' After we kissed he went to see them at the Bloodlands and—"

"Bloodlands? He used that word?"

Darcy nodded. "Somewhere north of Quebec. He was born there."

"Okay. Go ahead."

"And they said that he was wrong. They insisted he hadn't been bound to me, and that he needed to stay away from me and he'd get over it. But he didn't. And so he finally decided to come back." Darcy took a deep breath and sighed.

"He told you all of this?"

Darcy nodded.

"I've never heard of this. Seriously, kid. Nothing. Nada. Never." Willow looked concerned. "That said, he's full Métis and I'm only a quarter. I've never heard of *binding* or *Bloodlands*, but you better believe I'm going to ask my *Nohkom* about all of this. She's just as much Métis as Jack."

"There's more," said Darcy. "More that comes with the binding."

"Tell me."

"We Eyespeak."

"You what?"

"Eyespeak. If my eyes hold his, I can hear his thoughts and vice versa."

"Jesus. I've never heard of that either. What else?"

"The soul flight…going inside? That's him. It's related to all of this."

"Anything else?"

"His body temperature's higher than mine, I think."

"Anything else?"

"No." She decided not to tell Willow any more. "The way I'm telling you is making it all sound crazy, but it's not, Will. It's real. The binding. I…I can't explain it. But, it's real. I think—I mean, I think we belong to each other."

Willow stared back at her. Finally she ran a hand through her short black hair. "Okay. Let's say—for argument's sake—that you kissed Jack Beauloup once when you were fifteen years old and somehow became *bound* to him. Where's he been, kid?"

"Advised to forget me. Tried to forget me. Couldn't forget me.

Returned." *Control.*

"Listen, you know that I firmly believe that not everything can be seen and not everything can be explained. I'm just—I've never heard of any of this. Let me talk to my *Nohkom*, huh? Ask her about it? See if any of it rings a bell?"

"Sure," said Darcy, putting her napkin in her lap as their food arrived. Part of her wished she hadn't said anything. Being with Jack was like being in a bubble and sharing it all with Willow somehow felt like she wasn't protecting them.

"Hey…"

Darcy looked up, a fry halfway to her mouth.

"…to answer your question? Would it be crazy if you loved him?" Willow smiled gently, shaking her head. "It wouldn't be crazy. I think maybe you've been waiting for him to come back for twenty years. That's a long time to wait for someone. Why shouldn't that be enough to grow love? Seems like it grows on much rockier places than that."

"What's the deal with Amory?" she segued bluntly without preamble.

Willow choked on a bite of her sandwich and coughed, putting her glass to her lips for a long sip of water.

"What do you mean?"

"He *unclogged* the *thing*?" She gave Willow a look that said she wasn't buying it.

"The shower was clogged. Other than that, I don't know what you're talking about." Willow pursed her lips, taking another bite of her sandwich and looking out the window.

Darcy reached across the table and placed her fingers on her friend's arm. "*Attends-moi*, Will. That's what I'm talking about."

Willow jerked her head up to meet Darcy's eyes, working her jaw, her skin flushing uncharacteristically with color. Her almost-black eyes flashed with anger and confusion and…fear? Yes, fear too, in fearless Willow's dark eyes. Then suddenly, to Darcy's horror, they brightened with tears.

Finally she whispered, "*Je suis perdu.*"

I am lost.

And then, "He's too young for me, kid. In a million ways."

"Like that matters."

"It *does* matter," Willow insisted. "He's in his mid-twenties. He's never left Carlisle. I'm in my mid-thirties. I've slept with half of Boston. He's a contractor. I'm a doctor. He's your brother. I'd have no leeway. I couldn't make a mistake. I—"

"Do you love him?"

Willow swiped at her eyes before taking a deep breath and looking back out the window. "He kissed me."

"Today?"

Willow nodded.

"Damn, I *knew* it! I could feel it. It felt so *weird* when I got home. How was it?"

"Amazing," she breathed.

"And then what?"

"His sister came home."

"No! No! Oh, Will. I interrupted you two? Oh, no!"

"No, it's good. It's for the best, kid. He's with Faith. He *should* be with Faith." She covered her half-eaten sandwich with her napkin and took another sip of water, turning her glance back to the window. Her voice didn't change as she spoke in a dispassionate whisper, more to herself than to Darcy. "I'm not right for Amory. He's open and smiling and light and *faith*. And I'm battered and used and cynical and gray. He deserves more than me. Don't you see? He shouldn't love me and I shouldn't love him."

"Who are you trying to convince?"

"Me," she answered simply.

"But, Will," sighed Darcy, offering her friend a sympathetic smile. "*Il est déjà tard.*"

It's already too late.

Willow turned her face back to Darcy and nodded. Somewhere in those dark eyes Darcy could see the surrender, and she knew she was right even before Willow admitted it.

"Damn it, Darcy," she cursed softly. "I know."

Chapter 12

DARCY LOVED THE DRIVE SOUTH from Carlisle in the far north of New Hampshire, to Dartmouth, south in Hanover.

The first third of the drive was on Route 114, a rural two-lane highway that wound through some of the prettiest New England towns of New Hampshire, all of which Darcy knew well from her weekly commute over the past ten years. As she made her way further south, she admired the dogwoods and apple blossoms, just starting to explode with color. The fields were green and fertile and the sun shone down brightly on ancient stone walls and cheerful general stores.

But all of that lush spring beauty and rich history was lost on Darcy as her thoughts and feelings courted chaos in her head, and her heart stretched painfully as the distance from Carlisle, from Jack, lengthened. It was as though her heart physically remained in Carlisle while her body traveled south without it and the tendons and muscles strained against the growing expanse between them. By the time she reached the Moore Reservoir on the Vermont border, she pulled her car over at the North Littleton boat launch for the express purpose of deciding whether or not to turn around and go home.

She looked at her flushed, cherry-red cheeks in the rearview mirror then rolled down her window halfway. The cool, mid-morning air was bracing, and Darcy took a deep breath, soothed by the view of the vast lake before her.

As tears gathered in her eyes, she put her head back against the headrest and went inside.

D ARCY.
   Darcy. Darcy.

She could hear Jack's faraway voice, but the forest was covered in thick mist when she opened her eyes, and the stark, monochromatic palette was jarring to her. She rubbed her eyes and sat up straighter against the tree trunk where she found herself. Her legs were crossed in front of her, the edge of her white linen shift just touching her white-satin-slippered feet. Her fingers fluttered gently over something soft on the ground by her sides, and she looked down to see emerald green moss in spongy bunches, growing out of hard, white granite surrounding the base of the tree. The contrast made her blink—vibrant green and white in a sea of mist, softness growing effortlessly out of tiny fissures in the rock. *Leucobryum,* she thought absently. *Cushion moss.*

Darcy hadn't spoken inside for a long time, but she tried her voice now.

"Jack?" she breathed into the fog, and she saw the letters of his name in silver mist swirl from her mouth repeating as it dispersed, until the forest echoed softly with his name before falling silent, before the silver blended, forgotten, into the grey around her. "I miss you…"

She watched her words disperse and disappear again—*you, you, you*—until it was silent. Almost silent.

She realized something was coming closer. She heard the footfalls and inclined her head to the left as it came near. Her eyes widened as an enormous black wolf made his way out of the mist, sitting at the base of a tree not far from Darcy, training its glowing, yellow eyes on her.

Jack's voice was low and deep in her head:

I belong to you.

Her eyes opened abruptly, and she squinted, blinking against the sunshine sparkling on the water before her. A heavily bearded older man was rapping lightly on the lower half of her opened window.

"Girlie? You awake now? How about moving your car if you're not launching? Trying to get some fishing done." He hooked his thumb back toward his waiting trailer behind her.

"Oh! Yes! Sorry. I dozed off."

"You sure were out," he chuckled. "Beeped twice. Lucky thing *I* came along and not someone with untoward ideas."

Darcy looked at his grizzled face, her stomach turning over from the faint smell of gutted fish emanating from his lure vest. She cringed and he stepped back, offended.

"Just move your doggone car." He stomped away, and Darcy looked after him helplessly, wishing she could apologize for her expression, but it was too late.

She put her car in drive and made a wide turn out of the launching area and back toward the main road. She took a deep breath, feeling better. She hadn't seen Jack, but she'd heard his voice, and it soothed her.

The black wolf.

He appeared more and more in her soul flight…especially since Jack had reappeared. Darcy knew that the Métis claimed a special connection to the wolf. Willow's favorite t-shirt growing up had been silk-screened with the original flag of the Métis people: a wolf head in the middle flanked by feathers with the unity symbol underneath. Jack's surname bore some tribute to the wolf, perhaps making it totemic to him—she would have to ask him on Thursday.

As she pulled back onto the highway headed south, she thought about her conversation with Willow yesterday. It bothered Darcy. More and more.

Although Willow hadn't ruled out the possibility that it was a legend she wasn't acquainted with, Darcy knew that Willow's depth and breadth of Métis knowledge was vast and sound. It was unlikely there could be a whole sub-tribe of the Métis that practiced beliefs about which Willow knew nothing. It didn't make sense. Which left one alternative:

Jack was lying to her.

Of the many relationship deal-breakers in Darcy Turner's life, lying was at the top of the list. She would not engage in a relationship that wasn't built on honesty—at the hint of deceit, Darcy cut bait. As she had learned with Phillip, deceit led to secrets, to cheating, and eventually to heart-break. If Jack was lying to her about who he was, how he felt and what he believed, there was no room for him in her life. As much as it would hurt, she would rather turn her back on him now than have her heart broken in half later.

She didn't realize she was crying until a fat drop plopped on her shirt, making a blotchy wet spot on her chest. She reached up and swiped the rest away with the backs of her hands, desperately hoping that Jack wasn't lying to her.

Saying good-bye to him would not only be excruciating; if they were truly bound by some mystical force, there was a good chance it would be impossible.

"MM-HM, DARCY TURNER, YOU ARE a sight for these sore, old eyes!" declared Miss Kendrick, pulling Darcy into her thick, warm, brown arms.

The aptly named Fern Kendrick had been a fixture in the Life Sciences Greenhouse for as long as Darcy had been working there. She had started her tenure on the janitorial staff in the 1960s, but the administration had noted her fondness and care for the plants of the sciences department after a decade of extra watering, trimming, and babying of the various greenery they kept for research purposes. Over time, her janitorial duties were phased out so that she could be the full-time caretaker of the outdoor research gardens and indoor samples. When the modern greenhouse was completed in 1995, Annabelle Fern Kendrick not only cut the ceremonial ribbon but was the first person to enter the greenhouse and was often found by "Fern's Fountain," the affectionate name for the gurgling marble fountain set in the center of the large building where students and professors often met for impromptu lessons.

She was in her 60s now and without the benefit of a diploma or degree, Miss Kendrick couldn't be officially named to the Dartmouth faculty, but she owned the respect of every member and was consulted on botanical questions by educators and botanists all over New England.

"How are you, Miss Kendrick?"

"Darcy, we've been workin' together these ten years. When're you goin' to call me Fern?"

"Never," said Darcy, grinning at her and shaking her head. "Can't do it. Until I know more than you, I can't do it."

Miss Kendrick beamed at Darcy and pulled her over to a table of samples. "Come and see your babies."

Darcy looked at the beds of moss and lichen under the dim, lavender lights. "The *Parmeliaceae* lichen looks good, doesn't it?"

"It does."

"Did you try extracting the olivetol yet?"

"Yes, I did. And what exactly are you goin' to do with it?" she asked Darcy with a disapproving look.

"Not synthesize it into THC, Miss Kendrick." She rolled her eyes. *As if!* "But who knows what other helpful properties it might have, right? It's the responsibility of botany to help the world, if possible."

"Well, if you were goin' to test the psychoactive nature of it, I'd suggest mixin' it with somethin' acidic like fresh orange juice. You could bring a reaction to the olivetol with the essential oil from an orange peel in the presence of phosphoryl chloride. Or just react the olivetol with a-pinene, maybe."

"And that is why it will always be impossible for me to call you anything but Miss Kendrick," Darcy said without a shred of irony.

The older woman chuckled. "Somethin' else too as long as we're on the subject of things you can synthesize and smoke illegally. We been so busy with your lichen sample, we been ignoring the *Lycopodium,* the clubmoss. Now, I've been readin' up, and this stuff is like a super drug. Relief for arthritis, rheumatism, and other complaints."

She pulled a small tray closer to the front of the table, and Darcy leaned over it with a magnifying glass.

Miss Kendrick continued with a smile in her voice. "Native Americans called it Lost-in-the-Woods because in addition to the positive implications, it gave them a fuzzy, confused head if they dried it and smoked it. Which of course they did."

"Of course. What's the common name of this one? I know it's a *Lycopodium clavatum,* but—"

Miss Kendrick squinted over the sample. "Uh? That there's called wolf's-foot clubmoss. Also called wolf's-paw."

"Hmmm…" All roads lead to wolves today, she thought to herself, admiring the lime-green color of the tall moss. "I have to teach in twenty minutes. Will you gather together a few samples for me? The *Parmeliaceae* and the *Lycopodium clavatum?* I'm going to take them back with me."

"Aren't you stayin' over tonight, Darcy, honey?"

Darcy took a deep breath. Although her anxiety had lessened since going inside at the launch and with the company of Miss Kendrick, she still felt a strong pull to return home.

Why, Darcy? Jack's gone until Thursday. What's the point? Staying here will make the time go faster than waiting around at home for him to return.

"Have dinner with me at my place, sugar?" asked Miss Kendrick, with a wide, warm smile.

"You convinced me. I'll stay. I'd love to have dinner tonight."

Darcy kissed the older woman's cheek and hurried so she wouldn't be late for class.

IT HAD BEEN THE RIGHT choice to have dinner with her friend. Miss Kendrick entertained her with stories about the Dartmouth faculty and Darcy ended up staying with her friend instead of seeking a room in visiting faculty housing. Miss Kendrick's guest bedroom had the added benefit of housing several species of violets that greeted Darcy cheerfully in the morning. She considered staying over on Tuesday night too, but the pull to return to Carlisle was still on the spectrum of exhausting. She knew Jack wouldn't return until Thursday morning, but she thought that he probably wouldn't mind if she collected some samples in his woods while he was away, and even the thought of being at his house without him made her feel closer to him.

She had committed to dinner with one of the chemistry professors on Tuesday night, which meant a late start home, and Darcy hadn't been able to leave the campus until after nine o'clock. Still, the dinner had been worthwhile. She had discussed synthesizing the lichen and clubmoss samples to see if they had useful medicinal properties and Professor Jenkins had walked her through a rough sequence of steps for optimal integration. She wondered if the calming properties of the olivetol mixed with the healing properties of the clubmoss might make for an herbal remedy of sorts. But she could continue all of her research at home, and consult with Willow, of course.

Darcy scratched at her arm again as she made her way through the dark roads toward home. She had been surprised to find mild blisters raised all over her body on Monday evening as she was getting ready for bed. She remembered what Willow had said—that if blisters raised it was a burn, not a rash. And while it was just about impossible that it was a sunburn, Darcy's mind had wandered, trying to figure out what other sort of burn it could be. If it wasn't radiation, perhaps it was chemical? But, no, Darcy hadn't come into contact with any chemicals. Thermal, then? Electrical? None of it made sense.

Her a-ha moment came a few minutes later. Of course! Poison ivy! The answer to the riddle, "Name a rash that blisters." She must have come into contact with it in the woods. She would reconfirm with Willow, but of course that must be what it was. Much relieved with at least one answer to the many mysteries of her relationship with Jack, Darcy turned on the radio and let Mozart be her companion until she arrived home.

THE HOUSE WAS DARK WHEN Darcy got there, which wasn't altogether unusual as Willow was often at her office in town until quite late. That and she was one of the few remaining doctors on the face of the earth who made house calls, so it was possible she was checking on a patient or delivering a baby. That Willow's car was in the driveway meant she was probably at her office, though, since it was walkable from home.

Darcy picked through the mail on the kitchen counter then opened the freezer to find a carton of Ben & Jerry's. She cradled it against her elbow, rummaging in the dishwasher for a spoon. She set the ice cream on the window seat and wandered upstairs to change into her pajamas, then curled up in the picture window to eat her treat and wait for her friend. It wasn't a long wait until she heard a car pull into the driveway.

Now, this is interesting. Someone's driving her home at midnight? Why didn't she take her car?

Darcy hopped off the window seat, walking into the kitchen where she had a better view of the driveway. She gasped as she realized it was Amory's truck, with TURNER CONTRACTING written in bold letters on the side, and Amory's logo—a log cabin beside a fir tree—reflecting in the porch light.

Well, well, well. Darcy hurried back to the window seat, and after a few minutes she heard the back door open and close.

As Willow walked through the living room toward the stairs—

"So!" said Darcy. "You and Amory?"

Willow jumped a foot, placing a hand over her heart.

"AHRGH! DARCY? What are you doing? S-scaring people to death in the dark! Why are you home? You never come back until Wednesday!" Willow plopped down on the window seat beside Darcy, giving her an angry look. She held out her wrist. "Feel my pulse. Feel it!"

"Well, now, I *could* feel it, Will, but how would I know which Turner child was the cause of its thumping?" She pursed her lips and raised her eyebrows.

"And what's that? *My* ice cream? Nice. On top of everything, you're eating *my* ice cream. I'm getting a spoon."

Willow returned with a spoon and curled up on the window seat across from Darcy in the moonlight. She held out her hand.

Darcy looked at the small container then held it over her head. "Amory?"

"I'll tell you. Hand over the ice cream I bought."

Darcy offered it hesitatingly and Willow grabbed it away.

"We went for coffee," she mumbled.

"Sorry, *kid*," said Darcy, "I didn't catch that."

"Coffee. Coffee? Bitter? Dark? Much like me?"

"How did *that* happen?"

"Nail through hand. Puncture wound. Coffee."

Darcy gasped, cringing. "Poor Amory!"

"You're telling me. I hate injuries more than illness sometimes."

"Is he okay?"

"I won't lie," she said, taking another bite. "It was a bad one. Deep. Went down to the muscle. Sure you don't want more ice cream?"

Darcy shook her head no. She'd suddenly lost her appetite.

"I cleaned it up, plopped a bunch of antibiotic cream on it. Nothing to do now but hope it doesn't get infected." She took one last bite before putting the cover back on the pint. "Had to give him a tetanus booster too."

Darcy heard the sprinkle of sheepish humor in this admission.

"What are you not telling me?"

"*Technically*, you can have it in the arm, but…"

Darcy chuckled. "Where'd you give it?"

"Use your imagination," Willow said, eyes twinkling in the darkness.

"And *that* led to coffee?"

"Sort of. He was bent over, talking all fast and nervous while I took my time admiring, um, *prepping*, the…area. And he mentioned things had sort of petered out with Faith—"

"He mentioned this while you were staring at his ass?"

"Uh-huh. So, I told him it might pinch and asked him if he wanted to have coffee with me. I don't think he felt a thing."

Darcy smiled appreciatively at her friend. "I'll bet he didn't. So? Did anything *happen*?"

"Most sisters wouldn't want these sorts of sordid details."

"Are there *sordid* details to share?"

"We might've kissed again."

"Might've?"

"Do I look like one of those girls who kisses and tells?"

"You look exactly like one of those girls… Okay, we'll do it this way: How was the coffee?"

"It was good, kid. Really, really good," Willow murmured, looking up at the full moon out the window. "One of the better cups I've ever had in my life."

Darcy grinned, tapping the spoon lightly on the ice cream cover.

"So," said Willow, turning back to Darcy. "Why didn't you call me back?"

"What do you mean?"

"I called you this afternoon. After I talked to my *Nohkom*. I was sure you'd call me back right away."

"Nobody ever calls me. My phone probably died sometime on the ride. What'd she say?"

"Well, I was wrong…there *is* a binding legend. But, it's not Métis. I mean, it is, but it's not."

"Should I feel this confused?"

"Ready for a freaky Métis legend?"

"I guess…" Darcy recognized the ghost-story tone of Willow's voice, and knew she was in for one of Granny *Nohkom*'s whoppers.

"Long, long ago, the French settlers came across from Europe and with them, hidden on their ship, they brought a *terrible* creature. A werewolf. A full-blooded wolf creature, who roamed the woods of France for his victims, had snuck himself onto a ship bound for Canada.

"When the ship got there, the werewolf *ran* to the great north to hide and hunt, kidnapping four Abenaki sisters on one *dark, full-mooned* night. The oldest of the four, who was *wise* beyond her years, begged that the creature not kill them, and promised him something more precious in return.

"Nine months later, each bore a child. The children looked like Indian babies, until they each cut their teeth on the full moon, howling and fearful, and the mothers realized that they had each borne a monster. They took the children into the woods and left them there, abandoned to the elements.

"The Métis believe that the four children survived, growing into horrible creatures they called *Roux-ga-roux*. Unlike their Indian mothers or werewolf father, they lived in a state of half-creature. They appear as humans for most of the moon cycle but at the full moon, they shift back into *bloodthirsty* creatures, *skinwalkers* who hunt like their father for three…full…days.

"The skinwalkers have *razor-sharp* fangs, long, yellow claws, the face of a wolf, eyes that *burn*, and the *strength* of ten men. They carry little children off in the dead of night and eat their flesh, for the Roux-ga-roux can *never* have enough human flesh. It wants it. It *craves* it. Its fangs *drip* with the blood of its victims."

Willow was having trouble maintaining her composure, her lips trembling as she held back laughter. She cleared her throat and resumed her storyteller's voice.

"And…here's the part you've been waiting for, kid…

"Because *no one* but another Roux-ga-roux could ever love such a *hideous, abominable creature*, they must mate with one of their own. So, they are bound on the eve of their eighteenth birthday, one Roux-ga-roux to another, and spend their lives together…hunting…killing…and *mating*."

Willow stopped for a moment, her laughter finally getting the better of her. When she finally looked back up at Darcy, her eyes were glistening.

"*Nohkom* didn't actually say that part about the mating. I thought I'd add it. Oh! But she did have a caveat to the legend…apparently the Métis are safe from the creature. The Métis race was started when French trappers married Native American women, and the Roux-ga-roux race started when a French werewolf mated with Abenaki women. So even though they are different, they are both races of mixed blood who share the northern woods. By tacit agreement, the Métis don't hunt the Roux-ga-roux, and the Roux-ga-roux leave the mixed-blooded Métis in peace. They hunt the white man instead.

"*Nohkom* said that you should listen at the full moon, and you'll hear the howling cry of the Roux-ga-roux, Oh-oh-oh-Oh-Ooooooooooooooooo! Oh-oh-oh-Oh-Ooooooooooooooooo!"

Willow howled like a wolf, then grinned at Darcy.

"You know *Nohkom*. She always had a flair for drama!"

Darcy stared at Willow, then took a deep breath, clapping quietly. "Well done, Mistress Storyteller. But not so helpful. Did she say anything about a Métis subculture that fashions their marital beliefs on this Roux-ga-roux legend?"

"Nope. She'd never heard of any of the tribes practicing binding. But you said that Jack mentioned the woods north of Quebec? That's a big area, kid. I guess it's possible one of the tribes up there takes the legends a little more literally? Who knows?" She leaned forward and kissed Darcy's cheek. "I'm tired. I'm headed to bed."

Darcy nodded, feeling deflated. She'd hoped that Willow's grandmother would have some sweet story about a small sub-tribe that practiced wildly romantic notions about true love and first kisses. Instead, she'd gotten an old Métis ghost story about werewolves, kidnapping, rape, child endangerment, and death. *Great. Thanks a lot,* Nohkom.

She sighed in frustration. And she still had no answers to explain the soul flight, the Eyespeak, and losing hours of her life every time she was around Jack Beauloup.

Darcy had looked forward to Thursday with a sharp longing, desperate to jump into Jack's arms and love him all weekend long. Now, they'd be retreading old ground as she demanded answers and he sidestepped questions. Well, not this time. This time, she wouldn't be distracted by his beautiful body and hot, wet, toe-curling kisses. She would have her answers, or Jack would not have her. The longer she waited, the longer he'd wait. She'd get to the bottom of their connection. Her life—her heart—depended on it.

Chapter 13

DARCY DIDN'T ACTUALLY KNOW WHEN Jack was returning from Quebec on Thursday, but she woke up earlier than usual on Thursday morning, buoyant, hopeful, and relieved that what felt like a very long separation would be over as of that evening.

She dressed quickly and made a cup of coffee for herself before Willow even woke up, and headed up to her studio to work.

She couldn't concentrate.

Jack.

She couldn't think of anything but him, and she suddenly had an idea that being near his house, on the grounds of his property, might prove a balm to the longing she felt. She could just wander a while in the woods as they had on Saturday. Being in the woods and being at Jack's place would combine two of her favorite things in one place, and surely the fresh air would help her concentrate better on her writing when she returned home.

The wolf.

The memory of the gray wolf baring its teeth at her in Jack's woods made her think twice about her plan.

She took a small key out of her desk and opened a locked door that looked a lot like a coat closet. Inside, she used a second key to unlock a small trunk and removed her H&R single-shot centerfire rifle. Living in northern New Hampshire with all manner of wildlife meant that her parents had gifted Darcy the weapon at a young age, and they had gone to great lengths to ensure she knew how to fire, clean, and store the firearm. But Darcy still didn't like it. Even though she had lived amongst guns all her life, she wasn't comfortable with them; she didn't like the statistics on accidental shootings and guns finding their way into children's innocent hands. Further, she really didn't like the thought of killing anything. Heretofore she had only used the weapon for target practice—although she had been hunting before, when it came to actually pulling the trigger on a helpless animal, she hadn't been able to do it.

She couldn't remember the last time she used the gun, but she checked the bore and it was clean, which didn't surprise her. She could hear her father's words in her head: *If you're going to own a firearm, have respect for it.*

She looked out the window. It was turning into a bright, sunny day and Darcy didn't want the extra weight of the gun on her back, or the implication of needing it. She changed her mind, replacing the gun and locking the trunk and then the cabinet. She made sure her cellphone was charged and found some pepper spray in her backpack, just in case.

Thus armed, she made her way to Jack's place.

D ARCY PULLED INTO THE SEMI-CIRCLE driveway and put her car into park, closing her eyes for a moment. Part of her felt a little awkward now that she was actually here. She didn't have permission to be at Jack's place while he was out of town, although she couldn't imagine him objecting. Still, she felt a little silly and wondered if she should just turn around and go home.

But it felt so good to be back. She felt somehow closer to him, and she could hear the river babbling so cheerfully, she decided to take a quick look at the moss samples in the river, and then head home. A compromise. What harm could there be in that?

She got out of the car holding her coffee with one hand and slammed her door shut with the other. She took a deep breath, recognizing the familiar smells and sounds of the woods until her attention was drawn to the garage as she heard the unexpected sound of the door rising mechanically.

She jumped and turned, her pulse quickening as both garage doors opened simultaneously to reveal the Jeep and the sports car parked neatly side by side. Her mind had a series of quick questions:

Did he take a car service to the airport?

Or is he back early?

If not, who's here?

Her eyebrows furrowed, but her flight instinct didn't kick in. She stood frozen with a sort of surprised, apprehensive, confused curiosity, keeping her eyes trained on the front of the garage. *Could it be Amory?*

She perceived someone walking out of the shadows from the back corner of the garage, but her mouth dropped as he came into view. He came to the front of the garage and stood in front of Jack's Jeep, eyes squinted closed, face turned to the sun, stretching his arms up to the sky. It was a man. A very hairy man, well over six feet tall and completely naked. His body was dirty—almost covered in various shades of brown and maroon…what? Mud? His hair was matted and messy, but Darcy could tell it was black underneath. His beard was wooly and wild, black with a generous peppering of gray. Darcy's eyes were drawn up to his fingertips, which retracted in front of her eyes—long, yellow, claw-like nails shrinking back into his skin, as though pushed by sunlight back into darkness. He gave one long, low bellow of a growl to the blue sky before lowering his arms and head.

She couldn't help the sound that escaped her throat, halfway between a whimper and a scream, and the creature turned its head to her in surprise, glowing yellow eyes boring into hers.

Darcy.

Jack's voice. She sucked in a wheezing, desperate breath and felt her coffee splash over her shoes as her cup and keys fell to the ground. He blinked twice and his eyes turned brown.

Don't be frightened. I'm still me.

She couldn't breathe. She leaned up against the door of the car and watched as he approached her. One step. Two. As he came closer she could see how filthy he was. And no, he wasn't covered in mud. He was covered in varying degrees of dried blood.

**…they each cut their teeth on the full moon,
howling and fearful, and the mothers realized
that they had each borne a monster…**

"Darcy…" he started, and her eyes widened at the sound of Jack's voice in this thing's filthy, animal-like face. Her brain was a jumble, trying to process what was going on.

Why did Jack say he was away? Where had he been? Did she really just see claws retract from his hands? Why was he covered in blood?

"Darcy, what are you doing here?"

She couldn't catch her breath, and her hand fluttered over her heart, standing up against her car. "Wh-why do you look like that? What's going on? You w-were away on business."

**Skinwalkers who hunted like their
father for three…full…days.**

The world started spinning and she put a hand to her scorching hot cheek.

"Darcy. I can…I can explain."

"W-w-why are you c-covered in blood?"

**…razor-sharp fangs, long, yellow claws,
the face of a wolf, eyes that burn
and the strength of ten men…**

"C-calm down." He took another step toward her and she tensed. She thought about running, but she knew he could outrun her. She put up her palms in frightened supplication. The blood was rushing from her extremities, and her fingers felt like icicles. So cold, they might snap if bent.

"Don't come closer. P-please don't."

She was feeling dizzy. She couldn't think clearly. She stared at him desperately.

**Its fangs drip with the blood
of its victims.**

He flinched and froze, dropping her eyes.

Darcy sucked in a breath, trying not to faint. "W-where have you been? W-what have you…b-been doing…and whose blood is that?" Her voice was thready and high-pitched, and she felt the moisture of tears slipping down her cheeks. Her blood was pumping so fast it was deafening.

"I've been here," he murmured.

"In—in your garage?" She flicked her glance to the corner where he had emerged. To the metal door with the security pad. "That's not a wine cellar, is it?"

He didn't look up. He shook his head.

**No one could love such a hideous,
abominable creature.**

What was the name of the creature?

The Roux-ga-roux.

The mythical creature that ate flesh. The Métis werewolf. The monster. Words formed on her tongue and escaped her mouth before her brain could sanction their release.

"The were…wolf…the monster. Oh, Jack," she sobbed, her fingers shaking before her, wide-eyed and trembling. "You're…you're a Roux-ga-roux, aren't you?"

His eyes were burning and yellow when he raised them to meet hers. He closed them as his face crumpled in pain before he slowly bowed his head. Darcy knew the answer and her heart splintered with the pain of watching all of the puzzle pieces finally fit together with heartbreaking, terrifying clarity.

She wanted to run. She wanted to run away and hide before he answered her. She didn't want to hear the word that would destroy everything sweet and real between them. She didn't want to be in love with a monster.

But she couldn't move. She stood frozen, holding her breath, staring at his thick, black, dirty, wolf-like hair.

He raised his eyes and they were brown again. He looked so much like Jack Beauloup, Darcy wanted to die. She saw the pain there, the desperation, and then…the surrender.

"Yes," he breathed.

Her head lolled back and the world went silent and black.

For the first time in Darcy's life, she fainted.

SHE WAS SOMEWHERE SOFT LIKE a cocoon, and sighed with pleasure. It was warm and cozy and smelled like Jack. Jack, to whom she was bound. Jack, whom she loved.

Wait. Jack isn't…Jack.

Alarm bells were going off like crazy in her head as she remembered the creature from the garage and she jerked herself into a sitting position.

She realized that she was in his bed and he was sitting quietly in a chair bedside her, freshly showered and shaved, devastatingly handsome, looking exactly as he looked last Sunday morning when she said good-bye to him. He watched her carefully from his seat and she saw that his brown eyes were grief stricken as they caught hers.

"Don't be frightened."

Her glance darted to his hands but he kept them unmoving in his lap. Her breathing was shallow and ragged as she looked toward the bedroom door. He blocked her escape.

"I won't stand in your way if you want to go."

He looked up at her and she was shattered by the pain she saw there—she had never seen such misery, such anguish, such languid despair. Her eyes filled with tears of pity and grief, and even grudging compassion, as she stared at him. At Jack. At the face of this man whom she loved. Had loved? Still loved?

She didn't know. All she knew was that he held a terrible, terrible secret inside.

"Or we could talk."

His voice was a whisper, but she heard the glimmer of hope and it twisted her heart.

"Willow told you what I am?"

Darcy nodded once, drawing her legs against her chest, still leaning back against the headboard, her body tightly coiled, protecting itself.

"I need you to know—everything I said was true, Darcy. *Is* true. Everything…" He put his head down and ran his fingers through his hair, looking down at his lap, as his voice got softer. "Everything."

"Did you kill somebody in your garage?" She stared at him, and felt angry with herself for feeling relief when he shook his head back and forth. But it coursed through her body, warm and comforting.

"No. It was—"

"It was *what*?" she demanded in a whisper, relief cooling back to fear.

He looked up at her, his face twisted. "Fresh dead."

"What?" she demanded with a sob, repelled by this new, gruesome language. "What is *that*?"

"It was a—a buck I hunted on Sunday night."

"Deer. Willow said—"

He nodded. "Deer is…*atypical* for someone like me. Most of my kind prefers…"

Darcy swallowed. *Control.*

"This is what you meant? What you learned while you were away from me? You learned—"

"Yes. And more. So we could—so we could be toge…"

His voice trailed off in a tortured whisper. He didn't bother finishing the word, let alone the thought. He must have suspected how absurd it would sound to her right now.

Darcy looked down. She was having trouble understanding. Part of her didn't want to understand at all—just wanted to walk out of Jack's house, out of Jack's life forever. But while they'd been apart over the last few days, she'd felt a ceaseless, throbbing yearning to be with him again. She owed it to herself to understand who and what he was, before making the decision to leave.

"Do you know I love you?" he whispered, his eyes entreating hers.

"Tell me everything," she murmured, looking away from him, ignoring his words.

He didn't speak immediately and she sensed he was trying to figure out what to say. She had the insane urge to laugh at him. He'd had two decades—a veritable lifetime—to figure out how to tell her everything and now he was stalling. She hugged her shivering body. A moment later, he placed a blanket next to her feet. She stared at it and tears rolled down her face.

"You're cold," he said.

"I didn't think that," she said quietly in a small, broken voice.

"I know you didn't," he said gently, as she knew he would. "You shivered."

Darcy pulled the blanket around her body as he started talking.

"Willow was right. I'm a blooded Roux-ga-roux, which means by birth. I wasn't turned. A Roux-ga-roux, or um, we say a Roug...it's, um, it's a wolf-man hybrid. Also called a skinwalker by the Métis. My eyes turn yellow when I shift...or when I feel intense emotion, but I try to control it as much as possible. Your skin burned because when we had sex, my body threw off extreme heat. Not extreme for me or another Roug, but extreme for you, for a human. You lose time when we're together because we're on *my* time, which feels fast to you. *Soul flight* is the way Roux-ga-roux connect over time and distance with their mate. Except they don't call it that. They call it *Dansmatête,* which means 'inside my head.' Eyespeak is the way they communicate when they hunt together at night...only it wouldn't work with you because your eyes don't glow. We can only Eyespeak in the light. In the light." He said this slowly and wistfully, his voice breaking. He paused before continuing. "The binding. Darcy, the binding was irreversible."

Darcy blinked rapidly as more tears pooled in her eyes, spilling onto her cheeks in rushing streams.

"I shift for three days in every lunar cycle. Others of my kind shift more often, but I don't. I don't want to. I've learned how to control it almost all the time, but I can't control it when the moon is full. I have tried so many different ways, but I can't..."

Darcy looked at him and sobbed, "What else?"

"You don't need to know—"

"What else?" she persisted in a dead voice.

"It's the stuff of nightmares for your kind. Please—"

"The truth. Now."

He rubbed the back of his neck with his hand, looking down. She could hear him take two deep breaths before launching into it, cringing as he spoke.

"I have to feed when I turn, but I don't hunt hum—your kind. I'm bound to you so I refuse to hunt traditionally. So, I eat fresh dead instead. Animals. Big game. And three days a month I lock myself in a reinforced steel cage—a meat locker—under my garage with a dead—"

Darcy gagged then leapt off the bed like a gazelle, springing into his bathroom in time to vomit into the toilet. She retched and sobbed, holding her hair back with one hand until there was nothing left in her stomach and she sank down on the bathroom tile, sitting up against the tub where he'd held her hand on Sunday. *I can't lose you now.*

It made her heart clutch to think of his words.

"Are you okay? Can I help you?" he called.

"No!" *You stay away from me.*

She pulled a hand towel from the rack beside the sink and wiped her mouth, stalking out of the bathroom and sitting across the room from him on the edge of the rocking chair, by the windows where he'd kissed her so tenderly on Sunday morning.

"When were you going to tell me?" she asked, thinking that a lie of omission was just as bad as a bold-faced one.

"Darcy. I wanted you to get to know me. I didn't want it to…define me."

"It *does* define you," she whispered. "It *is* you."

"It's only a part of who I am."

"What if you weren't in the cage?" she demanded.

"I'm *always* in the cage at full moon."

"What if you weren't?"

He bit his lower lip shaking his back and forth.

"Answer me!" she demanded.

"I wouldn't hurt you," he said softly. "I would never hurt *you.*"

"You don't know that for sure."

"I do. I *can't* hurt you. It's impossible."

She believed him.

"Okay…but you could hurt someone else. Someone I love. Amory. My mother. Willow. My neighbors. Their children. You don't hunt because you lock yourself away. That doesn't mean you've mitigated the impulse. What if—?" She cringed, closing her eyes against the thought that her heart had lured such a creature to her town. Unintentionally, she had placed her entire town in danger. "You can't stay here."

"I can. I'm strong. I can control it."

Anger welled up inside of Darcy. For the kiss that had changed her world. For the confused years of soul flight. For the man who walked into her life almost two weeks ago, who she loved more deeply, more completely, than she had ever loved any other being, whom she knew she would love for as long as she lived. And anger bubbled up inside of her like spewing lava. Anger for his deception. Anger for his choosing her. Anger that he wasn't just a regular human man. Anger that his nature was so brutal. Anger that she loved him, but was also repulsed by him. White, hot anger—the type that made people say hurtful, unforgivable things.

Her eyes brimmed with furious tears as she stood broken before him.

"You're a fool if you believe that," she said evenly, holding his eyes with hers. "You're a *monster*."

His eyes flashed fire, narrowing at her words. Pain, and then fury.

"We're *bound*," he growled.

"I don't believe that." This was a lie. She wished she didn't believe it, but she did. No matter what he was, her heart belonged to him. She would deal with that later.

"Yes, you do…and you can't break it, Darcy. It's for life. We belong—"

"Maybe." She got up from her seat and crossed the room, picking up her shoes by the door and stuffing her feet into them. In her mind, she positioned a knife over her heart, took a deep breath, then pushed it in with all the strength she had. "But I can let it die inside of me. I can choose never to see you again."

He winced as if she had taken the knife to his flesh too. To *his* heart as she had to her own. He stood to face her, clenching his jaw and blinking his eyes quickly with emotion.

"*Please* don't do this."

"*You* did this," she lamented bitterly, biting back more tears. "I don't want any part of it. Leave Carlisle."

"I love you, Darcy. I'll love you until I die."

She swallowed, looking down, her heart bleeding out beside his.

"If that's true, then leave here. Please leave and never, ever come back."

"I belong to you, Darcy, and you—"

She stopped him with her eyes, which were shining with tears, angry and absolute.

"Belong to no one."

Then she turned and walked away from Jack Beauloup—out of his house, out of his life, away from his heart—without looking back.

Part 2:
Jack

The Binding

HE COULD FEEL HER EYES on the back of his head. Again. His heart pounded in his chest, thumping uncomfortably against his ribs, and it took every shred of his self-control not to turn his head to look at her green eyes and pinkish-blond hair.

Every shred. And for a seventeen-year-old skinwalking Roug, that's saying something.

Jacques Beauloup took a deep breath, slunk further into the theater seat and kept his nose in his book, reading. Or rather, pretending to read. He read the words but he was too distracted to actually process them or relate to them. She shifted in her seat, releasing pheromones, and her scent made him shudder and harden. He ground his jaw and closed his eyes, trying to calm down.

Auditioning for this play had been a mistake, but when he overheard her tell a friend that she was spending her summer attending the high school musical theater camp, he couldn't get the idea out of his head. He had no real interest in musical theater, but two months rehearsing for a play meant two months of seeing Darcy Turner every day. While he knew he couldn't *have* her—and heck, he barely *knew* her—he wanted to be around her as much as possible before things changed. Before he changed.

Speaking of mistakes, coming back to New Hampshire had been a mistake—a *huge* mistake—and Jacques couldn't help resenting his parents for their decision to try to reclaim the Southern Bloodlands. Others had tried to return and resettle in Carlisle, but it had never gone well. Jacques agreed with the pack elders—the land was irrevocably cursed and they should tear up the deed or sell the land back to the nefarious Proctors and be done with it. But Jacques's father, Dubois, was looking for a fresh start with Jacques's mother, Tallis, and had convinced her that they could find it in the woodland cabin still owned by the pack and located in the Bois Loup Garou.

The move really hadn't helped things at all. Aside from isolating their family from the support of the pack, Tallis Beauloup wasn't ready to forgive her cheating husband and could barely stand to glance at his infant daughter, Lela, whose care was mostly left to Jacques's less-than-enthusiastic twin sisters, Jemma and Jeanette. Jacques's five-year-old brother, Julien, escaped to the woods more and more often to evade the near-constant—and often explosive and bloody—battles between their parents.

On one topic all four siblings were in perfect agreement: their father shouldn't have broken the binding. His reasons for straying with Lela's mother didn't matter. His actions were indefensible.

Darcy cleared her throat behind him and his thoughts scattered like feathers in a tornado, his insides whirling with want for the pale-skinned, freckled, green-eyed girl a few rows back. He hadn't had a woman yet—what was the point? He knew that he wouldn't be able to reach any sort of climax with some random girl, so why get involved? Better to wait for the binding, which would happen by the Equinox on September 21, after returning to the Northern Bloodlands tomorrow.

And yet, imminent binding or not, he still couldn't get Darcy Turner out of his head. Not since the first moment he laid eyes on her.

He had initially noticed her in the library during the school year. Arriving a few minutes early on the first day of study hall, he found a seat at a table far from the circulation desk, away and alone. A few minutes later, the door had opened again as more students filed in, taking seats in small groups, joining friends, ignoring the dark-haired newcomer sitting on his own. Jacques, in turn, ignored them back, finding little in common with the white kids in this typical New England town, longing for the comfort and familiarity of his pack at home.

The door opened again and Jacques looked up in time to see the sun shift sideways in its course so that the angle from which it shined through the library skylight created a spotlight on the entryway and drew his eyes specifically to her. Blinded by the light, he couldn't make out her form at first, until a cloud passed slowly over the sun. She stood in the doorway in the fading glow, ethereal, like an angel, and Jacques watched her, breathless. Literally breathless—the air in his lungs was slowly expelled from his body until his diaphragm ached with emptiness. He felt his face go slack and his eyes water. He felt dizzy and weak until his body rebelled, sucking in a boatload of air and sitting up straighter. But he couldn't look away. She stared straight at him, locking her eyes with his, and he watched her pink lips turn up just slightly, her eyes soften as though in recognition. The mechanics of his heart were deafening in his ears, roaring with the rush of blood coursing recklessly through his veins, pumping at full speed as his eyes held hers.

"Darcy!" Her attention was claimed by a friend at a nearby table and he watched as she pushed her hair over one shoulder and sat down beside her friend. He stared at her body as she moved: her larger-than-average breasts, small waist and long legs made her look less like a girl and more like a woman to him. He watched as she folded her hands in front of her on the table after she'd hung her backpack on her chair, the graceful way her neck rotated to look at him one more time.

He had looked down quickly so that she wouldn't see his eyes. He felt the heat of them and for the first time in Jacques's life, he wondered if they were burning as he'd seen the eyes of the bound men glow. As a *lou-veteau*, a cub, his eyes only glowed at night or while feeding, so until now he had never felt the blinding heat in his eyes during the day. He risked a glance at the girl's light orange hair and then looked down quickly as a wave of hunger knocked the wind out of his lungs again. He'd never felt this sort of merciless pounding in his heart, never felt this sort of height-ened rigidity in his body, especially in his lap where his erection strained against his jeans, threatening to burst as he felt her turn to look at him. Between concentrating on not shifting and not ejaculating right there in the middle of the library, he didn't get even a second of studying done. He stared at the table with a fierce determination, waiting until she had left the room before he trusted himself to collect his things and stop off in the bathroom before heading to next period.

He found out later that she was two grades below him, the older child of two, in a family only outlasted in Carlisle by the Proctors. Jacques couldn't care less who her people were—his body burned for her in a way that was confusing and dangerous, but absolutely essential in its power and demand. Darcy Turner, the freckled white girl from the town adjacent to the Southern Bloodlands, was Jacques's first introduction to spellbinding, devastating lust.

His fingers twitched with the longing to touch her fair hair; his mouth ached to press up against her rosy lips; and her breasts tortured him at night as he lay in bed, trying to figure out why a human girl should have such an effect on him. After avoiding her eyes and fighting the attraction for weeks, he finally allowed himself to indulge his *longing* for her, as long as it remained distant and detached, fantasies housed in the privacy of his own mind. He promised himself not to speak with her and definitely not to become involved with her. He could admire her from a distance. He could want her in silence. Anything else wasn't an option.

And so Jacques watched her. He watched her in the library and in the school hallways. He memorized her schedule so he could watch her move from class to class. He auditioned for this ridiculous play so that he could see her over the summer.

Only once had he broken his promise to himself and spoken to her, but he considered it an exception to his pledge. Following her one afternoon, he watched in horror as she walked distractedly across the parking lot reading a book, and Jacques had grabbed her arm as a speeding car came around a curve. As his hand had touched her skin for the first time, it was like he was made of iron and she was a magnet, so terrible and forceful was the attraction between them. Every cell in his body stood at the ready to touch every cell in hers, and he'd had to push her arm away forcibly, or he might never have let go. The shock of it had confused and angered him, causing him to speak sharply to her and stalk away, hoping she didn't see the painful longing for her written all over his face.

Tonight was the final performance and tomorrow he would head north. For several weeks he would meet the eligible girls of his pack and the neighboring packs until he figured out the one to whom he should be bound. They would kiss, and if the binding was preordained they'd know it instantly. She would belong to him and he would belong to her. They would start their lives together—go to college or look for jobs together. Some even started families right away. They would inevitably hunt together. Eat, sleep, and drink together. Live free and die together.

At one time, Jacques looked forward to the binding with anticipation, for the pleasure he would find with his mate and the completeness her partnership promised him. But lately he couldn't think of anything or anyone but Darcy Turner, and he started to wonder if even the binding would be able to banish her from his heart and mind. Of course it *would*. It was the most powerful bond known to his kind. It was just that what he felt for Darcy was so all-consuming, he had trouble imagining how much different and more intense the binding could possibly feel.

Jacques finally got his body under control and followed the rest of the cast to the area behind the stage where they changed into their costumes before the performance. He put on the white pants and striped jacket quickly and went to stand at his favorite place on stage right. He felt her standing there watching him every night, saw her hopeful smile out of his peripheral vision as she tried to catch his eyes. He pressed his nose against the musty velvet curtains and inhaled, picking through decades of DNA to find hers and savor it.

A short time later Jacques found himself on stage singing "It's You" for the final time, when he felt a deep and sudden stirring inside. His body stood on stage singing, and if he had a soul, it would have felt the desperate, poignant melancholy of his dwindling time near Darcy Turner.

He thought of her walking into the library that first day, a beautiful, pale angel of blinding light walking into the murky, brooding darkness of Jacques Beauloup's Roux-ga-roux world. For the first time in his life, he admitted to himself that he despised that soulless part of who he was. The hunter. The killer. The monster. He cursed the unfairness of his birth. He wished for a moment that he was full-blooded human with a right to touch her, kiss her, take her out on a date, marry her, and father her children. Unlike others of his kind, he struggled against the weight of his dark destiny when he wanted her light in his life so terribly. He wanted her light. He wanted *her*.

His thoughts pressed further and he had a rash, passing notion, standing on that stage, that he would do *anything* to have her, anything—as impossible as it was to even dare to dream—to be bound to *her*. *I will do anything for the chance to love her and be loved by her.* And for that moment, the desperation in his heart echoed and reverberated off the walls of that old high school auditorium as the sheer power of his longing took flight.

The song ended and he bowed with the others, but something had changed inside of Jacques, and as he approached Darcy for the last time, he knew he wouldn't be keeping his promise to himself tonight. Just for tonight, just for one moment, he would act like a normal, human teenage boy. The binding would commit his heart elsewhere soon enough. Tonight it beat for Darcy Turner and he would surrender to his desperate hunger for her in these last moments they'd have together.

He watched as her green eyes lifted to his, twinkling in the near-darkness of the stage-right curtains. She seemed surprised by his frank attention after months of offering her his cool, disinterested glance. She stepped back as he approached, but once her eyes met his, she never looked away. Not when he breathed her name. Not when he touched the wild fluttering of her heartbeat in her neck. Not until his lips found hers in the darkness. Then he felt them finally close, her lashes fanning softly against his cheek as a single tear escaped the well of her eye.

If touching her arm weeks ago in the parking lot had felt magnetic, touching her lips with his felt like another force of nature altogether. Time stopped. The world around them disappeared. For a prolonged moment as their lips touched for the first time, Jacques's heart stopped beating. He felt it grind to a halt, the valves still and dormant, the blood stagnant in his dying body. Then he kissed her again. And as though his heart sought and found the rhythm of hers, the valves opened again with a whoosh and his blood started rushing. His heart had been re-born vibrant, alive…*bound*.

Though he'd never felt the sensation before, he recognized it with absolute certainty.

Jack drew back in horror to look at Darcy's face. She was a full-blooded human and he was a blooded Roux-ga-roux. *This is impossible.* He *couldn't* be bound to her. In the history of time and tribe, he could never recall a story of a binding between a Roug and a being of a different race. The members of his pack were only bound to one another—never, ever to an outsider, and certainly never to a full-blooded human.

"It can't be," he murmured, appalled by the permanency with which his actions, his broken promise, had just impacted both of their lives. But there was no escaping it. As Jack stared at her beautiful face, soft in the half-light, he felt the certainty of their fate. He could feel it. "It's *you*."

He wasn't the same person he was before he had kissed her. He was no longer a boy with a crush on a girl. He was a man staring at his woman. The deep, unerring, unrelenting longing he felt for her had been requited, had been transfigured into the unmistakable, undying love that accompanied the binding.

I belong to you.

Overwhelmed with tenderness, he gazed at her, allowing himself just for a moment to acknowledge the permanence of their bond and the fullness of his heart. For the first time in his life, he understood the binding as he'd never understood it before. It was the closest he would ever come to understanding what it was to have a soul. He would live for her. He would die for her. Her life was his and his life was hers.

On the heels of celebration, however, was confusion and fear. He trembled with the weight of the irrevocable contract he now had to her and turned away, but not before finding her hand in the darkness and lacing his fingers through hers. Her flesh pressed against his, cool and familiar, and he couldn't tell where her body started and his ended. His body accepted hers as an extension of his and only reconfirmed what he already knew.

And you belong to me.

He would have to leave her tomorrow. Now that it had happened, he needed to go home, to Portes de l'Enfer in the Faunique des Laurentides, also known as the Northern Bloodlands, to declare the binding to the elders, seek their acknowledgement and ask for their guidance. Surely there was a precedent. Surely he wasn't the first Roug to bind with a human. Surely they could explain to him how it happened and what came next. He would return to her as soon as he had some answers. His heart wouldn't let him stay away from her for long—a few days would be painful enough.

She looked up at him and he met her eyes in the shadows, fighting the urge to kiss her again. There would be plenty of time for that—a lifetime. He couldn't bear to be away from her for long. He placed her hand on his arm as they skipped onto the stage together.

He would get his answers and return immediately to his woman, to his love, to Darcy Turner.

F OR WHAT IS BOUND CANNOT be broken.

Chapter 1

JACK CROSSED THE ROOM AND stood at the window, willing Darcy not to leave. His fists were clenched tightly by his sides, and his fingers, whose nails had been clipped down to nubs an hour before while she was passed out, ached. *Look for me, Darcy. Look up and see me.*

He watched as she bent down beside her car, then stood up, holding wet, muddy keys, which she dragged across the thigh of her jeans. He could see that her face was wet from tears. She put one hand on the hood of her car and the other grasped the keys with white knuckles as she stood motionless. He watched the play of emotion on her face: sadness, revulsion, anger. She pushed her hair out of her face with the back of her free hand, took a deep, sobbing breath that racked her shoulders, and opened her car door. His eyes burned as he stood motionless at the window, lightheaded and unfathomably grieved, as he watched her drive away.

He watched until he couldn't see her taillights anymore and then he watched for a while more, staring in a daze at the muddy road that led back to town. He may have stood for an hour or more. He didn't know. He didn't care.

She didn't come back.

He felt his claws protracting from the pain in his heart and clenched his eyes shut, concentrating on anything but Darcy. Anything but her face as she stared at him. Anything but her words—*You are a monster.* He swallowed painfully and flexed his jaw as he tightened his fists.

I will not shift. I will not shift. I will not shift.

You knew things would come to this at some point.

I will not shift. I will regroup. I will not shift. I will regroup.

You're bound to her. Lean into that. Trust it.

I will regroup. I will regroup. I will regroup.

He felt his body start to relax and his claws retracted painfully. He looked down at his swollen fingertips, at the neat line of four bloody claw marks on each palm. His phone may have been buzzing for a long time, but he was only aware of it now as he came out of the immediate danger of shifting.

Jack looked down and sighed. *Lela.*

Disappointment washed over him and he realized that somewhere inside of him he had hoped it was Darcy. He definitely didn't feel like talking to his little sister right now.

His phone quieted and he held it loosely in his hand, away from the shallow puncture wounds that still bled. They'd heal in a few minutes and he could wash the blood away.

Buzz. Buzz. His phone started buzzing again.

"Damn it, Lela," he growled, staring at her smiling face flashing on the screen.

He touched Talk.

"*What?*"

"*What?* How about *Hello?* Bad mood much?"

Jack took a deep breath and sighed. What had happened with Darcy wasn't Lela's fault. Her life was tough enough without him taking it out on her.

"Not my best day. What's up?"

"Are you coming up? This weekend?"

"What are you talking about?"

"*Le Rassemblement, Jacques?*" *The Gathering of the Northern Bloodlands.* Shit.

He took the phone away from his ear, grimacing as he shook his head and cursed again softly.

"Is that this weekend?"

"Does a whore fuck in a whorehouse?"

"*Charmante, Lela.* You have a mouth like a sailor."

"I had a sailor *in* my mouth on Tuesday night…"

"Enough. I don't want to know."

"Still a sucker for the humans, huh? They'd kill us all if they had the—"

"I have to go."

"Wait. I'll stop. Don't hang up."

He kept the phone up to his ear, but didn't say anything. She knew better than to heckle him about hunting. Although none of his siblings knew the actual reason for his decision not to engage in hunting humans, they'd mostly come to accept it as eccentric.

"It's been years since you been up here for a Gathering. Tallis hates my ass, the girls barely talk to me and Julien's as growly as ever. I need *someone* who can stand me."

"What about Dad?"

"He's worse."

"How often is he shifting?"

"Almost never." Lela was tough, but Jack could hear the worry in her voice.

Once Jack's mother had decided she couldn't forgive his father, it was like something inside of him died. The binding was for life, but Tallis had abjured her mate in the most painful possible way for a Roug. They didn't sleep together, she blocked *Dansmatête*, they didn't Eyespeak, and they definitely didn't hunt together.

They still *lived* together, technically, but in a tense, furious silence that made the shared space claustrophobic and ate away at both of them. It made Tallis brittle, but strong. It made Dubois stupid and weak. Over the years, he'd become more and more problematic and a liability: shifting and hunting haphazardly without following the rules. Making messes someone else had to clean up. And when he wasn't hunting, he was drinking. Liquor and Dubois were not a good combination. Never had been.

"*Merde*," Jack growled.

"Just come for the Gathering? Please?"

Maybe it would be for the best. He felt uncomfortable leaving Carlisle at odds with Darcy, but mostly he trusted the binding—in theory, at least—and knew that eventually they would find each other again. Jack was committed to figuring out a way to be together, but she clearly needed a little bit of time to process things. Maybe he *should* get out of town for a few days and go to the goddamned Gathering. He could check on his family, and besides, he needed to talk to Tombeur about Darcy and see if he had any insight or advice.

"Yeah. I'll be there."

He heard her exhale in a rush of relieved breath.

"Thank you," she whispered.

"You bound yet, Lela?"

Silence. At twenty-one years old, Lela was three years overdue to find her mate, but she refused to be bound and as long as she could fend them off she could stay unbound. According to pack law, a man who couldn't subdue his woman didn't deserve her. At least twice, Jack had heard of young Rougs making a move on Lela. Both times they had at least one tooth knocked out of their heads by the unwilling object of their affection. She was young, but fierce, and other Rougs had thought twice before trying to kiss her.

"No," she snarled.

"It's going to happen, *petite soeur*, whether you want it to or not. It has to happen eventually."

"Never happened for you."

"You know it did."

"*Alors, qui est-elle, Jacques*? Who the *fuck* is she anyway? Why haven't we ever met her? What pack is she from and how come she's never come to the Gathering in all these years?"

"Never understood your stake in it, Lela."

"No," she muttered. "You never did."

He sighed. He wasn't in the mood to deal with his high-strung, over-emotional half-sister this morning. His quota of high emotion from women he cared about had already been met for today.

"See you tomorrow?"

"Fuck you, Jack. See you tomorrow." And she hung up.

Well, that was pleasant.

Then again, phone calls with Lela were rarely peaches and cream. He didn't blame her. Being raised by the woman who murdered your mother couldn't help but make you a little mean.

Jack vividly remembered the night that his father had returned with baby Lela. It felt like he'd been gone for ten years, even though it had only been one, because it had been such a terrible time. A year of watching his mother leave early for work and come home late. A year of hearing her weep and howl in her room, in agony to be parted from Dubois, humiliated by his cheating. Not that Jack's father had ever been a model husband—he was lazy and lacked imagination and initiative—but he was sweet and handsome, and whoever he was to anyone else, he belonged to Tallis.

Jack's mother was always the stronger one, and as she had risen in the pack, Dubois had become resentful of her, feeling emasculated even as she insisted that something good in her life meant something good for both of them. Finally, the night that Tallis was elected to the council, Dubois got drunk and slipped away with a young outcast, a half-Roug, half-Métis loner named Lynette. At twenty-two, Lynette still hadn't been bound, and she was known for offering her favors willingly to anyone who caught her eye, bound or unbound. Dubois was humiliated by Tallis's popularity and success and although he couldn't have found much actual physical pleasure in his dalliance with Lynette, he had been able to father her only child, Lela.

Upon discovering that Lynette was pregnant, Dubois and Lynette ran north with the intent to start over. But without the benefit of the pack around them, with its strength and protection, it was hard to find work, and with a few sloppy kills, it was easy for rogue Rougs to become the hunted rather than the hunter.

They eked out a miserable life before finally deciding to return to Portes de l'Enfer and throw themselves on Tallis's mercy. Since Dubois broke the binding, it would be up to Tallis to accept him back into her home and bed…or not. The fate of Lynette and the baby would be decided by the council on which Tallis sat.

It wasn't a good plan. They should have just stayed away.

LITTLE JULIEN HAD NUDGED HIS older brother, Jacques, awake. "I'm scared. *Réveille-toi!*" *Wake up!*

Jacques pushed his brother away, but the sound of loud voices in the small, adjacent living room made him sit up, rubbing his eyes.

The bathroom door between the bedrooms opened and Jemma and Jeanette entered their brothers' bedroom, looking to Jacques for comfort, awakened, like Julien, by the sound of fighting.

"I think Papa's back," sighed Jemma, biting her lower lip. "I swear I heard his voice."

"I think I heard a baby cry," whispered Jeanette, brown eyes big and frightened, bunching the sides of her nightgown in fists.

Jacques put his hands up to silence his younger siblings, pressing his ear against the bedroom door to listen to what the adults were saying.

"Tu…tu viens ici avec ta pute et ton bâtard et tu penses que je vais te souhaiter la bienvenue? Es-tu fou? Es-tu fou, Dubois?" Tallis spoke in a shrill, high-pitched voice.

You come here with your whore and your bastard and expect me to welcome you? Are you crazy? Are you crazy, Dubois?

Jacques looked at Jeanette's face, at her eyes closed and clenched shut against the shame of the words. Jemma began to cry softly and little Julien put his chubby toddler arms around her.

"Sors avant que je te tue!"

Get out before I kill you.

"Écoute-moi, *Tallis*..." his father began in a soft, cajoling voice, and Jacques's heart clutched to hear his father say his mother's name, Tah-lee, so tenderly, beseeching her to listen.

Jacques gestured again to his siblings to stay quiet and slowly cracked open the door. The light was dim in the simple, rustic living room. The desk lamp where his mother had been paying bills was on, but the fire was petering out. His mother stood in the center of the room with her hands on her hips, her black hair falling down her back in curls and tangles, her chin held high. Jacques's fifteen-year-old heart swelled with pride. She looked like a warrior.

He turned his glance to the door. A young woman in a simple dress and shawl stood against the door holding a bundle in her arms, her eyes down. He recognized her as Lynette Reynard. Reynard. The Fox. The surname the Roux-ga-roux gave to half-breed skinwalkers; to be a Reynard was a mark of shame. It would be especially embarrassing to his mother that his father had cheated on her with a Reynard.

Jack looked more closely at Lynette, even feeling a little sorry for her until he looked closer and perceived a smile on her lips. His brows furrowed. She was smirking with her little beady fox eyes narrowed. Why was she smirking?

His father stood in front of the girl, looking much older and bigger than she, his once jet-black hair peppered with grey, wild and long. His face was a mixture of emotions from angry to remorseful to...Jacques sucked in a surprised breath. Oh my God. *Love.* He saw love on his father's face as Dubois gazed at Tallis, and it softened the anger and the remorse. Despite everything, his father still loved his mother.

Jacques looked back to his mother's face to search it more carefully. Fury, check. Disgust, check. But there. There on her mouth he saw it in the way her lips didn't tighten into a thin, white line. They stayed soft and open, in spite of her words, and Jacques thought to himself, his heart skipping hopefully, *She still loves him too.*

A snarky giggle distracted Jack from their intercourse. He looked at the girl. She placed the bundle gently on the chair beside the door and pushed Dubois out of her way, stepping forward, toe to toe with Jacques's mother with her hands on her hips.

"The great Tallis who couldn't hold on to her man! So busy with your council meetings, he came to me. And he liked what he found between my legs." Lynette cupped the part of her body she was talking about and Jacques felt his cheeks flush hot as he watched her.

His mother's eyes brightened to a burn then narrowed and Jacques swallowed nervously, recognizing her expression. This girl was making Tallis very angry.

"I don't blame him. You think he wants your smelly old dried-up prune cunt? What man would want that, when he can have this?"

Jacques's mother looked up and down the girl's body slowly, her nostrils flaring with fury, her lips a thin, white slash. Suddenly her eyes flicked to Dubois and Jacques knew that they were Eyespeaking. He could see it between them, heavy and serious.

Finally, Dubois stepped forward and put his hand on Lynette's arm, holding Tallis's eyes with his. "That's enough, Lynn. We're leaving. *Maintenant*. Now."

Lynette yanked her arm away, turning to him. "Are you scared of her? Of this old lady? Fuck you, Dubois, you half-man weakling. I'm not scared of her."

Tallis dropped Dubois's eyes and focused hers with razor-sharp precision on Lynnette. They burned bright yellow, but Lynette didn't seem afraid. Jacques felt a bead of sweat start behind his ear and make its way down his neck. Flicking his gaze lower, he noticed his mother's claws, sharp and yellow, protracting quietly from her fingertips. He wanted to yell to Lynette to run, but his throat was so dry, he couldn't make a sound. He was stricken, frozen.

Lynette put her hands back on her hips and smirked at Tallis with confidence and swagger. She took one finger and poked Jacques's mother in the chest, above her breasts. "He's done with you. *We're* done with you. Your binding is broken, Tallis Beauloup. It's dead. I belong to Dubois Beauloup and he belongs to—"

Jacques gasped in horror. He watched as his mother swiped a single claw with deadly precision across Lynette's neck, severing her jugular with one fatal, well-positioned blow. Blood, red and bright, sprayed into Tallis's face but she stood unmoving as the younger woman lurched forward, falling into his mother's chest, then slowly slipping down the front of her body to the floor.

Dubois screamed, falling to the ground beside Lynette, keening, holding her slippery head in his blood-saturated lap.

Tallis's arms fell softly to her sides, and Jacques heard the whispered word, "*Moi.*"

Tallis appeared dazed for a moment before glancing down at her rash handiwork. She stood still, her tired, broken eyes turning brown as she stared down at her husband clutching the body of his dead lover. "*Il m'appartient.*"

Me. He belongs to me.

JACK TOOK A DEEP BREATH and shook his head, trying to scatter his painful memories, and then he checked the time and put his phone in his back pocket. It was before noon. If he left this afternoon, he'd make it to Portes de l'Enfer by evening, but the Gathering really wouldn't start until tomorrow. Besides, he had to figure out what to do about Darcy.

Darcy.

He sat down, pushing back on his hands until he rested against the headboard of his enormous bed where she'd sat a little while ago, her horror-stricken, grave eyes fixed on his. Jack bent his knees against his chest, closed his eyes and inhaled; her scent surrounded him, sharp and sweet from so much recent lovemaking on these sheets. It made his heart twist and ache.

To come so close to having her in his life only to have her walk away—*run* away—made his eyes burn with frustration and the unfairness of it. She had no idea the years of discipline and planning that had gone into controlling his impulses to the extent that he could live comfortably and safely among her kind. All for her. All so that he could be with her. And she had turned her back on him.

It didn't matter to his heart. His poor, stupid heart loved her more than ever.

After having sex with her, feeling her naked body pressed up against his, clenched tightly around his in pleasure, he was more firmly bound to her on a conscious level than he'd ever been. He'd always known it was likely that sex with Darcy would prove addictive and essential once he'd experienced it, but he was unprepared for the strength and absoluteness of his need for her now. It wasn't only unbelievably painful, but almost impossible, to imagine his life without her.

He thought of her green eyes rolling back in her head, the softness of her perfect breasts, her light hair spread out like a halo behind her head as his body entered hers, her nails raking across his back, her voice whispering *stay* so that they fell asleep intimately joined together. The way his own body had recognized hers, trembling and shuddering its pleasure, the words *I love you* falling from his lips over and over again like a vow, an oath, the only truth he'd ever known.

His memories switched to this morning—the fear and disgust as she realized what he was. The way she fainted when he confirmed it. Watching her bolt off his bed to vomit when he admitted he fed on fresh dead. Her eyes, so betrayed and disbelieving and hurt.

You're a monster.

I can let it die inside of me.

Leave Carlisle.

Her words tortured him with a pain so specific and overwhelming, his heart clutched and his breathing became ragged as a vise squeezed his chest. He bowed his head and covered his face with his hands. What if he couldn't win her back? How could he bear the pain of it? *Better to die than live without her.*

He clenched his eyes shut.

He pulled her inside.

HE DIDN'T HAVE A LOT of time. He felt the cool ground under his pads as he searched for her in the dim light of dusk. He was up high—on a hillside or mountain peak. He stopped and turned his nose up, inhaling deeply to find her. When he did, her scent was wispy and thin…she didn't want to be here.

She was on lower ground. He took off at a full-speed run toward her. *Darcy. Darcy. Darcy.*

He heard her name echo off the tall pines as he repeated it in his mind over and over and over again, as he rushed over fallen logs, through brambles, his only mission to find her before she slipped away.

He ran down through the towering trees until he finally found himself in a meadow with high grasses and saw her standing in the middle with her back to him, the white fabric of her dress moving softly in a half breeze, her fingers touching the prickly tips of the grass as she had when they walked through Dooley Meadow. He made his way carefully, quietly, closer and closer until he was almost beside her.

One more step and he felt her fingers lightly fan the bristly fur of his back with the same distracted rhythm she'd touched the grasses. He closed his eyes at the gentle contact and took a deep, relieving breath of cool air, which soothed his aching lungs. She didn't pull away. Once, twice, he felt her fingers graze the ruff of fur at his neck. He raised his eyes to hers and she turned her graceful neck to look down at the wolf at her feet as diamond tears fell from her eyes, landing with soft *plops* in the downy fur that surrounded his face.

My heart is broken. Her lips didn't move but he heard her voice—the dazed, heavy lament in her tone that mirrored the grief of her face.

I belong to you, Darcy, and you—

He jolted back, his palms by his sides, flat on the sheets of his bed. They curled in frustration as he realized it was over.

"DAMN IT!" he bellowed, grabbing the pillow beside him and chucking it across the room as hard as he could. It hit the rocking chair by the windows and exploded, a shower of feathers rising up into the air before falling softly on the chair, the bed, the bureau, the floor. It wasn't enough. It wasn't enough, damn it.

He wanted her *here*. He wanted her here in his bed, writhing under him, arching her back to meet his thrusts, touching his scarred chest with her delicate fingers, screaming his name as her body exploded against his. He wanted her musical voice, her inquisitive green eyes, her strawberry-blonde hair, her freckled face. He wanted her working on her book in the study over the garage that he'd built for her, he wanted her coming and going, making coffee in his kitchen, eating Coq au Vin in front of the fire, taking hikes and collecting samples. He wanted her to wear his bathrobe when they got caught in the rain, and to fall asleep in his bed every night and wake up there every morning. He wanted her in his life. He wanted her in his life the way he'd imagined it a million times as he mastered control over his body and planned a way to be with her. He had worked for her, planned for her...he loved her, worshipped her... he would die for her, but he wanted to live for her. And damn it, he had waited long enough.

And now...now...all she could see was a monster. She didn't want him. And even if she did, she wouldn't give into her longing.

He sobbed at the unfairness of it, in frustration and with deep grief, bowing his head and resting it on his knees in despair.

She didn't call you a monster.

It was a small voice that rose from the fragile depths of his battered heart.

WHAT?

When you were inside…she didn't call you a monster again.

SHE SAID HER HEART WAS BROKEN.

It isn't. If it was, yours would be too.

SHE TOLD ME TO LEAVE CARLISLE.

She's upset.

SHE SAID SHE'D LET IT DIE INSIDE.

It can't die. You're bound. For what is bound cannot be broken.

He ran his hands through his hair in despair.

She didn't call you a monster again, the small voice insisted.

SO WHAT?

So, there's hope.

He got out of bed and stalked to the windows, considering this, seeing the possibility in it. She had looked so sad, so deeply grieved standing alone in the tall grasses. But she had touched him gently, not recoiled. She had met his eyes, not drawn away. She hadn't looked disgusted or frightened. He recognized her expression, in fact. He'd seen it somewhere, once upon a time. Where? Where had he seen it?

And then he knew.

Darcy's lips had been open and soft, in spite of her sorrow. Just like his mother's had been the fateful night his father returned.

She still loves me.

His eyes burned and he closed them, taking a deep, cleansing breath— the first he'd managed since Darcy left him this morning.

So, there's hope.

He took yet another deep breath and felt himself surrender to the binding. It was strong. It would hold. He would give her space. And eventually they would find their way back to each other.

Chapter 2

To SAY HE DIDN'T SLEEP well would have been a gross understatement.

He didn't sleep at all.

The tricky thing about the word "hope," he realized as he stared at the shadows of branches on his bedroom ceiling for most of the night, was that it was laced with as much uncertainty as positivity. And by midnight, "hope" had become Jack's least favorite word, his enemy. "Hope" meant that Darcy wasn't by his side, meant that for the foreseeable future she *wouldn't* be by his side, meant that things might not work out for them in the end, regardless of their attraction, regardless of their feelings, regardless of the binding.

Damn you, hope.

I want my woman.

A little after midnight, the overwhelming urge to shift or pull her inside again was so all-consuming, he decided to take a run. He pulled on sweatpants and a t-shirt and slipped his phone in his back pocket. Forest running as a human couldn't hold a candle to forest running as a Roug, but shifting fully while in a heightened emotional state was absolutely unthinkable. The absence of moonlight made it a pitch-black night, so he used his nightsight, allowing his eyes to burn bright so that he could see in the darkness, but that was the only thing he shifted.

When Jack shifted fully, aside from his burning eyes, long, sharp claws protracted from his fingertips and his lateral incisors, canines and bicuspids all dropped like fangs from above, while his incisors and canines erupted and sharpened from below. His body thickened in muscle mass and height, giving him increased strength and speed. His feet widened and toughened into leather-like soles that could run comfortably over the rocks and branches of the uneven forest floor. His hearing, smell and taste were far superior to a bloodhound. His skin was covered—almost everywhere—by a thick coat that receded when he shifted back to human form, with the exception of his hair and beard, which he groomed immediately after.

There were two types of shifting: *Métamorphose Commune* and *Métamorphose de Pleine Lune.* In English, Common Shifting and Full Moon Shifting.

In both cases, the physical changes were about the same. For Jack, the biggest difference was in his ability to control himself.

During a Common Shift, when the moon was anything but full, his lust for flesh and blood was well controlled. As long as he wasn't heating up his blood with high emotion like anger or sorrow, his human impulses and moral code remained intact and could overwhelm the darker Roug impulses. He could use his nightsight or even allow his claws to drop. He could shift fully, if he wanted to Roug run. He needed to be sure he stayed under the radar, of course, but he could control himself almost completely during a Common Shift.

Not so during the Full Moon Shift, at which time his human moral compass was completely marginalized and his Roug urges came to the fore. Although Jack was able to satisfy his cravings on animal flesh and blood when he was locked away without other options, it would be difficult for him to resist a human kill if he found himself in a heavily populated human area. His lust for flesh and blood was all-consuming.

No shifting. No shifting. No shifting. His sneakered feet still ran swiftly, even for a human, helped by seeing the forest as clearly as if he were wearing night-vision goggles. Especially tonight, immediately after a *Pleine Lune* shift, Jack wouldn't generally have any problem with rogue shifting, but his heart ached from losing Darcy and he didn't trust himself not to shift with such intense feelings feeding his darker side. The only factor that could possibly compromise a Common Shift, besides intense emotion, was the smell of human blood. If blood was involved, it increased the difficulty of his control. Which, of course, made him think of Phillip, Darcy's college boyfriend.

When Jack saw Darcy at her cousin's wedding two weeks ago, it wasn't the first time he'd seen her in twenty years. In fact, Jack had seen Darcy many times over the years; he had just taken great pains to ensure Darcy never saw him.

Of all the places she had lived, his favorite was Boston, where she had attended graduate school and where she had a small studio apartment in a pre-war building that had a fire escape outside her window. During Darcy's high school years he'd spent most of his time working for the Council in the Northern Bloodlands, forbidden to see her or contact her in any way. It was for the best. At that time, Jack didn't even have rudimentary control over his impulses and being around her would have put her in danger. But by the time he turned twenty-five, thanks to Tombeur, he had mastered the basics of control. And although he still honored the decision that he should endeavor to forget her, the pull to see her, his curiosity to know her, became too great to ignore. In direct and flagrant disregard for Tombeur's proviso that Jack try to forget Darcy, he decided he *had* to see her.

Much as he had in high school, he made an agreement with himself. If he could track her down, he could *observe* her. Watch over her for a few hours. Get a fix. He wouldn't approach her or let himself be otherwise known to her. He just needed to see her.

Tracking her down hadn't been difficult.

H E'D BEEN WAITING IN HIS truck in the back of the parking lot at Young's Grocery for two days, hoping that Cassie Turner would turn up to do some shopping. As soon as he saw her, he hustled into the store, grabbed a basket and "accidentally" bumped into her, offering an enthusiastic hello.

"Hey there, Mrs. Turner!"

"Well, hello," she'd said, giving twenty-five-year-old Jack a perplexed, albeit friendly, smile.

"I knew your daughter Darcy. We were at Carlisle High together, ma'am. We were in a play together. *The Music Man*."

"Oh, yes, of course…," she'd murmured, still trying to place him. Suddenly she beamed, pointing her index finger at Jack's face. "Lloyd, wasn't it? Lloyd Brenner?"

"See?" he'd exclaimed. "You remember me!"

Fifteen-year-old Amory rolled his eyes, throwing a case of Coke in the carriage and giving Jack a bored stare under reddish lashes. Jack stared at Amory's green eyes for a moment, flinching. It was the closest he'd come to looking into Darcy's in eight long years.

"Well, Lloyd. How are your folks? They moved back east, right?"

"They're very well, ma'am. Back in Boston," he added, hoping she hadn't kept up with the Brenners, whoever they were.

"That's right! Boston!" Her eyes lit up. "Well, that is a coincidence. You must look up Darcy the next time you're home visiting your parents!"

Bingo! "Is Darcy in Boston? Good for her. How's she doing?"

His heart rate had sped up at her name. Hell, his heart rate had sped up just standing near her mother and brother, as it sharpened his memories of her eyes, her lips, her skin tone, and especially her scent.

"She is just doing great, Lloyd. She's getting her master's degree at Harvard."

He could barely breathe, but struggled to keep his face lightly and politely interested.

"Is that right? Musical comedy major?"

Cassie chuckled, shaking her head. "Oh, no. Botany. Plants and flowers. Can't get that girl out of the woods."

Jack's nostrils had flared with this information. He couldn't help but hope that her comfort in the woods was an unconscious manifestation of her connection to him. It made his heart thump louder in his ears, and he rubbed his eyes, worried that his feelings were getting so intense that his eyes would start to burn.

"Oh, no! I think my contact shifted," he said, eyes down, still rubbing.

"Can I help?" Cassie put her hand on his shoulder and he stepped back from her. He needed to get away.

"No, ma'am. I'll just go wash it out. Great running into to you, Mrs. Turner."

"Oh, you, uh, you too, Lloyd. I'll tell Darcy…" He heard her voice over his shoulder as he practically sprinted out of the store, dropping the basket in a pile by the door.

His truck was parked in the back of the parking lot and he jumped in, turning over the engine. Catching his eyes in the rearview mirror, he saw he was right. They burned yellow. But it didn't matter now that he was alone. He knew where she was. Boston. Harvard. Botany. He could find her. He pointed his truck south and started driving.

HE BLEACHED HIS HAIR BLOND, just in case, and dressed in a Boston College hoodie, hood pulled low, before finding a seat on a bench outside the Botanical Museum at Harvard, where he sat waiting for two days. The second day, he saw her. Well, in all honesty, he smelled her first.

Her scent had changed the slightest bit from eight years ago. It was less girl, more woman, and infinitely more distracting to fully matured Jack. He'd been sitting on the bench cracking peanut shells open with his teeth when the wind had changed, drawing his attention to the walkway coming from the academic buildings.

Darcy.

Darcy Turner.

Mine.

His eyes felt drugged and heavy watching her walk toward the museum. She was alone and walked quickly, her flip-flops thwacking the pavement with each step she took. Her hair was still straight and long, still strawberry blonde, the color of cantaloupe melon. She wore denim cut-off shorts which showed off her long, tanned legs, and a moss-green, scooped-neck t-shirt that hugged her prominent breasts, which had filled out as she matured. He stared at the shadowed, tan valley between them, clenching his eyes shut against the waves of lust that were starting to overwhelm him, and then quickly opened them, not wanting to miss a moment when she was in his sight. As she entered the building, he checked out her waist, which was small, and her hips and backside, which were womanly and rounded. As the door closed behind her, he let out the breath he'd been holding.

His body was rigid with need, his erection bigger and harder than he could ever remember. Every muscle coiled with the need to spring after her, touch her, taste her, mate with her, make up for the long, lonely years without her. He swallowed the lump in his throat painfully, bending his head and resting his elbows on his knees. He'd seen her. The plan was to see her and go directly home. But now that he'd seen her, he needed to see more. Even if he couldn't touch her. Even if he couldn't speak to her. He had to see more.

People came and went from the museum as the afternoon wore on, until the door opened again and Jack looked up to see Darcy exiting in the building. He sat up straighter on the bench, watching as she turned her neck to smile at someone behind her, and his heart leapt to see her lips tilt up in a smile. He drank in the sight of her standing in the afternoon sun and felt his body involuntarily start to stand, pulled toward her by a force stronger than him. But Jack's heart soon took a dive, crashing onto the pavement at his feet, when the object of her smile followed her out of the building and put his arm around her waist. The interloper pressed his lips to Darcy's, smiling at her, and Jack threw up in his mouth, turning away from them in loathing.

While he had worried about her safety and general happiness, one thing had never occurred to him, and seeing it now soured his stomach and made him feel faint:

His woman had a boyfriend.

OUT OF BREATH BY THE speed of his run, Jack stopped for a minute, looking around to orient himself. He'd run clean across six miles of preserve deep in thought. He was coming up on Dooley Meadow then Beaver Pond, and then he'd come out in the field behind the Second Congregational Church. He slowed his pace, his fingers fanning out over the high grasses as Darcy liked to do, and he turned his thoughts back to Boston.

Jack walked by the bench where they'd sat together playing *quid pro quo*, and made his way out of the woods, finding himself on the field behind the church. He looked up at the white steeple, brightly lit by a spotlight on the ground, and felt the old anger toward the institution that had forced his people from their lands so long ago. He took a deep breath, turning on to Main Street, remembering the soft light that would filter out of the window from her apartment in Boston.

HE HAD EVENTUALLY GOTTEN HIMSELF under control enough to follow her and the man home. He recognized the man from his year at Carlisle High School: Phillip Proctor, of the nefarious Proctors, whose ancestors had forced the Beauloups and other Roug families from their land. He clenched his jaw, hating Phillip—even hating Darcy a little. He braced himself to watch Phillip follow Darcy into her apartment, but was relieved when they kissed good-bye at her doorstep while Jack squatted across the street, pretending to tie his shoe.

"Can't I come in, gorgeous? Philly wants to come out and play," he'd whined, touching her cheek with his bony, patrician fingers. Jack wished he could break those fingers one by one. *Snap. Snap. Snap.* As for Philly? There were dark things Jack would like to do to "Philly."

"Phillip," she'd said, smiling gently, pulling back from him to find her keys. "I have to write up my notes and I have a big paper due tomorrow. You'd be a distraction."

Jack didn't like the implications of this and looked down again as his eyes started to burn.

"You're no fun," Phillip pleaded, tracing her lips with another finger. "All work and no play—"

"Means Darcy graduates!" she finished with a chuckle. She winked at him and hurried into her building, pulling the door shut behind her and leaving Phillip panting after her on the stoop.

That's my girl, thought Jack. He looked up at her address. He'd be back later. He had other business for now.

Phillip stood in front of her building for a moment, as though he couldn't decide what to do next. Then he pulled out his fliptop cell phone and started dialing. Jack crossed the street to follow a few feet behind him. He watched as Phillip glanced back at Darcy's building one last time before speaking.

"Michelle? Phillip Proctor. Yeah, from Saturday night. Uh-huh. Are you as hot as I remember?" Phillip chuckled. "Scorching, huh? So, I was wondering what you're doing now? Is that right? All alone…I could fix that if you wanted some company?" Phillip chuckled again. "Okay, gorgeous. See you in ten? You bet." He flipped the phone shut and hailed a cab.

Jack had seen and heard all he needed to know. It would have been one thing if Phillip was a highly principled, caring, attentive boyfriend who put Darcy's needs and wants before his own. Oh, sure. Jack still would have hated Phillip's guts, but he also would have grudgingly respected his place in Darcy's life while he was unable to claim her.

But Phillip—and Philly, for that matter—were cheating on Darcy. Cheating on the sweetest, smartest, sexiest, most amazing woman in the world. Jack's blood boiled and he darted into an alleyway as his claws protracted from the blinding fury in his heart.

Phillip was going to pay.

FROM HIS FAVORITE SPOT ON the fire escape, Jack felt like he was a part of her world. He had meant to remain in Boston for a few hours—just to see how she was doing and then return to his life working as an enforcer for the Council. At this point, he was two days overdue to return and knew his disobedience could carry a heavy punishment, but he couldn't seem to tear himself away.

As the days went on, it was easier to control his body, although his hunger for her was ceaseless. But his years of loneliness were somewhat assuaged by being close to her. Even if his lips couldn't speak to her and his arms couldn't hold her, his heart knew how close she was, and he drank her in with his eyes. It wasn't enough, but it was something, and now that he'd experienced being around her, it was hard to imagine letting go.

Jack figured out that Phillip worked for a bank and they mostly saw each other on the weekends, so in the four days that Jack had been following her and sleeping in the far corner of her fire escape, Phillip hadn't been around. Perhaps "scorching" Michelle had proven more hot than Phillip could handle. God willing, she'd burned a hole right through Philly.

Darcy's life became familiar to him the longer he stayed. He watched as she walked around her apartment in some silky boxers and a matching tank top that was totally wasted on her cat, Frank, who wove in and out of her long, tan legs and occasionally spat at the window if Jack leaned forward too close.

She heated the water for tea, taking a tea bag out of a box, unwrapping it, and placing it in her teacup. She liked tea in the evening and sometimes white wine, never red. Her long hair undulated against her back as she moved and his fingers twitched. He took a deep breath, leaning back, staring up at the waxing gibbous moon. Whether he wanted to stay longer or not, this would be his last night in Boston. He needed to be back up in the safety of the Bloodlands before he shifted at the full moon. A city was no place for a lone Roug.

She poured the boiling water into the cup, and then he watched as something caught her attention. She put down the kettle and made her way to the speaker beside her front door. One delicate, white finger pressed down on a red button, speaking into the speaker on the wall. She stepped back and grimaced, looking down in thought, then pressed the button again. Suddenly she threw back her head, scrunching up her shoulders and giggling, and pressed the green button. After she unlocked the door, she disappeared for a moment to grab a silky bathrobe off the back of her bathroom door, reappearing slightly more covered, but almost sexier.

Jack leaned closer to the window. Who was here? It was almost ten o'clock on a Thursday and she had tea to drink, teeth to brush, and studying to do before bed. She opened the front door and Phillip staggered in, steadying himself on a bookcase beside the front door. Darcy stepped back, looking surprised, and tilting her head to the side in disapproval.

Phillip struggled out of his leather jacket, throwing it on the floor, and fell back onto her sofa. Darcy picked up the jacket, hung it on a hook beside the door and asked him a question. He nodded and she walked back into the kitchen, took another cup out of her cupboard and found a new tea bag. She poured some hot water into Phillip's tea and walked back toward the sofa, handing it to him. He glanced at it then gestured to the coffee table, where Darcy placed it in front of him.

As soon as the cup hit the table, Phillip's arm reached out and snaked around Darcy's waist, pulling her down onto his lap. She shook her head, chuckling as he buried his face in her hair, presumably kissing her neck, although it was hard for Jack to see.

Jack could feel his claws dropping, bit by bit, and he was powerless to stop them. The sight of this bastard pawing his Darcy was almost more than he could bear to watch, so he was relieved when she pulled away from Phillip. Still sitting on his lap, she leaned back, picking up the tea and offering it to him with a gentle smile.

Phillip looked at the proffered cup then smacked it out of Darcy's hand, sending its contents flying across an end table and pieces of the shattered cup as far as the kitchen. Darcy leaned back in frightened surprise, her eyes furrowing in understanding as Phillip took hold of her flimsy bathrobe, ripped it open, and pushed his face into her breasts. Jack leapt up and tested the window with the palms of his hands to see if it would open, but realized it was locked shut.

He could hear Darcy's voice through the window, higher pitched as she pushed at Phillip's head, trying to get off his lap.

Jack started to panic. He felt his eyes burning and the prickly hairs pushing through his skin. A full shift had started and Jack was paralyzed for the few seconds until it was finished.

Phillip's arms were like an iron band around Darcy, even though she struggled and fought to get away from him.

Faster, faster, faster. Jack stared at the moon, pleading.

Darcy finally wrenched one arm free and reached back to smack Phillip's face, but Phillip caught her arm and pushed her backward, hard. Darcy fell over the coffee table and landed on her back, her head cracking the floor loudly. With Darcy unconscious at his feet, Phillip staggered up, pushing her head lightly with his foot. In the absence of response, he shrugged then moved his hands to his pants, unbuttoning the top button and unzipping his fly. He reached down and pulled down her silky boxers until they lay tangled around her knees. He licked his lips, smiling, then stood back up to pull down his pants.

Jack flexed his enormous muscles, his long twelve-inch claws protracted to the hilt, and he howled at the moon, fully shifted. He put his back to the window, then with one big push, he hurtled his body through it, shattering the glass of the large pane and rolling unharmed onto Darcy's kitchen floor. Lithe like a wolf with burning eyes and snarling fangs, he jumped to his feet only to see the terror in Phillip's eyes as Philly was neatly castrated by a Roux-ga-roux claw.

S O DISTRACTED BY HIS MEMORIES of Boston, Jack found himself walking up the sidewalk that led to Darcy's house, which wasn't at all surprising. From the moment he tied his sneakers, his heart had been pulling him here. After years of finding her surreptitiously, Darcy acted like a homing device for his heart. Even being in the vicinity of wherever she lived proved soothing to Jack more times than he could count. He detoured off the sidewalk and slipped into the woods adjacent to her lot, walking stealthily through the thicket until he had a good view of the window seat in the picture window.

Somehow he knew she'd be there, curled up with a cup of tea, knees pulled up to her chest, staring at the darkness out the window. He blinked to be sure his eyes didn't glow, then stepped out of the dark woods and walked closer to the window. She couldn't see him through the glare of soft light on the glass.

Her face had a faraway expression, but her eyes were heavy and sad as she traced the rim of the tea cup. He checked the driveway for Willow's car, but it wasn't there. She was all alone with too much heaviness on her mind. His longing to knock on her door and try to talk with her was overwhelming. Just seeing her sent ripples of pleasure through his body, even as it made his heart ache to see her so sad.

He took his phone out of his pocket, careful not to flash the screen toward the window as he checked the time. *1:31 am. Aw, Darcy. You should be sleeping, baby.*

He looked down at the phone again and then back up at the face of the woman he loved. He couldn't stop himself. He dialed her number.

Thank God her roommate was a doctor, which meant that early morning callers weren't cause for panic or alarm. She got up to grab the phone, then returned to the window seat and pressed Talk.

"Hello?" Her voice was raspy and tired. She'd been crying. A lot.

"Darcy," he started, watching her. Her shoulders drooped and she covered her eyes with one hand, but she didn't hang up. "It's me."

She stood still with one trembling hand over her face. He wished he could see her expression. After a moment, she moved her hand and took the phone away from her ear. She crossed her arms over her chest and sat down on the window seat with her back to him.

But she didn't hang up. Finally she put the phone back up to her ear.

"Darce?" he whispered.

"What?" Her voice was thready and thin, laced with tears, and she shifted back into her favorite position so he could see her in profile. He watched her swipe the back of her hand slowly over one eye.

"I know it's a lot to process, baby," he murmured.

She nodded.

"If I could come over, we could—"

"NO!" Her back straightened and she was shaking her head no, even though they were on the phone. "No, Jack. Don't come over. I can't—"

"I won't. It's okay."

"I mean...p–part of me wants..." She started crying softly.

"Please don't cry, baby. Please don't." It was killing him to watch her, unable to offer her comfort. "I never wanted to hurt you."

"It was too good to be true," she whispered.

He swallowed. "I love you. That's true. Nothing feels as good as being with you. That's true too."

"But, you're—"

"Yep. That's true too. I'm not exactly who you thought I was."

"It's like a lie, only worse."

"You'd never have seen *me* if I told you. We never would have had last weekend. And last weekend was..."

He watched as she put the phone down, wiping tears away with both hands. Thoughts of last weekend were affecting her as much as they were him. Her shoulders rose as she took a deep breath then picked up the phone again.

"You have to leave, Jack. You have to leave Carlisle."

"I am."

Her mouth dropped open and her brows furrowed. He watched as her tongue darted out to wet her lips and then she pressed them together.

"When?"

"Tomorrow. I'm going north."

She nodded and he could hear the tears start again. Her shoulders trembled and she put the phone down again to wipe her eyes with the corner of her bathrobe.

"Oh," she finally murmured when she was able to speak.

"Darcy." He paused and took a deep breath. "Do you want me to come back?"

She looked out the window, and his breathing caught as he saw her swollen, tear-stained face. "I...I...I don't..."

"Wait," he said, cutting her off and swallowing the lump in his throat. "Don't answer that."

She sobbed, taking a deep, shaky breath and nodding. He watched her, trying to think of what to say, how to convince her that the man speaking to her now was the same man with whom she spent last weekend. He swallowed then began softly, gently, beseeching her to love him again.

"Listen to me. I love you. With everything I am. With everything I'll ever be."

"Jack—" she sobbed.

"That's all I wanted to say. That's all I wanted you to know. No matter what happens between us, Darcy Turner...I love you forever."

"I can't do this. Good-bye, Jack." He watched as she lowered the phone from her ear and touched the End button, and then she hung her head and wept.

He let out the breath he was holding, clenching his jaw with the force and fury of his longing, his frustration. To have come this close to having her, only to lose her...it was mind-boggling in the worst kind of way. He turned back toward the woods then took one last look at her window. She had her cheek cupped in one hand; the other still held the phone. He could see a necklace, a shiny infinity sign, catch whatever dim light was shining in from her kitchen. His fingers twitched from the memory of its shape and texture. For so many years, it had been his.

THE BLOOD FROM PHILLIP'S INJURY made Jack consider feeding, but the sight of Darcy's unconscious, exposed, injured body on the floor overwhelmed almost any other instinct. Almost. For a moment he stared at the soft, pinkish triangle of curly hair between her thighs, smelling that intimate part of her, his own body hardening in response. His breathing changed from the fury of anger to pure, unadulterated lust. His nostrils flared as her scent washed over him again and again, and he closed his eyes, feeling his Roug part assert itself.

She's yours. Take her. She belongs to you.

He opened his eyes slowly, and the first thing he saw was the gash on her face, breaking through the thick haze of his desire. He growled in frustration and forced himself to shift back to human form to survey the scene.

What a fucking mess.

Next to Darcy, Phillip lay crumpled and unconscious on the floor, his pants covered in blood and his severed penis beside him.

I'll deal with you in a minute, motherfucker.

He gently pulled up Darcy's shorts, grazing the skin of her thighs with the backs of his fingers, and shivering from the slight contact with her body. Then he picked her up off the floor, cradling her limp, warm body in his arms, and carried her to her bed. He closed his eyes, memorizing the weight of her, her scent and softness, before regretfully lowering her to her bed. Pressing his ear against her heart, he was relieved to find a strong, steady heartbeat. He inspected her head. There was a golf-ball sized bump and a small, nasty gash, but he was pretty sure she'd be all right. When he left with the scumbag, he'd call an ambulance and leave her apartment door unlocked for the paramedics.

He sat down on the bed next to her for a moment, surprised that her safety overwhelmed his lust for her body or Phillip's blood. He stroked the light orange hair off her forehead, feeling his heart expand with love for her. The binding had held for eight long years.

For what is bound cannot be broken.

It didn't matter that she was full-blooded human and he was full-blooded Roug. It didn't matter how long he stayed away. His love for her was as constant as ever. Forever. For life.

He picked up her hand and pressed his lips to her palm, inhaling deeply with closed eyes, then placed her hand gently on her chest. Something shiny caught his attention. A silver necklace, an infinity sign on a silver chain, sitting on her bedside table that he'd seen her wear several times while he was in Boston. He touched it gingerly and then shoved it in his pocket, turning away from her.

He had to go. Although he didn't care if Phillip lived or died, he wasn't going to murder him in Darcy's apartment and connect her with that sort of sordid investigation. No. Unfortunately Phillip needed to stay alive, which meant they needed to have a word before Jack returned home. Jack took some dental floss out of Darcy's bathroom and tied a tourniquet over Phillip's stump, and then pulled the rug out from under the coffee table and wrapped up Phillip, which took care of the blood in Darcy's apartment and made him easier to carry. Jack called 911 to request an ambulance for Darcy, threw Phillip over his shoulder, then made his way down the stairs. He placed Phillip's body in the bed of his truck and started the engine, idling on Darcy's street until the ambulance arrived. Satisfied that she would be cared for, Jack headed north again.

He reached the Lakes District in New Hampshire ninety minutes later. Stopping at the town park in Wolfeboro, across from a building with a large red cross reading "Lakes Region Medical Center," he pulled a ski mask out of his glove compartment and walked around to the back of the truck, where Phillip Proctor lay moaning in pain.

Jack jumped into the truck bed and nudged Phillip's face with his foot just as Philip had done to Darcy.

"Hey, fuckhead. Can you hear me?"

Jack leaned down and unrolled the rest of the carpet that held Phillip then picked him up by the lapels of his shirt and dragged him to the edge of the truck bed. He opened the gate and dragged Phillip out of the truck, settling him in a half-conscious state on a nearby park bench; then he squatted in front of him, pinching his arm. Phillip's eyes opened in pain and widened when he looked back at Jack's covered face.

"It—it—it was a…a *m-monster*."

"Listen to me, shithead. If you ever—and I mean ever—go near Darcy Turner again, you better want to die slowly and painfully. You hear me, Phillip? Because the monster will be watching. And he'll come back and finish the fucking job he started tonight." Phillip swallowed, nodding painfully, in a daze. "Let me make myself clear: the only reason you are alive is because she doesn't deserve to be mixed up in the bullshit of your murder. Anyway, you can never hurt another girl like that again. I made damn certain of that, you fucking eunuch."

Jack got back in his truck and drove away. Somewhere in northern New Hampshire, Philly and the area rug found a new home together in a never-heard-from-again dumpster.

When Jack got to Quebec he scrawled a postcard to Darcy.

It read: *You are a beautiful, amazing woman and you deserve far better than me. I'm sorry for everything. Good luck, Darcy Turner. –Phillip*

Chapter 3

JACK TOOK THE LONG WAY home, walking the twelve miles from Darcy's house slowly, arriving back at the lodge close to dawn. There was no sense in trying to go back to sleep. Better just to pack a bag and head north. Away from Darcy. For what felt like the hundredth time in his life.

He tried to look on the bright side. She hadn't hung up the phone at the sound of his voice and she didn't call him a monster again. Part of him wondered if he should have pressed his advantage and knocked on her door, but building up trust with her again might take some time and Jack didn't want to blow it by pushing her too hard too soon.

He thought back to that night on the Carlisle High School stage. That fateful night before his eighteenth birthday when he kissed a human thinking it would be harmless and somehow became bound to her. If he'd known what fate his actions would set into motion, would he have stayed away? In a million years he wouldn't have wished this fate on her. But there was no way he could have known. The reality is that it had never happened before, and as far as Jack knew, it hadn't happened since. Their binding, legitimate and strong though it was, was also an aberration. He couldn't have anticipated it, but he had been horrified when he looked into her sweet face and realized that eventually their road would lead to yesterday morning. Eventually she would have found out who—and what—he really was.

He flattened his hands on his kitchen counter, bowing his head.

You didn't make *it happen. It just happened. You can't do anything but trust it. The binding will hold. The binding will hold.*

He set the coffee to brew, took a long, hot shower, got dressed and threw a few things together in a backpack. Then he poured himself a cup of coffee, washed out the pot, turned off all the lights and locked the front door.

His phone buzzed as he pulled out of the driveway. He looked down, hating the fact that his throat tightened and his body tingled, hoping it was from Darcy.

It wasn't. It was from Lela.

Two words.

Dad's missing.

It felt a little dramatic to send a text advising Jack that his father was missing when his father had regularly gone missing throughout his life.

Dad's missing. Also known as Friday. Or Tuesday. Or July.

Always the drama queen, Lela.

His phone buzzed again and Jack picked up his phone to read the second part of the message.

Tallis can't even find him.

Now Jack's eyebrows furrowed. No matter how much distance separated a Roug from her mate—or how much bad blood—she should be able to pull him inside. Lela's message meant that his father wasn't just physically missing. It meant one of two things: that his father was unconscious…or his father was dead.

He had a four-hour drive ahead. Jack stepped on the gas.

Affter AN HOUR, JACK FOUND himself across the border in Canada as he drove north on Route 108 through the *Parc National de Frontenac*. He passed through the small town of Lambton and sped through Beauceville where he generally stopped for gas and food. He kept his foot on the gas. He needed to make good time.

Jack was so focused on driving, he jumped when his phone rang. He picked up the phone to look at the caller ID and was surprised to see the name "Willow Broussard, MD" pop up on the small screen. The phone rang again and Jack looked out the window, a sour expression reflected back at him. He could tell Willow was very protective of Darcy, which meant that this was going to be a spectacularly unpleasant phone call. The phone rang again. He'd lost his girl and his father was missing. Now this? Jack took a deep breath and pressed answer.

"*Bonjour?*" Maybe he could throw her off.

"*Jacques? Préfères-tu parler en français? Très bien. C'est Willow.*"

Shit. He'd forgotten she was fluent. And if her tone was any indication, she was pissed. And the answer to her question was no. He didn't really want to speak to her in French or at all.

"Willow," he said, low and even. "What can I do for you?"

"You can leave my friend the fuck alone."

Here we go. "Can't do that."

"Yes, you can. You can walk away from her and leave her alone. You're off to a good start. So I just wanted to say thanks for leaving and don't come back."

"I'm bound to her, Willow."

"Yeah. I heard."

He heard the sarcasm in her voice. He hadn't expected that. Not that he'd necessarily expected her to embrace his nature and lifestyle, but he did think there was a good chance she'd believe it was true.

"It's true."

"Are you fucking crazy? It's a *legend.*"

"Legends come from somewhere. Did Darcy tell you what she saw yesterday morning?"

"She said she saw you walking out of your garage in the form of a monster, passed out on your driveway, and when she came to, you looked like yourself again. She said you admitted to being a…a—I can't even say it, and it doesn't matter anyway because it's bullshit. She can't stop crying. She can't work. She's confused. She's taking an ancient legend and mixing it up in her head with old feelings for you. And you're encouraging it."

"You think she's crazy?"

"You know what, Jack? Yes, she appears delusional and emotionally unstable to me. That's my medical opinion. My *personal* opinion is that you need to stop fucking with her head and *LEAVE HER ALONE.*"

Jack swallowed, his heart twisting at Willow's description of Darcy. "She's not crazy."

"Really, Jack? Really? You're some sort of mythical skinwalking creature of the night? Do you think I'm a total moron? I don't know what your game is, but—"

"I think you know that there are unexplainable things in the world."

She didn't dispute this. "Please just stay away from her. She said you're going north. Please don't come back." Her voice had softened as she pleaded with him and it gave him the opening he needed.

"Willow…" he started, and then stopped, wondering if he was making the right decision. He had no other choice. He needed her to believe him, which meant he needed to have this conversation. "What do you know about Phillip?"

"The douchebag who assaulted her then dumped her by postcard while she was at Harvard?"

"That's the one."

"How do *you* know about Phillip?"

He ignored her question. "Tap into the medical records for the Lakes Region Medical Center. September eighth, 2002. Late night or early morning on the ninth. Check for someone admitted who'd had a very *specific* accident. Someone who seemed frightened but wouldn't share any details about his accident. He may have used an assumed name. Read the records. Then we'll talk."

"You know, Jack? You show up here and you make these wild, crazy assertions about yourself and you mess with my friend's—"

"Listen to me," he growled. He took a deep breath and lowered his voice. "I know you love her. I do too. I would never hurt her. I would do *anything* for her. Anything. Check the records, Willow. Let me know what you find."

He heard her sigh. "She was really, really happy with you, Jack. Last weekend? I'd never seen her so happy. She asked me, 'Would it be crazy if I loved him?' I've never seen her like that. Not with anyone else."

Jack's throat felt thick and his eyes burned. It wasn't lost on him that while he had declared his love for Darcy many times, she had yet to return the sentiment, and while the wait wasn't exactly painful, hearing her say the words was something he wanted, something he was longing for.

He cleared his throat. "What did you tell her?"

"What?"

"What did you tell her? When she asked if it would be crazy?"

"I told her it wouldn't be crazy. I said you'd waited a lifetime for each other. I told her that love had been known to grow in rockier places."

Jack's eyes shuddered closed with relief and gratitude, and he knew deep in his gut that if Willow Broussard ever needed anything from him, he'd be the first to offer her his help.

"Thank you," he murmured. "Check the records."

"Fine." She sighed. "I'll do that, Jack."

He heard the phone click as it hung up, and he rolled down his window, appreciating the fecund humidity that rose out of the rain-soaked forest. It smelled like rotten wood and moss and earth and Darcy and everything that was familiar and good. It smelled of rocky places where good things could still grow.

JACK HAD TO FILL UP his tank in Quebec. He also called his mother to let her know he was about ninety minutes away.

"*Jacques?*"

"*C'est moi, Maman.*"

"*Je ne le trouve pas.*" *I can't find him.*

"*Je vais t'aider à le chercher.*" *I will help you search for him.*

She continued in French. "I try to feel him, but I can't. I don't feel him anymore, Jacques. It's just cold and black when I go inside."

"Hasn't this ever happened before?"

"No." He heard her sob. "Never. Not in forty years."

"We'll find him...either way."

"I don't hate him. I could never—"

"I know, Mom. I'll be there soon."

"Wait! Before you go. Did you see her, Jacques?"

He took a deep breath and sighed, feeling very tired and very sad.

"Yeah. It didn't, uh, it didn't go so well. I, uh, I'll be there soon."

He pressed End before she could reply and Jack stared at her picture on his phone for a moment. It was an old picture of her from his childhood—she was wearing a parka and the fur surrounded her face, with her tangle of thick, black hair spilling out the sides, down her shoulders. There were snowflakes caught in the strands, white crystals against the inky cast of her hair. Her cheeks were red and her dark eyes were shining while her lips tilted up in a surprised grin. His father had taken the picture long ago and Jack had always loved it best of any photo taken of her before or after. She was hopeful then. She was happy. It was one of the last times Jack ever remembered his mother being happy.

She had been exonerated for the murder of Lynette Reynard, of course. Jack had even testified on her behalf, confirming that yes, Lynette had challenged the binding between Tallis and Dubois. It was an open-and-shut case.

The Roux-ga-roux's sacred text held a long explanation about the inviolable nature of bindings in their culture, ending with the words, "for what is bound cannot be broken." Jack and every other blooded Roug held those words as sanctified, as absolute. Bindings were a preordained contract in the Roux-ga-roux nation, and challenging it on any real level was a valid cause for self-defense or defense of mate. When Lynette uttered the words "Your binding is broken...it's dead," she'd given Tallis cause to retaliate. Her actions were excused as a crime of passion in emotional self-defense, and the matter was summarily dropped. However, Lynette's death left one very inconvenient, loose end.

The Council gave the motherless child, Lela, to Dubois and Tallis to raise, and because she would be raised in a full-blooded household—and as remuneration for her mother's murder—she was elevated from the surname Reynard to the surname Beauloup.

The humiliation of not only raising Dubois's bastard, but also having to honor her status as a full-blooded Roug was difficult for Tallis. No one actually heard the bells at the time, but the death knell rang for Dubois and Tallis's bond that day. And after that, there were no more photos with shining eyes and snowflakes in her hair.

Jack's mother, who sat on the council with the other pack elders, was the only member of his family who knew about Darcy. Jack hung up the gas nozzle, got back in his car, and pulled away from the service station, vividly remembering the night he told her about his binding.

AS JACK DROVE FURTHER AND further away from Darcy, from the high school auditorium where he'd kissed her hours before, from the small-minded town where he'd never really fit in, he felt his heart stretching painfully.

Tallis had returned to Portes de l'Enfer with the girls and Julien as soon as the school year was over, leaving Dubois, Jack, and Lela in Carlisle. His mother missed the pack too much to stay. She missed her role as a council elder. She didn't want to live amongst the humans, Southern Bloodlands or not. And the bottom line was that she couldn't bear to look at Lela, who was a constant reminder of Dubois's infidelity.

When Jack arrived in Portes de l'Enfer in the middle of the night, several days earlier than expected, Tallis was delighted to see him but perceived the differences in him almost as soon as she embraced him.

"Jacques! Vous êtes trois jours plus tôt que prévu!" You're three days early!

He leaned back, holding her eyes in the darkness, and his mother gasped, grabbing his arm and hurrying him into the small living room where she had killed Lynette Reynard. She stood with her hands on the hips of her jeans, staring at his eyes, her face concerned.

"Your eyes are burning, Jacques."

He nodded briefly, suddenly worried to tell his mother the extraordinary truth of what had happened between him and Darcy.

She took a close look at his face and clothes. They showed no evidence of a hunt, but she still asked uneasily, "Did you just come from hunting?"

He shook his head slowly no.

"There were no She-Rougs in Carlisle."

He shook his head slowly no again then swallowed, looking up at his mother submissively from downcast eyes.

Tallis glanced nervously at the girls' bedroom, pressing her finger over her lips as she pulled their door tightly closed. She took Jack's arm, leading him into her bedroom, behind the kitchen, on the other side of the cabin. He sat down on the foot of her bed and she stood before him, hands on her hips.

He could hear the panic in her voice. "Jacques…"

"She's human." He blurted it out.

Tallis gasped, her hand covering her mouth as her eyes widened. She shook her head quickly, staring at his face.

"That's not—that's not…possible."

Tears pricked his teenage eyes and he dropped her gaze. She put her hand under his chin and lifted it. He watched as her face transformed from surprised to horrified as she saw the truth in his eyes.

Finally, she sat down beside him, staring straight ahead. She took his closest hand in hers and squeezed it reassuringly.

"You must tell me everything."

He told her about the sun shifting course to shine on Darcy that first day in the library. He told her of his endless yearning to be near her. Tiny details about how she looked and how she moved now spilled out with such precise, intimate description, in such a devoted tone, it was as if Darcy Turner stood before them in the flesh and he merely pointed out the obvious. He didn't hold back the details of their kiss, and when he described the stillness of his heart between their first kiss and their second, his mother had suddenly tightened the grip on his hand and bowed her head. Jack suspected she was working to hold back tears.

"You've been bound," she finally whispered.

"Yes," he answered. "She belongs to me and I belong to her."

Tallis dropped his hand and shook her head.

Jack continued. "I've come to tell the council. For the acknowledgement."

The acknowledgement was the second part of the binding. It wasn't necessary that every binding be acknowledged, but it made the contract official in the eyes of the pack and afforded both members the status of full-grown, or mature, Roux-ga-roux with rights to vote, work, and establish a household.

In a flash, his mother had raised her eyes to him and he could see they were desperate and grave.

"Oh, Jacques. Don't be a stupid child! If you do, they will kill her."

"But, all bindings must be respected, must be ack—"

She placed her hands on either side of his face, silencing him. Her grip was painful, the bones of her fingers rigid against his skull in a way that made him grimace.

"You listen to me, Jacques Beauloup. I have no love for the humans. None. But the Council will not believe you. And if you convince them as you have me, they will hunt her down and kill her so that you can be re-bound to one of our own kind."

His eyes had burned again with confusion and fear. "That can't happen. I love her."

His mother flinched, her hands slipping from his face. When she met his eyes again, hers were fathomless in their grief. "This is a *terrible* thing."

Jack stood up, crossing his arms over his chest, and growled at his mother. "She's mine."

Tallis rubbed her hands on her thighs, regarding her son.

"Then there's only one option. You must turn her," she finally sighed.

Jack shook his head quickly. "I won't."

Turning a human was a crapshoot and Tallis knew it as well as Jack. It was possible, but the death toll was high, plus there was another, more important reason that Jack refused to turn her. Turning a human to a Roux-ga-roux was like a rebirth on every level…which meant that while Jack would remain bound to Darcy, there was no guarantee she would remain bound to him. In Jack's mind, it was unthinkable to risk the binding.

"Jacques, if she's not one of us, she's a threat to us."

Jack thought about Darcy walking into the library, about her light and goodness. The thought of turning her dark like him made his stomach turn. "I won't do it."

"You can't stay bound to a human."

"Why not? Just because it's never happened before? I don't care. I'll... I'll leave her at the full moon...I'll come north to hunt...I'll—"

"And when she bears your children? How will you explain when they cut their teeth? When they long for the flesh of their own mother? How will you explain the Eyespeak? And Jacques, you don't know yet, but when your eyes burn for her, your skin will burn her too. How will she accept you when you shift? How will—"

"I don't know! We—we won't have children. I'll only shift when the moon is full. I'll—I'll—"

"Jack...this can't be what you want."

"She belongs to me. Exactly the way she is. I won't let her go and I won't turn her. I'll figure it out."

"It *can't* be figured out."

"*IT MUST BE!*" he snarled at her, baring his fangs, his eyes burning hot.

She stared at him, searching his eyes, unflinching.

"It would take a lifetime."

"Then it'll take a lifetime," he growled back at her.

She started to say something else then shook her head, and Jack knew that she was accepting the absoluteness of his decision. "Think hard, son. Think about what you're doing. We can have someone take care of her."

Jack sprang to his feet, facing her, eyes burning and claws dropping. "I will kill the person who ends her. Then I will kill myself."

His mother's eyes were burning too, but her fangs and claws remained sheathed. Her voice was calm, but firm. "Sit down."

He remained standing. "I mean it."

She nodded once, keeping her eyes down, and his fangs and claws retracted slowly.

"Are you sure this is what you want?" she asked in a leaden voice, meeting his eyes.

He nodded once.

"Are you sure? If she can even come to love you, Jacques.... How will you protect her? From yourself? From others who would harm her?"

"She belongs to me." He ran a hand through his hair, resting it on the back of his neck. "No one will hurt her. No one will ever find out about her."

Tallis stood up and placed her hands on his broad shoulders, tilting her head, her sad smile and tired eyes beseeching him to reconsider. She still didn't understand that his binding was as solid and irreversible as her own.

"I saw you that night…with Lynette Reynard. You know better than anyone, *Maman*. It can't be broken." He looked down for a moment to collect his thoughts before recapturing his mother's eyes. He clenched his jaw together, his mouth a thin, white line. "I am bound to Darcy Turner. Me. She belongs to me."

Tallis had taken a deep breath then raised her eyebrows at him as he used her own words, the words she'd used after the murder of Lynette Reynard. Finally, Tallis nodded her head in acceptance.

"Then so be it. For what is bound cannot be broken. You need two council members to acknowledge the binding before the Solstice. It will be me, of course, and the only other I trust is Tombeur Lesauvage. He's young and liberal. A forward thinker. He was the one who encouraged us to try to resettle the Southern Bloodlands. I will speak to him and if he agrees, we will acknowledge in blood tomorrow."

She cupped his face with her hand.

"Oh, Jacques. You're choosing a terrible path. I wanted so much better for you, my son. A fine binding with a good hunter. Not this. Never this. I see so much heartache and pain ahead. How I wish…I just wanted—"

Jack pulled away from her, feeling the ties that bind a child to its parents strain and snap to dangle helplessly between them.

"It doesn't matter what you wanted, *Maman*. *I* wanted *her*."

AFTER TOMBEUR LESAUVAGE HEARD THE whole story, he agreed to acknowledge Jack's binding, combining his blood with Tallis's and Jack's then inking the initials D.T. next to Jack's name in the sacred text.

But Tombeur had strict conditions first, which—if not met—would result in him alerting the council to Jack's aberrant bond and initiating the process of hunting down Darcy. Jack bristled against the conditions but grudgingly agreed.

Failing to convince Jack to turn Darcy, he insisted that because a Roug-Human binding was unproven and untested, Jack was to stay away from contact with Darcy for a period of ten years. He made it clear that he hoped that because the binding wasn't with one of his own kind, it would fade over the course of a decade. Jack had protested bitterly, but without recourse and fearful for Darcy's safety, he was forced to agree to the condition.

Tombeur further stipulated that, during that ten years, Jack would agree to live in the Northern Bloodlands and work for the council, steeped in the culture and traditions of the pack.

"Hoping you can brainwash my binding away, Tombeur?" he'd asked bitterly, but Tombeur had only raised his eyebrows, remaining quiet and waiting for an answer.

Jack had reluctantly nodded.

Tombeur went on to insist that if Jack somehow reached the age of twenty-eight still determined to make a life with Darcy Turner, he would be responsible for outlining a plan to reenter her life without exposing the pack or otherwise placing it in jeopardy.

"She can't live here, so you'll have to live among her kind, and although I've tried to advocate living in some kind of harmony so that we could reclaim the Southern lands, I've never heard of a Roug willfully living *with* a human. And while I don't give much of a fuck about your precious pet either way, I will hunt her down myself if she becomes a liability for my kind, Jacques Beauloup. You'll have to figure out how to control your impulses. I don't know how. But this is your road, not mine."

Jack had leveled his eyes with Tombeur's.

"That's right. It's mine. *She's* mine."

"I'm not going to bullshit you, *louveteau*, I fully expect for you to relinquish this binding over time—"

"*Je ne suis pas un louveteau. Je suis un Roux-ga-roux ligoté.*" *I'm not a cub, I'm a bound Roux-ga-roux.*

Jack held Tombeur's eyes in a show of courage and equality and wouldn't look away or down, regardless of Tombeur's fierce stare and the aggressive stance of his far more muscular body.

Tombeur finally looked away with a grin and rubbed his chin. "I'll give you this: you got steel balls, son. Good thing, 'cause you're gonna need 'em."

Tombeur had put out his hand.

Jack eyed it, wishing his life was different. But he saw the wisdom in Tombeur's insistence, even if his body cried out to return to her immediately. He would stay in Portes de l'Enfer for a decade and work for the Council until his twenty-eighth birthday. And until he had a viable plan to protect his pack and his woman, he would not return to Carlisle.

"I agree to your conditions."

Jack shook Tombeur's hand then watched as Tombeur blended the blood and scrawled the initials D.T. beside the name Jacques Beauloup. The binding was complete, but Jack's journey back to Darcy had just begun.

Chapter 4

JACK TOOK A DEEP BREATH and exhaled loudly, exhausted by the force of his memories. At the time, he'd had no idea it would take almost twenty years to come up with a viable plan and return to her.

And look where it got you, Jack. Great job.

He wasn't more than ten minutes from home now, and after he greeted his family he intended to grab Julien, who knew the woods better than anyone, and find their father. He was sick of sitting so long, and after the long drive he'd welcome the run. A Roug run. It had been a long time. He almost sighed in anticipation.

He glanced at his phone and was surprised to see that he had a text message. So deep in his own thoughts, he hadn't heard the phone ping.

Found the records you were talking about. When can we talk? Willow

He slowed down the car on a straight, wide road so that he could text back:

Almost home. Need to deal with family business. Tonight. Jack

He hit Send then impulsively wrote again:

Tell her I miss her.

And hit Send again.

As he pulled into the parking area adjacent to his parents' cabin, he checked his phone again and was disappointed to find a single reply.

Tonight. W

Not a word about Darcy.

"*JACQUES!*" LELA RACED OUT OF the cabin and threw her arms around her older half-brother.

"Hey, Lela." Jack clasped her smaller body in his arms, looking down at her braided hair.

When she finally leaned back and looked into his eyes, Jack was surprised by how mature and womanly she appeared. Lela had always been good looking, her skin and eyes a touch lighter than most Rougs, owing to her quarter-blooded human ancestry, but the last time Jack had seen her was three years ago and she'd still been a teenager. She'd certainly filled out since.

"Are you checking me out?" she asked, looking up at him from under heavily lashed eyes.

He pushed her away. "Quit flirting. I'm your brother."

"Half," she said, eyes challenging, hands on her hips. Jack had a sudden flashback to Lynette standing the same way before Tallis.

The door opened and Jack's brother Julien appeared behind Lela. Again, Jack was surprised by how much his siblings had changed in the three years he'd been away. At twenty-six, Julien was almost as tall and broad as Jack with a thick head of jet-black hair, void of the grey Jack sported at his temples. But Jack could see the sorrow around his eyes.

Julien was a *Veuf*. A widower. Bound at eighteen to his sweetheart, Natalia, she'd been killed on a hunt last summer, hit by a truck when they were crossing the road during a hunt south of Portes de l'Enfer. Julien had dispatched the driver quickly, leaving the truck abandoned, and returned to the pack carrying the limp body of his mate.

Jack dropped his eyes to see Julien's little daughter, Delphine, appear at his side. The four-year-old had black hair like her mother and big, brown eyes tinged with tiny moss-colored flakes like her father. Since losing Natalia, Julien and Delphine had moved back in with his parents and Lela.

Lela turned around and grabbed the child, adroitly swinging her up on one hip with a bright smile.

"You know who this is, *louveteau?*"

Delphine shook her head no, looking from her aunt to eye Jack warily.

"This is your Uncle Jacques. Papa's brother."

"Uncle Jacques from the Southern Bloodlands?" she whispered.

Julien stepped up, peeking around Lela's shoulders to wink at his daughter.

"The same."

He smiled at Jack and put out one large paw of a hand, which Jack shook with a big smile.

"Good to see you, *petit frère*."

"*Petit* means small," declared Delphine, with furrowed brows. "My papa ain't small."

Jack chuckled. "He's small to me, *louveteau*. And so are you."

"A'course I am," she replied with a very cross face. "I'm a little girl."

Lela smiled at her half-niece and put her down, telling her to go find her *grand-mère* Tallis and tell her Jacques was home. The three siblings watched her scamper off toward the garden and Jack turned back to Lela and Julien.

"Any news?"

Julien took a deep breath and shook his head.

"*Maman* is crazy with worry."

"In addition to being *just* crazy…" Lela added.

Jack gave her a warning look.

"Hoping you wouldn't mind shifting and helping us search," Julien inclined his head to Lela then looked at Jack expectantly.

"Is Lela up for this?" he asked his brother.

Julien looked surprised at first then grinned, and Jack saw the softness in his little brother's eyes. "Have you *met* Lela?"

Jack flicked his eyes to Lela. Hers burned in indignation. She looked as fierce as a warrior, as fierce as his mother had looked in her prime.

"It's going to be a hard run," he said, deciding not to dwell on the quick tell of emotion he'd seen in Julien's eyes, but wondering if there was something between him and Lela. Although half-brother/half-sister bindings weren't necessarily encouraged, they weren't prohibited by the pack either.

Lela smirked like a fox.

"Then try to keep up, boys."

JACK, JULIEN, AND LELA HAD no luck on their run, even though they covered a huge swath of forest fully shifted. By the time they returned to the cabin, the sun was setting and they were dirty, tired, and hungry. Jack and Julien slipped back into pants they'd left waiting at the side of the cabin.

When Jack rounded the corner of the house, Lela stood naked by the front door, clothes in her hand by her side.

"Good run," she said to Jack, her voice deep and soft.

Jack stopped in his tracks, surprised, and couldn't help but sweep his eyes quickly over her body. Black hair brushed the tops of her shoulders. He dropped his eyes and noticed her nipples standing at attention in the night air. Her waist was small and tight over small hips, and the junction of her thighs was covered in a triangle of dark, curly hair. He looked away and his eyes unfocused without a hint of interest or attraction as he thought of Darcy.

He missed her. He clenched his eyes shut to keep from going inside, to keep from finding her. He wanted to wait until later when he was alone. Then he'd try to connect with her, and hopefully she—

"Jesus, Lela!" Julien hurried around Jack, holding out the shirt he'd been wearing earlier, and putting it over her shoulders. He clutched the sides together until she reached up and took them from him.

"You're a prude, Julien."

"Only because you're acting like a slut."

Jack's head had whipped up as they argued and now he was surprised to see Julien's eyes burning as he looked away from an unaware Lela, who called him a "fucker" as she quickly let herself into the cabin.

Julien stared at the door, cursing softly under his breath. Jack touched Julien's arm and spoke gently.

"She's our sister."

"*Half*-sister. Which doesn't mean anything to the pack."

"Doesn't it mean anything to you?"

"Why should it?" Julien's eyes narrowed but changed from burning gold back to brown. Jack could see the confusion there.

"I can't help it," he admitted in a whisper. "She doesn't *feel* like a sister to me."

Jack took a step back, staring at his younger brother, unsure of what to say. Regardless of pack rules, they'd grown up with Lela. She wasn't a contender for binding. She was their sister, their family.

"She's so good with Delphine. And she's around all the time. I hear her sleeping in the other room. I hear her breathing. I hear it when she turns over in her sleep. I smell her scent. Everywhere I turn, there she is. I—"

Jack put his hands on Julien's shoulders. "I know it's not forbidden, but it's wrong, it's…"

"I *know!*" When Julien looked up, his eyes were angry. "I haven't made a move on her, have I? I haven't kissed her. Christ, you come back every couple of years and think you have all the answers for us peons."

"I don't have all of the answers, Julien." He thought about Darcy—about the otherworldly pull he felt to her, even before he kissed her. So much of what Julien said about Lela felt familiar to Jack. Still, it wasn't right. Maybe it was Julien's grief over losing his wife, and Lela had offered him comfort, confusing him. "I was sorry about Natalia. I know how much you loved her. Maybe you're just confused about—"

"Fuck you, *Jacques*," said Julien and pushed past his brother into the cabin. "You have no idea what you're talking about."

Jack stood outside by himself for a moment, shaking his head. Things were messier at home than he'd anticipated, but Julien was wrong—Jack had no answers. Not for his own life, and not for those of his family. He was the last person in any position to give advice. He ran both hands through his hair and followed Julien into the cabin.

Their mother was sitting in a rocking chair by the fireplace, a sleeping Delphine on her lap. She didn't look up as they entered.

"*Pas de chance. Je peux à peine le sentir maintenant.*" *No luck. I can barely feel him now.* She finally looked up at Jack and gave him a wan smile from her bony, sunken face, and then tilted her head to the side and continued in French. "You look good, son. Strong."

Lela stood in the kitchen, holding a mug with one hand, and the ends of Julien's shirt over her breasts with the other, eyes down. How Lela and Tallis had managed to share the small cabin for all of these years was lost on Jack. He couldn't imagine the strain on both of them.

"Lela, I said wash up. Delphine needs to be put to bed. *Maintenant.* Don't make me wait."

Lela nodded once then quickly crossed the room, heading to the bathroom between the bedrooms on the left side of the house.

"She should have left the search to you two. To my boys." She looked up at Julien and her shrewd look wasn't lost on Jack. "Were you distracted by her?"

"No, *Maman*," Julien answered, but he evaded her gaze.

Tallis took a deep breath then sighed, staring at the fire. "Bane of my existence, that girl. If she'd bind herself, I could finally get her out of this house but she finds fault in every available male. That they want her at all is a mystery to me. She's nothing but a filthy Reynard bastard, even if she goes by Beauloup."

"It's not her fault—"

Tallis raised her eyes to Julien and they burned yellow to match his.

"We won't discuss it. You go wash up. Use my bathroom."

Tallis watched him cross the room and waited until he had closed her bedroom door behind him before she gestured to the seat across from her, encouraging Jack to sit.

"Did you see her? Your human?"

Jack nodded, sitting on the edge of his father's rocking chair across from his mother, then looked down at his hands.

"And?"

"Didn't go well, *Maman*. She caught me shifting."

"That wasn't the plan."

Jack rubbed his eyes with his hand. "I'll go back after the Gathering. I just want to give her some time."

"Are you still bound to her? Did you…"

"Yeah, we are," he said quietly. "And yeah…we did."

His mother gave him a sad, gentle smile. "I could see it on your face."

"I have to get her back."

"We'll see." She tilted her head. "And the rest?"

"It worked. The vault. The fresh dead. It all worked. If she hadn't seen me…"

Jack rubbed his jaw, frustration and hunger causing the bile from his stomach to spew into his mouth. He swallowed it back with a grimace.

"How I *hate* zis Darcy from Carlisle," his mother declared in heavily accented English in a low growl.

"Well, that's too bad, because I love her."

"Who is Darcy from Carlisle?" asked a sleepy Delphine, stretching her arms from the comfortable cocoon of her grandmother's lap and yawning.

Jack's eyes flew open and met his mother's in a panic. Aside from Tombeur, no one knew Darcy's name or location. Although a few had asked about Jack's binding over the years, both Tallis and Tombeur had protected the identity of Jack's mate.

"Who is she, *Grand-mère*? And why do you hate her?"

Tallis took a deep breath and gave Delphine a cheerful smile, answering her in French. "A legend, *louveteau*. Just a silly old legend."

Jack shook his head in anger, holding his mother's eyes. It had been careless of her to say Darcy's name out loud, and although the child seemed pacified with the simple explanation and too sleepy to actually absorb the information, it made Jack realize how much danger he put Darcy in every time he came home.

Lela came out of her bedroom, running her fingers through her long, black, wet hair. She was dressed in jeans, a t-shirt that hugged her breasts, and bare feet. He tried to see her through Julien's eyes and her appeal wasn't lost on Jack. She was trim and attractive with a feisty spirit, and Delphine's face brightened the moment her aunt entered the room.

Lela approached Tallis and reached her arms out for her niece. "Come on, Delphy. *Tante* Lela will put you to bed."

Jack watched as the sleepy little girl was transferred lovingly from Tallis's lap to Lela's arms. Whatever bad blood ran between the two women, it was good to see them keep it under control in front of Delphine.

"Night-night, *Grand-mère*," the little one called, resting her sleepy head on her Aunt's shoulder.

"*Bonne nuit, ma chérie*," her grandmother replied.

"What about Dad?" Jack asked, as Lela shut the bedroom door with a quiet latching sound.

He watched in horror as his mother's steely eyes filled with tears. "Barely a thread now. Not even. I can't find him inside and my heart feels him slipping away."

Jack took a deep breath and reached out his hand to hold hers. "We'll look again tomorrow. Maybe he's just injured. Coming in and out of consciousness."

"*Non, mon fils.*" His mother turned back to the fire, tears streaming down her face and rocking softly. "*Tu ne le trouveras pas. Il est perdu pour moi.*"

No, my son. You won't find him. He is lost to me.

JACK WANTED TO TALK TO Tombeur, but he also needed to talk to Willow. After dinner with his mother, Julien, and Lela, he said he wanted to take a drive over to Tombeur's place and wouldn't be back until later. Although Tombeur sat on the Northern Bloodlands council, he wasn't part of the Portes de l'Enfer pack. His cabin was a hard drive northeast, a little under an hour away on the eastern end of adjoining packlands. Tombeur was the leader, or alpha, of the Lac Noir pack.

After about thirty minutes of driving, Jack pulled over onto the shoulder of the road and dialed Willow's office number, hoping she'd still be there.

She picked up on the third ring.

"Doctor Broussard's office."

"Willow?"

"Jack." He heard the tired sigh in her voice. "Let me close my office door. Unlikely anyone would come at this hour, but just in case…"

"How's Darcy?"

"She's sad. Fragile. She's also getting pretty angry at the whole situation. I checked on her this afternoon. I don't think she's left that damn window seat since she got home from your place yesterday morning. She's pretty much a mess."

Jack clenched his jaw, feeling his chest tighten. *Darcy, Darcy, Darcy*—

"So, listen," Willow continued. "I tapped into the New Hampshire medical system records and using the date you gave me, yes, I found a very, um, *unusual* case matching the dates and location."

Jack took a deep breath and refocused his attention on the conversation with Willow. "Just to be sure we're on the same page, can you describe the injury you were alluding to?"

"Severed, um, *limb*. Neatly severed."

"Any other details?" she asked.

"It had a tourniquet. Tied with dental floss. Green."

"Goddamn it," murmured Willow, and he could hear the grudging acceptance, under layers of shock, in her voice.

"He was going to rape her, Willow."

Willow didn't speak and Jack went on in a rush.

"He was s scumbag piece of shit and he was cheating on her. He came by one night to see her, late. And she let him in and he was drunk. And she made him tea and he started to assault her. I was out on her fire escape so I shifted into Roug form and I broke through her kitchen window and…well, I…"

"You cut off his dick."

"Yeah," sighed Jack. "He's lucky I didn't kill him. I wanted to. Darcy was lying on the floor—"

"You called the ambulance?"

"Yeah. I put that shitbag in the back of my truck and waited until the ambulance got there, then we drove north. Check the almanacs. It was a waxing gibbous moon that night. I had to be back up in the Bloodlands before—"

"Before the following night. Full moon."

"Yeah," Jack whispered. "I am who I say I am, Willow."

She ignored this. "But Darcy never mentioned seeing you—"

"She never saw me. I spent three nights on her fire escape. In the corner. Frank saw me. Didn't like me much, either. I followed her to and from school. I watched her. I was there on the fire escape when fucking Phillip came that night and I—"

"You rescued her," breathed Willow.

"I'd do *anything* for her."

"Anything else? About that night?"

"I took something. I just…I just wanted something that belonged to her. It was a silver necklace. A Métis eternity symbol. You know, the figu—"

"I know the necklace you're talking about."

"You do?"

"I gave it to her, Jack. She lost it. In college."

"She didn't lose it. I took it." He may as well come clean. "And I returned it last week when I left flowers for her on your porch swing."

"You came into our house?"

"I put the necklace in her jewelry box and left."

"Jesus, Jack. That's trespassing. And pretty creepy."

"I'm sorry. I don't have a good excuse. I couldn't give it to her, and I'd waited a long time to return it."

There was a long pause on the other end and Jack worried Willow had hung up.

"Willow?"

"You know, I—I want to believe you."

"Then, please, *believe me*. We kissed when we were kids, the summer before my eighteenth birthday. It bound us together. Her to me and me to her. It shouldn't have happened. It should have been impossible, but it happened. And yes, I have to shift when the moon is full. For three nights. But I don't hunt. I lock myself away. I wouldn't hurt her. I wouldn't hurt any of her kind."

"Where do you lock yourself?"

"Under my garage," he answered. "You want to see it? You can go there and see it."

"How do I get in?" Willow asked.

"Garage code is DARCY on the alphanumeric keypad. Back of the garage you'll see a metal door and another keypad. That one is ROUG78. You'll be able to see the control room and if you flick the cameras on, you'll be able to see the vault. I'm sorry, but you can't go in. The only way to get into the vault is combined retinal and fingerprint scan, so you'll have to take my word for it. But, there's no escaping, believe me. Once you're in, you're in until the door unbolts automatically, which, for me, is generally 72 hours. Go see it."

"This is some crazy shit, Jack."

"It sounds crazy, but it's true. Your tribe's legend is my pack's history. Is that really so unbelievable, Willow?"

There was a long pause as he waited for her to answer. He heard her sigh.

"What a life you dragged my friend into. Wanting you for decades. She finally gets you, and surprise! You're a werewolf."

He heard the very, very slight tone of humor in her voice and it made his muscles relax. He spoke calmly. "Not a werewolf. A Roux-ga-roux. Full-blooded, not turned. And I had no idea that kiss would be binding. I never would have—"

"I can't believe I'm having this conversation."

"You believe me, Willow?"

"Sort of. My *Nohkom* said…" She paused. "It doesn't matter. I'm going to check out your…vault. Hey. How'd you get Amory to build something so creepy for you?"

Jack smiled. "I told him it was a wine cellar."

"Figures. Amory loves his wine."

"From what I hear, Amory loves his Willow." He blurted out the words without thinking then cringed, recognizing the likelihood that he'd offended her, overstepping the very fragile limits of their relationship.

She paused again and he heard the sharpness in her voice when she finally spoke. "We're not that good of friends yet, Jack. I'll be in touch."

She hung up. The call was gone and he hadn't had the chance to ask about Darcy again. His longing for her surged up inside of him. He had to connect with her.

He looked in the rearview mirror, but the road was quiet. No one coming or going. He locked the car doors, closed his eyes, and put his head back against the headrest.

Then he pulled her inside.

COLD AND WET.
   Her moods were influencing their forest. Cold and wet was the

worst.

He hated the feeling of the cool wetness under his paws, squishing between the fur of his toes, the hard, constant rainfall making his fur stink. He hated knowing that she was so sad that she made their sky weep with her sorrow.

Where is she?

He looked up at the moon and howled, breathing in deeply, catching the faintness of her scent. South.

He ran, slipping over wet leaves on the forest floor, sliding through mud, his body twisting around trees, leaping over wet logs, and through thorny brambles. He couldn't remember ever having to run this hard and this long to find her. He stopped, inhaling. He was having trouble tracking her. It was as though she was on the move too, and the rain came down in furious torrents, making the forest dark and slowing his pace.

He finally came to a lake and padded around the water line, bedraggled and exhausted, searching for her.

Darcy! Darcy! DARCY!

He could smell her, but couldn't see her until he turned his gaze toward the lake itself. She was in a small boat out in the middle of the water, at least a quarter mile from the shore. Her hands rested lightly on the oars and her chest moved up and down rapidly as though she'd been hard at work.

He locked his yellow eyes with hers.

Come back.

Stay away.

He heard her voice, steady and sure. Hard like steel or iron or anything else that can be fashioned into a weapon to filet something soft.

Please, he begged her. *Come back to me.*

She put her head down, working the oars, her little boat skimming the water, moving further and further away.

He whined in frustration, padding back and forth across the shoreline before putting a paw in the clear water. Bitter cold seeped into his fur, numbing his paw with pins and needles. He looked up again and watched her pulling hard on the oars to place distance between them. He put another paw in the freezing water, his eyes narrowing with the sharp pain of the cold through the thick pads. He turned around and ran away from the water then faced the lake and ran full speed into the water, jumping to get as far from the shore as possible before swimming.

Cold. Bitter, Arctic cold.

He pumped all four legs as fast as he could, moving his heavy, wet, exhausted body through the icy cold water.

Darcy.

He struggled to keep his head above the water line but after miles of running followed by unfamiliar swimming, his body was starting to give out. The rain fell mercilessly, surrounding him from down below and up above. He could barely feel his legs and paws anymore and the paddling rhythm he had established at first started to falter. He tried to tread water but without the vigorous paddling, he quickly lost feeling in his legs entirely and felt his body dipping lower.

He lifted his head, searching for her boat, but it was so far away now he couldn't really see it at all. Depleted of strength, he finally stopped fighting and let his weary body relax, falling into the dark, cold water alone, his last thought,

I belong to you, Darcy, and you—

His eyes jerked open and he gasped, taking in mouthfuls of air into his burning lungs. He turned the key slightly in his car and pushed the button to lower the window. It wasn't enough. It was crushing his chest. He opened the door of the car and staggered out, into the street, unable to get enough air into his depleted lungs, the pain in his heart overwhelming the aching pain of his body.

She left you to die.

You're losing her.

He felt shocked, dumbstruck, confused. She left him to die.

He leaned up against the car, a desperation building inside of him, white hot and depraved, more brutal than he had ever felt before. His eyes burned and his claws dropped. His fangs protracted until the long, jagged points gnashed against each other in furious sorrow, his fur prickling through his skin, covering his body in thick, padded armor. It had been years since Jack had shifted from his emotions alone, but he didn't fight it.

The binding isn't holding. You're losing her.

He flexed the taut, rippling muscles of his fully shifted body, lifted his claws to the sliver of silver moon and howled with anguish.

Chapter 5

IT TOOK LESS THAN FIFTEEN minutes on foot to make it the rest of the way to Tombeur's cabin. Jack approached the small cabin, trying to control the impulse to turn and hunt with every step he took. *Hunt a human, hunt a human, hunt a—*

"*Assez proché, Peaumarcheur!*" *Close enough, Skinwalker.*

Jack whipped his head to the right and found the butt of Tombeur's rifle pressed up against his cheek.

"Downshift. *Maintenant.*" It wasn't a request. It was a demand.

Jack took a deep breath and closed his eyes, concentrating. His claws and fangs began to retract. The prickly fur receded back under his skin. His blood rushed, hot and unfulfilled, fighting the downshift, but losing. A moment later he stood dirty and naked next to Tombeur in the woods behind his cabin.

"*Jacques?*"

"*Oui. C'est moi,*" he replied through clenched teeth.

"Well, damn. Why'd you come shifted?" Tombeur asked in English, his familiar twang welcome in Jack's ears. He lowered the gun and turned to face Jack. "That ain't friendly, son."

"I…" Jack took a deep, steadying breath then looked down, feeling ashamed. "I lost fucking control."

"Whew! Guess so." Tombeur raised his eyebrows and nodded. "Wait here. I'll get you some pants. Don't want you scaring my girls."

Tombeur headed back to the cabin and Jack put his hands on his knees, finally catching his breath for the first time since he went inside.

She left me to die.

She's just angry.

SHE LEFT ME TO DIE.

Yes, she did.

The voice stepped back into the shadows. It didn't have a move. There was nothing left to say.

He didn't want to talk to Tombeur about Darcy. He didn't want to think about her right now. He was angry and hurt. He was scared that the binding wasn't holding, after all.

"Here you go." A pair of jeans fell at Jack's feet and he picked them up and pulled them on, buttoning the top button. They were a little big and slipped down his waist to rest on his hips.

"Where'd you leave your car?" asked Tombeur.

"Halfway down the road from Portes de l'Enfer."

Tombeur nodded. "I'll drive you back down in a bit."

"Thanks. Sorry about that, before."

"You came all the way up here tonight? You know I'll be down for the Gathering tomorrow. Got something under your skin, Skinwalker?" Tombeur grinned, tilting his head to the side. "You want to come in and have a beer?"

Jack nodded and followed his friend through the rest of the woods toward his cabin. At forty-nine, Tombeur had more grey than Jack remembered him having, but he was still as big as ever. Easily six feet, five inches tall, broad-chested and covered in sinew and muscle, Tombeur was one of the fiercest, most respected, most forward-thinking Rougs in the Northern Bloodlands. He was also Jack's mentor and more of a father figure than Jack's own father had ever been, despite a relatively small twelve-year age difference. Tombeur had insisted that anything he asked Jack to do, he'd do himself too, and together they'd learned the limits and boundaries of control.

Jack followed his friend into the dimly lit cabin that smelled of cinnamon and cloves.

"Chantal made some sort of bread. Pumpkin, I think. You want?"

Jack's mouth watered and he nodded, taking a seat by the fire as Tombeur opened two beers and brought them over.

"Chantal, honey, you remember Jack?"

Tombeur's sixteen-year-old daughter gave Jack a shy smile from the kitchen as she cut two large slices of the bread and brought the plates over to the men, and then retired into her bedroom.

"She's pretty, huh?"

"Very," answered Jack, tearing off a piece of the warm bread. "She have a mate in mind?"

"Between you and me, I wish she'd spark with Julien."

Jack looked into Tombeur's eyes and noticed—for the first time—the flecks of moss green lodged in and among the fiery brown. Unusual. Jack realized he'd seen that unique eye coloring somewhere before. Recently. *Where?*

"Julien, huh?"

"He's good stock. Your mama's one of the best hunters I ever known."

"Yeah. But my Dad—"

"Can't win 'em all. He's got a good heart. Used to have, anyways…"

Jack nodded, thinking of his mother's smile in the snowy parka.

"He's available, right?" Tombeur continued. "Julien?"

Sort of, thought Jack, averting his eyes.

"You got something to say, son?"

"I think he's still confused. Grieving."

Tombeur sat back taking a deep breath and letting it out slowly. "That was some nasty business with Natalia. Shocked all of us that she'd be so reckless."

He remembered Julien's words: *You have no idea what you're talking about.*

"Reckless? What do you mean?"

"Oh! You don't know? You gotta come home more often, hoss. Natalia was all lit up on something that night. That truck didn't hit her, she rushed it. Maybe she thought those big ol' headlights were eyes and was charging for a kill? I don't know. She got in with one of the packs north of here. Stopped showing up for work, left Julien with the little 'un for days on end. Only came back at *Pleine Lune*. Finally did her in, whatever that stuff was. Awful shame about the little 'un, though. Motherless little thing like my girls."

The little 'un. Delphine. Suddenly Jack remembered where he'd seen the unusual, moss-colored flecks. In the eyes of his niece, Julien's daughter.

"Thank God for your mother. First Lela, then Julien's girl. She's quite a woman."

Jack swallowed uncomfortably, looking down, running through dates and places in his mind. Jacques, Jeanette, and Jemma had been born within two years of each other. Then ten years later, along came Julien—about a year after Tallis first started working for the Council.

Jack thought of Julien's frustrated sigh: *She doesn't feel like a sister to me.* No wonder.

As impossible as it seemed to imagine, those eyes were like a red flag and Jack's heart processed the truth in vivid clarity: Julien was Tombeur's son and Delphine was his granddaughter. Jack fought the bile that rose in his throat at the realization that his mother had broken the binding four years before his father had. She had been unfaithful first. He wondered if his father even knew.

But Tombeur hoped that Chantal would "spark" with Julien. Did that mean he supported half-brother/half-sister binding? No. Tombeur was modern. He'd be against that. In all likelihood, Tombeur didn't know Julien was his.

Jack sat back in his chair, leveling his eyes at Tombeur, deciding whether or not he should say anything. He decided to keep talking about Tallis.

"Quite a woman, huh?"

"Sure is."

Jack's eyes narrowed. "You see her much?"

Tombeur's eyes looked down and he sighed. "Just council meetings."

"How about Julien? Ever see him?"

"Once a year about. Never got to know him as well as you. Awful sorry how things worked out with Natalia."

Jack nodded quietly. For how long had his mother and Tombeur carried on? It couldn't have been long—they'd been discreet. And what was still between them? The questions swam around in his head but with Darcy rejecting him and his father missing, Jack had enough on his plate. He decided to leave it alone for now.

"I had no idea about Natalia."

"Some sad shit. They're a bad pack, Jack."

"You heard about my father?"

"Aw, shit. Did he go back up there again? I already dragged his ass back to Tallis once. Goddamn that man—"

"Wait. What?" Jack's plate clattered to the floor as he sat up on the edge of his seat, holding Tombeur's eyes.

"How do you think Natalia got into that shit?"

"My father?"

Tombeur nodded.

"Does Julien know?"

"I have no idea. I assumed so."

Jack stood up. "You're saying my father got Natalia into that shit?"

"I'm pretty sure. They worked at the store together. Drove in and out of work together."

"Fuck," Jack snarled, running his hands through his hair. "What a goddamned mess."

Tombeur furrowed his brows, looking up at Jack. "This what you came to talk about?"

"No. But that…that'll have to wait. My dad's been missing for days. My mom can't find him."

Tombeur nodded solemnly. "You think he's up there?"

"I do now. Where's that pack? The bad one?"

"They're up by Lac du Coeur. Twenty-five miles or so, as the crow flies. No good roads for driving, though, Jack. We're better running."

"We?"

"Now, you didn't think I'd let you go alone, did you?"

Jack huffed once and nodded, relieved to have Tombeur's company and glad he hadn't shared his suspicions about Julien's parentage. He knew how unhappy his parents had been and anyway, Jack loved Tombeur like a father. Their secret would keep for another day.

ROUG RUNNING WITH TOMBEUR WAS—NEXT to being with Darcy—Jack's favorite thing in the whole world. The rush of wind through his fur, the intense smells of the forest—animals, plants, even humans far away. He could hear every creeping sound, every footfall, every howl and growl. Huge, heavily padded feet rushed over the ground bipedally and his eyes kept him safe from obstructions. He followed behind Tombeur as he had a million times before.

But unlike other runs when he was totally focused on the forest, the ground, the smells and the sounds, tonight his head was a jumble of human thoughts that couldn't be quelled by the shift.

His mother had broken the binding.

His father had broken the binding.

Tombeur had broken his binding too.

Jack thought of Darcy rowing away from him, faster and faster, and his heart hardened.

For two decades Jack had thought of no one but her, his whole life driven by his belief in the sanctity of the binding. He had stayed away for her. He had learned control for her. He had devised a plan and amassed the funds to make it work. Every moment of his adult life had been spent in pursuit of realizing his connection to her, being with her, figuring out how to live in her world. Every moment spent nurturing and encouraging the love he felt for her. Every moment living for her.

For what?

He was surrounded by others who had been unhappy, who had abandoned their mates, broken their sacred bond. What was he holding on for?

For the first time in his life, he thought to himself, *Maybe you should let her go.*

His feet hit the ground in a rhythmic rush, wet branches caressing his body or swiped away with his powerful claws.

You're a monster.

Leave Carlisle.

Belong to no one.

I can't do this.

It started to rain—a bitter, angry, sideways rain that pelted him from every angle, making it harder to see. Tombeur stopped ahead of him, raising his nose upward and inhaling. He lifted one massive, hairy arm and pointed straight ahead and Jack nodded, downshifting.

In a moment they stood naked, in human form, in the rain. Unless they wanted a battle, they couldn't arrive in shifted form.

Tombeur stood next to Jack and whispered, "We're less than a mile away. It's late and it's dark and the Gathering is tomorrow. Shouldn't be a rowdy night. They'll be saving that for tomorrow's celebration."

"What's the plan?"

"Let's case the village. The junkies aren't native pack members. They'll be together somewhere. Find them, we'll find Dubois. We'll carry him out together and then shift once we're a little ways away. Better we avoid the pack, if possible. They're not the friendliest."

Jack nodded and fell into step behind Tombeur. His human form feet were calloused and tough, but the forest floor was rugged and rough on his bare skin.

"Do you know what the stuff is? That they're selling?"

"It's called 'Dub,' short for W. Not totally sure what it is, but I've heard it's some sort of synthesized Wolfsbane."

"Wolfsbane!"

Every Roux-ga-roux knew about the dangers of Wolfsbane. It smelled and tasted delicious, but it was poisonous to the Roug digestive tract. In very, very tiny, stabilized doses, it acted as a depressant, diminishing impulses, causing a Roug's heart to slow down and breathing to deepen.

It was only *occasionally* used as a relaxant when the regenerative powers of their bodies weren't working and medical intervention was necessary. But in anything but a miniscule, controlled dose, it was a dangerous drug that would lead to certain death.

The thing about Wolfsbane, however, was that it generally caused violent, painful vomiting if consumed. Jack's eyes looked up at Tombeur in question.

"It's Wolfsbane mixed with something that stabilizes it and keeps it down."

Well, that answered that.

"But it's a depressant. Why would it make Natalia rush that truck?"

"It starts off making you mellow. You forget your worries, it's all trippy and sweet, like candy that makes you all high and relaxed. So, you keep going back for more. You don't want to run. You don't want to mate. You just want to chill out. Then *Pleine Lune* comes around and your body wants a kill. So, they have to go off it to get up the energy to hunt, and I guess the withdrawal makes them crazy. Shakes, hallucinations, fangs and claws and no restraint. No rules. Crazy stuff."

"Natalia went off it to hunt?"

"That's my guess. She was acting crazy enough with that truck."

"And then?"

Tombeur shrugged. "And then they're all jacked up after the hunt, they want to come down, so they go right back on the Dub. And here's the thing...if you're on it long enough, you can't go off. Even for *Pleine Lune*."

Jack's stared at Tombeur, shocked, incredulous. "Are you saying they eventually *miss* the hunt?"

Tombeur nodded. "They do. And a Roug can't miss the blood for more than a cycle. Two at the most. Can't survive."

It all came together in Jack's head with blunt precision. The reason his mother couldn't feel his father is that he'd missed the hunt. Maybe more than once. Dubois was either dead or very close to it.

The soft glow of the village lights came into focus as they rounded a bend.

"You go to that way. I'll go this way. We'll meet at the back."

Jack walked stealthily along the tree line, looking at the dilapidated cabins surrounded by mud and garbage, nothing like the orderly village at Portes de l'Enfer where his mother had gardens and flowering trees on her property. Jack had grown up close enough to a town to attend school with Métis kids, unlike this remote village where the kids were likely homeschooled, if at all. Jack wrinkled his nose at the smell. Unconsumed, rotting human parts. This was a messy, sloppy pack, which also made them dangerous.

Toward the back of the village, about twenty feet from the forest where he lurked, Jack spied a lean-to next to a dirty, muddy playground. Several Rougs were scattered around it in various states of undress, lying across a beat-up picnic table, on the bottom of a slide, and there, propped against a rusted jungle gym, sat Dubois with glazed eyes open, staring up at the sky.

Jack winced, clenching his jaw. His father was wasted to nothing with sunken cheeks and hands shaking in front of him, held at an awkward angle, as though they been broken at some point, and reset badly.

Jack stood at the edge of the woods and waited until Tombeur joined him.

"Found him?"

Jack nodded and gestured to the jungle gym. None of the Rougs had yellow eyes—all had that vacant, dazed stare. You'd barely know they were alive but for the occasional ragged breaths they took.

"You see any pack?"

"I don't think so. I think this is where the *visitors* hang out."

"He might fight us."

"He'll lose. He's smaller than Delphine."

Tombeur looked at Jack, holding his eyes. "I'm sorry, Jack."

"Let's just take him home."

They approached the cluster of wasted, softly groaning Rougs. Jack knelt down beside his father and twisted his head to face him.

"*Papa, c'est moi. Jacques. Me reconnais-tu?*" *It's me. Jack. Do you know me?*

Dubois's head wobbled uncertainly on his neck and he tried to focus his runny brown eyes.

"*Jacques?*"

"*C'est moi, Papa. Je vais te ramener à la maison.*" *It's me. I'm going to take you home.* "*Pour maman. Pour Tallis.*"

"*Tallis…Tallis, mon Tallis…*" he murmured, tears trailing down his sunken cheeks.

"*Oui, Papa. Tallis.*" He looked up at Tombeur. "Take his legs. I'll take his shoulders. We'll get him into the woods and then shift and take him home."

As they hefted Dubois's body and started for the woods, they heard a noise coming from the closest cabin to the playground. A Roug came out of the cabin with a shotgun in hand.

"*Où allez-vous tous les deux?*" the voice demanded. *Where are you two going?*

Tombeur hurried his pace, catching Jack's eyes and shaking his head briefly. Jack read his message. *Don't shift yet. Try to make it to the woods.*

"*Où amenez-vous ce vieil homme?*" *Where are you taking that old man?*

Jack heard the hammer pull back, and the explosive sound of gunfire ripped through the air as a bullet sailed by Jack's ear. They still had about five more feet until the woods where they could safely shift and run.

Another hammer pull and another shot, but this time the bullet ripped clean through the muscled flesh of Jack's upper arm. He bellowed in pain, feeling his fangs dropping, his claws unsheathing under his father's shoulders. Pain and fear were making him unstable; his blood was heating up, his claws weren't retracting.

He didn't want to think about Darcy and yet hers was the face his mind seized upon to distract him from the pain ripping through his body. Her pale skin, her blonde hair, the freckles across her nose, the lips that he loved to kiss. He concentrated on her face. He had to make it through tonight no matter what. He had to see her again.

"Don't shift," snarled Tombeur. "We're almost there. *Control, Jacques!*"

Jack heard the hammer pull back one last time, just as they reached the tree cover of the forest, but the roaring of the gun and whizzing bullet wasn't forthcoming. Surely the loss of one old junkie wasn't worth a chase? Jack kept moving, but didn't look back over his shoulder. He caught Tombeur's face in the moon and it had relaxed. Jack took a deep breath then, panting in relief. They'd made a successful escape.

About a quarter of a mile into the woods, they propped Dubois up against a tree and Tombeur took a look at Jack's arm. He grimaced.

"It's not pretty. Going to leave a hell of scar, Jack."

Jack looked at his bloody arm, black and shiny in the darkness. It throbbed like crazy, even though it would heal quickly once he shifted. But Tombeur was right. Without sewing it up in human form, it would heal jagged and angry. He thought of Darcy's reaction to the misshapen flesh, how her eyes would soften as she surveyed the ugliness.

She doesn't want you, stupid. You've got no one to look pretty for.

He clenched his eyes shut, remembering her loving gentleness as she kissed the scars on his chest. The memory made his heart hurt worse than his arm.

"I'm ready to shift when you are," he said bitterly and Tombeur nodded.

Once in shifted form, Jack carried the body of his barely conscious father over his shoulder for the entirety of the run, past Tombeur's cabin, back to his abandoned car.

In Roug form, with over twice the muscle mass he owned in human form, his father's unconscious, wasted body barely made an impression on him as he ran swiftly through the woods. He couldn't help thinking about his parents' failed binding. Tombeur's too. Maybe he'd been foolish all these years to believe that his would be different—that he could some-how make a human understand who he was and still want him.

His feet pounded against the rocks, twigs, and uneven paths of the for-est floor, but he didn't feel a thing. He wished his heart had been as well protected. He was still reeling from the ugliness of tonight's *Dansmatête*. He could still feel the sharp, pricking pain of the freezing water, like a million needles under his fur, numbing his skin. His chest remembered the terrifying pressure as it ran out of air, the unavoidable pull of the dark, swirling water, tugging him down into the watery depths. He wasn't cold, but he shivered. She had left him there. She had rowed away with all her might, leaving him to die.

He caught sight of the moon up ahead, over Tombeur's shoulder, and he howled with the pain of her rejection, her words on Thursday morning and her actions tonight as she abandoned him to a freezing, dark, watery death. She didn't love him. She'd never said it, no matter how much he hoped he'd seen love in her eyes. He howled again in pain and anguish.

Bindings are broken.

She doesn't want you.

Let her go.

He increased his speed, bypassing Tombeur, even with the weight of his father, relishing the wind in his fur as he raced through the forest, knock-ing away branches, ripping boughs from tree trunks, howling at the moon with the force of his sadness, his fury, his despair.

By the time they reached Jack's car, his anger had given his sadness a good, hearty kick in the ass.

She doesn't want you? She wants you to die?

Fine. Don't go back. You don't need her.

They shifted back into human form and settled Dubois on the backseat. Jack turned the car around, southwest toward his mother's cabin.

Jack was filthy and naked, and when he looked at his arm, he saw that Tombeur had been right. Where the bullet had torn through his arm was now a ragged, angry mess of pinkish scar tissue about the size of a silver dollar. He glanced in the backseat at his father, who seemed to be sleeping, but it was hard to tell. His eyes were finally closed.

"You okay?" Tombeur sighed beside Jack, his beard caked with mud. He'd heard the pain in Jack's howls. "How's your arm?"

"Doesn't hurt."

"Sure is ugly."

Jack glanced over at his friend. "Thanks."

"You want to talk about it, then? What's got you emo-shifting and howling like a banshee?"

"Not really."

Tombeur ignored him. "You saw her? Darcy Turner?"

Jack nodded.

"How'd it go?"

"Not good," answered Jack clenching his jaw.

"You always knew it'd be a tough haul, Jack." Tombeur rubbed his chin. "I have to ask. Is she a danger to us?"

Jack deeply resented the protective surge he felt in response to Tombeur's question. He sighed and shook his head. "I don't think so. She's angry. Confused."

"Keep on top of it, Jack. Our agreement stands. If she's a threat to us, we have to—"

"I understand," Jack interrupted in a tight voice. "She's not."

Tombeur was quiet for a while, probably deciding whether or not to take Jack's word. Jack sat rigidly, waiting to hear what Tombeur would say next. He finally relaxed when Tombeur asked, "What're you going to do?"

Jack's first instinct was to insist, *I'll go back and work on it. I'll make her want me. I'll make her love me again.* Then he saw her face in the boat, the timbre of her voice, so cold, so hard. His lip twitched with betrayal and anger.

"I don't know," he answered honestly. "She doesn't want me."

He couldn't force her to love him. They'd be bound forever, but they could live separate lives. He couldn't be re-bound, but he could find a *Veuve*, a widow who needed protection and care. He'd never love her, but he could care for her, and maybe they could even have children one day, full-bloods like him. He never had to return to the Southern Bloodlands. He never had to return to Darcy Turner. He could stay away, as she had demanded. *Spend my life amongst the other monsters.*

Even as his thoughts drifted in this direction, somewhere inside he knew it was impossible. His heart. His eternally hopeful heart loved her. Loved her most of any other being living on the face of the earth.

Jack took a deep breath, hating his heart, hating his binding, hating Darcy Turner most of all.

Tombeur's question lingered. *What're you going to do?*

"Go back to her," Jack heard himself murmur. "Someday."

"Never saw a binding as strong as yours." Tombeur nodded beside him. "And with a human, no less."

"What about *yours?*" Jack asked sourly, wishing to hell the human who was supposed to love him hadn't left him to drown.

"Mine was…" Tombeur's voice trailed off.

"Was what?"

"Complicated," said Tombeur, turning his neck to glance at Dubois again.

"By *what?*" asked Jack, hearing the challenge in his tone, already knowing the answer, but wanting to hear it from his friend's lips.

"She was sickly. She couldn't be a true mate. Made me long for things outside of the binding."

"I don't. I don't long for anything but Darcy and she can't hunt at all."

"Like I said, strongest binding I ever seen." Tombeur took a deep breath and sighed. "You think we should call Tallis? Warn her he's coming home?"

"Don't need to." Jack shook his head, putting the car in gear and turning around toward Portes de l'Enfer. "She'll feel it."

They rode in silence for some time until Tombeur glanced around at Dubois's limp body lying on the back seat. "He's in real bad shape, Jack."

"Yeah," Jack nodded, clenching his jaw against the sudden wave of sadness he felt. For his father's wasted life. His mother's betrayal. Darcy's rejection. The list was getting longer and longer.

"Almost at your mama's now, Jack. You focus on your folks now."

Jack pulled into the parking area adjacent to the cabin, noting the dim light of the living room still on. His mother opened the door, her face awash with tears.

Jack pushed opened his door in time to hear his mother's faint, grief-stricken voice.

"*Il est trop tard,*" she said, opening the back door of the car to look at the body of her husband, before falling on her knees in the mud beside him. She bent her head forward until it rested on Dubois's thin, grey mop of hair, then wailed, "*Il est déjà parti.*"

It's too late. He's already gone.

JACK STARED UP AT THE ceiling, lying in his childhood bed. Julien had helped him bring in their father's dead body and lay it gently on the kitchen table. Tallis would spend the night with him, preparing him for burial in the morning, and Tombeur insisted on staying with her.

Julien lay in the other twin bed next to Jack.

"She knew," he said. "About half an hour ago she started clutching at her heart and crying. She knew he was gone."

Jack breathed through his nose, blinking back weak, useless tears. His father had likely died as he and Tombeur sat in the front seat discussing complicated bindings. How incredibly pathetic.

"I remember from when Natalia…" Jack heard his brother sniff lightly. "Ah, it was painful. The unbinding. But then…suddenly? It's just…gone. After feeling the connection so sharply, so strongly, so absolutely, it's just gone. Not like it was never there, because you know it was…but like a very old, sweet memory from a long, long time ago."

Jack clenched his jaw together until it hurt.

"I'm just trying to say that *Maman* won't be in pain by tomorrow. She won't be in agony anymore."

"You think it's agony to love someone?"

"To be bound to someone who you're losing? Who you've lost? Who you want even though you can't have them? Yeah," his brother breathed into the darkness of their childhood room. "I think it's *agony.*"

Jack knew that Julien was speaking of Natalia. Or of their parents. But Jack could only think of Darcy. He saw her eyes, bright and green. Her hair, so shiny and silky in his hands. The single, whispered word: *Stay.*

Agony. Jack knew a little bit about agony too. He turned away from his brother, squeezing his eyes shut as his feelings assaulted him from every angle.

His father was dead, his mother was unbound, and he felt lost.

He knew it was too soon and weak as hell, but he couldn't help himself. He pulled her inside.

I T WASN'T RAINING ANYMORE.

It was dark, though. It was night and Jack knew there was a good chance that she was asleep. He hoped so. He counted on it.

He padded softly, orienting himself. Sniffing the air lightly, he caught her scent, but he didn't race to her.

He walked stealthily over pine needles, cushiony and flat like a mattress or blanket, gingerly making his way closer to her. Her scent was stronger and stronger as he crossed a meadow into a pine haven, tall trees creaking softly like a lullaby.

She lay on her side, curled up on a pillow of bright green moss, her body covered in a simple white sheath, her feet bare. Moonlight shone down on her hair, making it glow like a halo around her head, and her light skin seemed even whiter in contrast to the darkness that surrounded her. Her chest rose and fell with deep breaths and her mouth was lightly open in sleep.

Jack swallowed. He had never seen anything or anyone so beautiful in his entire life.

He watched her shiver lightly in her sleep and his breath caught.

You're cold.

She took a deep breath through her nose, and though her eyes remained closed, he was surprised to hear her voice, sleep-muffled and slight, as if escaping from a dream.

I didn't think that.

He couldn't help the way his breath came out in a sob at the welcome sound of her gentle voice. He padded over to her body and lay down at her feet, careful not to touch her, but unable to refuse what small comfort she didn't withhold. Listening to the sound of her breathing, with his terrible longing for her soothed by her presence, his eyes finally drifted closed and the last thought he had before he fell asleep was,

I belong to you and you—

Chapter 6

COUNCIL MEMBERS AND REPRESENTATIVES FROM all eight packs of the Northern Bloodlands started arriving at dawn. From a distinct triangular territory in the central, forested part of Quebec, as far east as Fremont, as far west as Wemindji and as far south as the woods just north of the great city, the packs descended on Portes de l'Enfer in the Faunique de les Laurentides for the annual Gathering.

Each of the other seven packs were allowed to send up to twenty-five pack members, including their five council members, to the Gathering. The Portes de l'Enfer pack, as hosts, encouraged all pack members to attend the meeting.

Some of the packs, like the one from Lac de Coeur, came on motorcycles, loud and gregarious, despite the early morning. Others, like the pack just south of Jack's in the Cap Tormente National, arrived civilly in cars, dressed like natty humans. Some of the packs who were spread out over the far northwest had come shifted in the night and were still naked and dirty in the morning—and Jack was pretty sure some of them might even stay like that all weekend.

The ancient log Gathering Hall, built two hundred years ago when the Natio Luporem established itself in the Northern Bloodlands, was a massive, oval-shaped longhouse that held three hundred Rougs in bleacher-style seating with the forty Council members seated at a large horseshoe-shaped table in the middle of the open, sawdust-covered floor.

Tallis had left early to arrange for Dubois's tribute on the day's agenda. He would be buried at sundown.

From what Jack could tell over breakfast, Julien had been right.

The sunken, pallid mask gone now, his mother's face had filled out in the night and her skin tone was healthier, with a glow in her cheeks. Her eyes sparkled like a woman ten years younger and there was a bounce in her step as she moved around the kitchen making breakfast. She even had a kind word for Lela, complimenting her on the pot of morning coffee, and winking at Tombeur as he took a sip, focused, with a searing intensity, on Tallis. Jack watched his friend and mentor—he didn't even need to be subtle in his observation, for Tombeur didn't seem to realize that anyone but Tallis was alive—following his mother with his eyes, churning and hungry. Jack wondered how soon it would be before Tallis and Tombeur were bound. Not long, he guessed.

Jack walked to the Gathering Hall with Julien, Delphine, and Lela, who held his hand. He felt very bad for her; while Tallis had moved on from her broken binding swiftly, Lela was grieving the loss of her father. Jack could feel the heaviness of her heart as she walked beside him.

"He's not suffering anymore," he offered, speaking quietly and squeezing her hand.

"Oh, I know," said Lela. "It's just…he was unhappy. He was so unhappy." Jack nodded.

"And he was all I had," she continued in a small voice. "I have no one to love me now."

"That's not true," countered Jack, stopping their walk and looking into his sister's eyes. "*I* love you."

Her eyes widened and her face—which had been so sad a moment before—brightened perceptibly. "You mean it?"

"Of course," he said. "And so does Julien. Delphine is crazy about you."

Her eyes clouded over and her shoulders suddenly deflated as she sighed loudly, turning away from him.

"Will you at least stay for a while, Jack?" she asked hopefully.

Jack thought of Darcy's cold, frightened eyes. The boat rowing away. Although he wouldn't be able to stay away forever, no matter how much he wished he could, he also wasn't in any rush to return to Carlisle.

"Yeah, Lela," he said, chucking her gently under the chin. "I'll stay a while."

She smiled at him, lacing her fingers through his.

They entered the Gathering Hall and looked for the area reserved for their pack. It was getting pretty full, but Julien and Delphine had reserved seats for them on one of the higher rows.

As they crossed the central floor, passing by the Council table, Lela turned to Jack, stopping him, placing her hands on his chest. Her eyes searched his. Her voice was breathy and anxious.

"You love me, Jack? You really love me?"

Jack furrowed his brows. "Of course I do."

She held his eyes and nodded, that happy brightness softening her features again. Then she turned and took his hand, pulling him toward the steps of the bleachers.

"SO LET IT BE KNOWN: There will be no more hunting on the road between Tadoussac and Saguenay. Too many accidents there. We're drawing attention to ourselves.

"One kill per *Pleine Lune* shift. I don't care if you want more. You and your bound mate get ONE, so make it last, and don't hunt in the same place more than twice a year. Stretch your legs. Go for a run. The kill zone needs to be wide and deep so that we don't draw attention.

"Camping season is upon us. It is unwise to hunt populated campgrounds where tourists have cameras on their person at all times. We don't need any media attention shifting to the Bloodlands. Be stealthy. Be clever. Ample food will be available, so use judgment when selecting your prey.

"And as we repeat every year…the Métis in Mistissini and Chibougamou are strictly off limits. We respect the old order. We don't hunt other half-breeds. They pretend not to see us and we LEAVE. THEM. ALONE."

Tombeur scanned the crowd as he read the minutes from the meeting toward the middle of the afternoon. Some of the packs in the northwest heckled him and his eyes burned yellow in their direction.

"You don't like it? The Council will help you see the value in following the rules."

The Council Enforcers stationed around the enormous lodge moved over to stand in front of the bleachers where the hecklers quickly quieted down.

The crowd hushed.

Jack recognized many of the older members of the CE. He himself had been a Council Enforcer for years as part of his contract with Tombeur, and hunting down rogue Rougs was nothing new to Jack. Keeping order was imperative. Without it, the Roux-ga-roux would have exposed themselves and become extinct long ago.

Even as his tenure on the CE had been necessary, some of Jack's work on its behalf had been chilling. He closed his eyes. He preferred not to think about it. The skills he'd learned there had allowed him to contract work as security for the humans. It had taught him a marketable skill that led to a profitable career, and gave him unrestricted access to learn how to live among them.

"Now, our Senior Council Elder, *Le Premier Loup*, Marcus Saint Germain, will read the names of the fallen."

Jack sighed and stood up with everyone else. It had already been a long day. New business was always first and had taken up much of the morning followed by the rules and regulations review, which Tombeur had just finished. Then the fallen. Then the bindings.

Marcus Saint Germain was one of the oldest elders, holding the title First Wolf, the last alpha, a position of the utmost respect and authority. He had read the lists of the fallen and the bound for as long as Jack could remember, although Jack's binding had never been read aloud at a Gathering. His mother and Tombeur had seen to that. Better not to draw attention, his mother had explained.

Saint Germain was halfway through the list of the fallen when Jack's parents' names grabbed his attention.

"...Dubois Beauloup joins the fallen, leaving Tallis Beauloup unbound..."

Jack heard the hushed murmurs of surprise among the pack members who didn't know Dubois had died during the night. He looked over at the Lac de Coeur pack, coldly, as they looked uncomfortably away from the Portes de l'Enfer pack. Catching his mother's reaction, he saw her wince lightly as her late husband's name was announced. Jack doubted anyone else noticed, but as soon as the next name was read, she raised her eyes to find Tombeur across the table, staring at her. Jack watched as Tombeur's eyes grew into a goldish green, before he hastily looked back down at the table. If he kept staring at her, everyone in the Gathering Hall would know his intent. And then Jack guessed that's exactly what he wanted because he raised his eyes again to Tallis, golden-green and furious as he held her gaze. Tallis sat up straighter in her seat and Jack watched as her eyes turned quickly to molten lava, copper flecks burning bright.

Others started to notice too, because Jack heard the faint rumble through the crowd. "Tallis..."

"Look at Tombeur…" "Tombeur and Tallis…"

They held each other's eyes without looking down, without faltering or failing.

Unaware of the stir caused by Tallis and Tombeur, Saint Germain finished the list of fallen with the familiar words, borrowed from the Cree: "…ah tey wa chee un kink tay." *…and again I will see You.*

The white-haired old man bent his head, clasping his hands in front of him, and the room went respectfully silent in tribute. Finally, Saint Germain lifted his head and howled up at the large cutout in the ceiling of the meeting house, and was quickly joined by the howls of the other pack members who raised their voices in final tribute.

Jack sat back down and looked at his mother, whose eyes were back to brown. He flicked his glance to Tombeur, whose eyes were also brown again as he resumed his seat at the council table.

Saint Germain picked up a different list from his seat at the table and turned slowly, smiling at the packs, and Jack could feel the familiar anticipation. This was everyone's favorite part. Not only was the meeting almost adjourned, which meant drinking, food, bonfires, forest running and celebration, but everyone liked hearing the names of the newly bound couples, who would stand and kiss if they had attended the Gathering in person. And the *most* exciting part was the end, when Saint Germain would ask for any Gathering bindings to be witnessed, at which point a male and female Roug could stand in the center of the Council table and kiss for the first time. Even if the female wasn't interested in the male, she couldn't refuse and vice versa. It was a gamble, of course, to see if they'd become bound or not, but very exciting if the mates had chosen well.

There were sixteen new bindings to acknowledge, though only nine of the new couples were in attendance. They all stood when their names were called and treated the Gathering to a kiss, ranging from chaste to passionate, the female half of one couple already showing a sizeable *louveteau* bump under her breasts.

The crowd whooped and hollered with every kiss, anticipating the end of the Gathering and the possibility of a live binding.

Finally Saint Germain placed the list of new bindings on the table and walked slowly around the hall, looking up into the bleachers with midnight dark, focused eyes.

"And now I ask, as I do every year, are there any here who would ask to be bound? Any woman who seeks a man? Any man who seeks a woman? Remember, if your name is spoken you must join your potential mate in the council ring. You may not refuse. Anyone? Anyone?"

Jack could feel the electricity in the room—the excitement as pack members looked around the room, many of their gazes settling on Jack's mother and Tombeur who had made such a scene a few moments before.

"Don't be shy, now. There's no way to know if you're meant to be bound until you give it a try. Don't any of you young bucks have a pretty thing in mind who's spurned you once or twice? Come now. Here's your chance. Look around…"

Jack grinned with the rest of the crowd, looking for any sign of movement. He saw his mother clench her jaw and lightly shake her head, looking at Tombeur, who was trapped in her gaze. Jack was so transfixed on them he didn't notice Lela rise beside him.

"LELA BEAULOUP!" Saint Germain hurried from the opposite side of the room to stand before the set of bleachers that held Jack and his pack. Jack's neck snapped to the side and jerked up, looking at his little sister standing beside him. She smiled down at him, expectantly, hopefully, and an awful feeling made Jack's stomach flip over. He turned to look at his brother Julien, who gazed longingly, tenderly at the back of Lela's head, putting his hands on the bench, ready to stand and accept her offer.

"Who is the lucky Roug?"

"My half-brother…" she declared in a firm, proud voice, and Jack felt Julien's knee nudge his back as he began to stand. "…Jacques Beauloup!"

A flurry of excited mutterings rippled like waves around the Gathering Hall as Jack whipped his head around to look at Julien's crestfallen, quickly angering face. He turned back to Lela, looking at her disbelievingly, and shook his head no, mouthing the words "I can't."

"JACQUES BEAULOUP! PLEASE RISE!"

This is insanity. I'm already bound. My binding was acknowledged.

Jack stood on shaky legs, finally towering over Lela beside him. She took his hand in hers and squeezed it. Jack pulled his away, furious with her.

"I'm bound, Lela," he growled to her, his face flushing and eyes burning with embarrassment and confusion.

She smiled prettily at him and shrugged.

Jack turned his eyes to Saint Germain, standing on the floor several rows beneath them.

"This is a mistake, Monsieur Saint Germain," he declared in a strong, clear voice. "I was bound twenty years ago. *For what is bound cannot be broken.*"

Saint Germain's bushy, gray eyebrows rose into his hairline as another titter moved through the crowd in fascinated, entertained currents.

"My mother and Tombeur acknowledged the binding in the sacred text."

Jack's mother and Tombeur stood as Saint Germain turned to them.

"This is so?"

Tallis and Tombeur nodded solemnly and Jack expelled a breath he didn't realize he'd been holding.

Saint Germain's eyes narrowed as he looked back up at Lela. His voice was falsely light with strong undercurrents of irritation.

"Lela Beauloup. You waste my time, *louveteau*. You cannot bind yourself to an already bound man. You should know this—" He turned away from her, dismissively.

"WAIT!" she exclaimed, and Saint Germain turned back to face her. "None of us have ever *seen* his mate. Not in twenty years. If he can't produce her, I submit that she must have died. I want him to spark to me."

The crowd murmured, taking in this mew information and processing it.

Saint Germain wrinkled his forehead and turned to Jack. "*Can* you produce her? Your mate?"

Jack's nostrils flared, thinking of Darcy. "Not now. I—"

"Perhaps she is ill. Can you produce her within one week? One month?"

Jack took a deep breath and finally answered through clenched teeth. "I cannot."

"You say you have a mate, but you cannot produce her. I don't doubt you *had* a mate. I would never question the word of Tombeur Lesauvage or Tallis Beauloup, honorable council members. But, perhaps she died, as Lela Beauloup suggests. Perhaps a new woman is too much work and you prefer to remain unbound?" He waggled his finger at Jack and smiled merrily. He tapped his finger against his lips, considering the case for a moment before gesturing to the council table with a flourish. "I am skeptical about your claimed binding. You will join Lela Beauloup in the council ring and you will let her spark to you to see if you may be bound to her."

Lela had been holding her breath and now she released it, looking up at Jack with a happy smile. Jack sneered at her, his face sour. Not only was this a waste of time because she wouldn't be able to bind to him, but it was drawing attention to his situation—a situation he'd successfully kept private and silent for all of his adult life.

He reluctantly followed a bouncy Lela down the stairs and onto the floor, directed by Saint Germain to pass through the narrow walkway in the open horseshoe of the table, into the center of the council ring.

They stood before each other.

"This is madness, Lela," he whisper-growled. "You know I'm bound."

"AH, AH, AH! Our male doesn't appear too pleased!" teased Saint Germain to the delight of the crowd.

"It's the only way I'll know for sure," she breathed, her eyes wide and hopeful, burning for him, even as his stayed a dull, neutral brown.

"Let's just get it over with," he muttered through clenched teeth. "Close your eyes."

She complied, closing her eyes and leaning her face toward him. The crowd quieted down immediately.

Saint Germain waited until the room was silent before reciting the ancient words:

"IF SHE BE FOR ME, LET MY HEART STOP BEATING. IF I BE FOR HER, LET IT BE BORN AGAIN."

Jack took a deep breath and sighed, looking at Lela's upturned face, then gently pressed his lips to hers as the crowd watched in breathless anticipation.

After a moment he stepped back from her and her eyes opened in disappointed brown to regard his.

"I told you," he said quietly, sorry for the shattered, confused look in her eyes. "I'm already bound. *For what is bound cannot be broken.*"

The crowd grumbled in disappointment. There would be no passionate kiss in the ring today. No binding to celebrate tonight with catcalls and pranks.

Jack turned his back to walk away from her, out of the council ring, when her voice stopped him.

"I DEMAND A RE-BINDING!" Lela demanded in a loud, desperate snarl that reverberated off the rafters of the old hall.

Saint Germain, who had been watching the proceedings with stunned interest, furrowed his brows at Jack, motioning him to return to the center of the council ring. The crowd went wild with buzzing noise, both at the spectacle that Lela had created and Jack's reaction.

Jack strode to his mother, whose face registered regret and grief, her fingers curling into fists on top of the table. "What's a re-binding? *Maman?* What's a re-binding?"

Tallis lifted her head and held Jack's eyes. He could see that whatever it was, it wasn't going to be good for him and Darcy. She stood up and the crowd noise dimmed so that she could speak.

"Demanding a re-binding is equal to calling Tombeur Lesauvage and Tallis Beauloup liars. We acknowledged this binding many years ago. I pledge to you that it is still intact." She shot Lela a look that would wither live blooms, but Lela smirked and looked away. "My daughter is grieving the loss of her father. She doesn't know what she's—"

"I DEMAND A RE-BINDING!" Lela howled, throwing her head back, to the delight of the crowd who started chanting, "RE-binding! RE-binding!"

Jack's eyes burned as he stared at Lela, feeling betrayed, his claws protracting as he considered doing her real harm. He let them drop a little, staring at her with menace.

Saint Germain joined Jack and Lela in the council ring and put up his hands to quiet the crowd.

"Sheath 'em," he growled softly at Jack.

Jack concentrated on retracting the claws, nostrils flaring in frustration and anger as he stared back at Saint Germain.

The older man tittered once Jack's claws were hidden. He raised his voice to the crowd, every bit the showman. "Very unusual. This is very, very unusual. We haven't had a demand for a re-binding for as long as I can remember. But, you're right, of course. Bindings should not, cannot, be hidden—they are our most sacred honor on which our way of life depends. If they are ever in question, we must all have a chance to feel the power of their singular energy." He looked up and down at Lela with a look somewhere between amused and admiring. "A re-binding. You're a clever girl when you want your way."

Tallis slammed her hands on the table in front of her. "This little bitch is disrespecting the council. She is a Reynard! An outrage!"

Saint Germain turned to Tallis with a hostile glare. "You will be seated and remain in order, Tallis Beauloup, or the CE will escort you outside."

Tombeur stood opposite Tallis, his fiery eyes focused on Saint Germain.

"Sit down, Tombeur, or you'll go with her."

He turned his back to Tallis and faced Jack and Lela.

"A forced re-binding. Hm. You say you can't produce your mate in one month's time, but how about two?" Saint Germain looked back and forth between Lela and Jack, rubbing his chin. "The council will vote immediately. All those in favor of the re-binding of Jacques Beauloup to his mysterious mate, stand."

Jack watched in horror as various members of the council stood, raising their hands. One, two three…twelve, thirteen, fourteen…Damn it, no! Twenty. Twenty of the forty council members stood around the table.

"Goodness gracious. We're tied, which means the Council Elder gets a vote." He looked at Jack and raised his eyebrows before turning to Lela and slowly, dramatically raising his hand.

The crowd erupted with stomping, clapping, and calling. Since the most exciting thing to happen at a Gathering in most of their lifetimes was to witness a live binding, this was unprecedented. Saint Germain quieted the crowd by waving his hands then turned to Jack.

"You have until the Summer Solstice to produce your mate, Jacques Beauloup. That's eight weeks. If you cannot, not only will the binding will be considered broken, but we shall have to investigate the circumstances of your…*phantom* mate." He smiled at Jack and winked at Lela, rubbing his hands together. Then he turned slowly, addressing all of the packs at once in a booming voice that ended the Gathering. "That is all. *C'EST FINI!*"

The crowd erupted yet again, stomping their feet on the bleachers and howling in approval. Jack looked at Tombeur, who shook his head and swallowed, looking down. He shifted his gaze to his mother, who winced and turned away.

Then he looked at Lela. Only Lela held his eyes. Lela, who smiled like Lynette the fox, who had twisted his fate and put him in an impossible position.

JACK, JULIEN, TALLIS, AND TOMBEUR sat around the kitchen table while Delphine napped in the room she shared with her *Tante* Lela. Lela knew better than to come home after the scene she made at the Gathering.

"I'd like to kill her," snarled Jack, his fangs and claws kept in check, barely.

Julien shrugged. "No one's ever met your mate, Jacques. She had the right to ask for—"

"NO!" screamed Tallis at her younger son. "You will NOT defend her for this. Not this time, Julien!"

"I'm just saying that any pack member can ask for a re-binding. The council voted."

"Son," started Tombeur, looking at Julien with thoughtful eyes. "No one's saying she didn't have a right. But, she's brought down a mess of trouble on this family. On your Mama. On me. Most especially, on your brother."

Julien turned to Jack. "Well, as long as we're on the subject…WHY haven't we ever met your mate? What pack is she from? Where do you live with her? Why are you gone for a year or two at a time, and you always come home without her?"

"Back down, Julien," warned Tallis.

Jack's eyes felt hot and he knew they were burning with outrage.

"I'm not trying to start trouble. I'm trying to understand."

Jack turned to Julien, blurting the answer out with a growl. "She's human."

Julien's eyes widened to saucers and he started to speak, but no words came out. He shook his head back and forth, searching Jack's face.

"That's impossible," he finally murmured.

Jack nodded. "Yep."

Julien turned to his mother and Tombeur. "You knew about this? You *acknowledged* it?"

Tallis's eyes filled with tears and she looked down at the table. Tombeur reached over and covered her hand with his.

Jack pulled his eyes away from them and turned to Julien beside him. "It happened the summer we lived in the Southern Bloodlands. In Carlisle. I kissed her the summer before my eighteenth birthday. It bound me to her. It bound her to me. I came home for the acknowledgement and promised to stay away from her for a decade. I worked for the Council Enforcement. I lived here. But I never forgot her. When I was twenty-eight, I left. Tombeur helped me find a job working in private security for the humans. I earned money, I learned how to blend in. I renovated the cabin on the Southern Bloodlands into a lodge so I could live there with her. I had a vault built for me."

"How do you hunt?"

"I don't. I lock myself in a room with fresh dead. A deer or moose. Three days later the door unlocks, and there's almost nothing left of the carcass."

"You're satisfied?"

"Are you asking if I miss the hunt?"

Julien jerked his head up and down once.

Jack did. Sometimes.

"I don't have a choice. I love her. I'm bound to her. I'm not going to hunt her kind."

"You feed on animal flesh? Only?" Julien asked this thoughtfully, surprised.

Jack nodded. Julien shuddered, bunching up his face in disgust. Finally, he shrugged before speaking again.

"This is bad, Jack. You can't bring her here for Solstice. You can't, they'd tear her apart. But, if you bring anyone else, they'll know immediately she's not your mate. We can feel it…when the kiss is true."

Jack looked at his brother and nodded grimly.

"You'll have to turn her," said Julien softly.

"Out of the question," growled Jack.

"You don't have another move. She's human. You're Roug. You're bound to each other. You can't bring someone else for Solstice—every Roug in the Gathering Hall would know she was an imposter the second you kissed her. You have to bring the human. But she can't come as a human—there's no way you'd be able to protect her. If you don't bring her, they'll declare you unbound. Or, God forbid, they'll convene an Inquisition and investigate. You only have one move, Jack. You have to turn—"

"I *won't*—"

Jack heard a door creak open and stopped short, turning his attention to little Delphine who appeared at her bedroom door, rubbing her little hands in her eyes. "Where'd *Tante* Lela go?"

Julien got up from the table and walked over to his sleepy daughter, swinging her up on his hip and kissing her dark hair. "She didn't come back from the Gathering yet, baby."

"Yeah, she did. She was just here. She was goin' tell me a story."

"What are you talking about, baby?"

"I opened my eyes and she was kneeling by my bed. She had her backpack on and she said she might not see me for a while, but did I want a story before she left. And I said, Yeah. And she said, Which one? And I said, Tell me the legend of Darcy from Carlisle who *Grand-mère* hates and Uncle Jack loves."

Jack's eyes shot open and he stared in shock at his niece.

His mother gasped then jumped up from the table, rushing to Julien and Delphine.

"Delphine, this is very, very important. What did *Tante* Lela say after you asked for your story?"

"Bad words."

"What words?' demanded Jack, panic rising.

"*Tante* Lela said, Fucking Carlisle. And then she sort of growled, I'm going hunting. And I felt worried, so she kissed my cheek and she said I'd have a better story later when she came back. Then she kissed my eyes and told me to go back to sleep. But I didn't go back to sleep. I peeked. She went out the window." Delphine looked over her father's shoulder at the shocked faces of her uncle and Tombeur, and then shook her little head. "Where is she, Papa? I thought she was coming right back."

TALLIS SPREAD OUT A MAP on the kitchen table.

"Away from the Bloodlands, she can't shift until dark," said Tallis. "I don't know that she could make it all the way to Carlisle shifted anyway. My guess is that she's going to hitchhike. Either that or she could catch a bus in Quebec City."

Julien shook his head. "I know her. She loves shifting, but she wouldn't risk it alone. She's hiding right now. She'll head to QC with one of the packs leaving tomorrow morning then she'll hitch south. We can beat her there."

Jack whipped his head up from the map to look at his younger brother. "We?"

"We."

"Take care of her." Julien shifted his daughter to his mother before leveling his eyes at Tallis. "When I come back with Lela, you'll have to bury the hatchet, *Maman*."

"And why would I do that?"

"Because I'll be bound to her when I return," said Julien.

Tallis gasped. "NO! NO! She's your—"

Julien narrowed his eyes, raised an eyebrow, and flicked his glance to Tombeur's bowed head, his meaning clear. Jack watched as his mother's face segued from indignation to understanding to red with shame. Julien pointed to his eyes, then to Delphine's, then glanced back down at Tombeur, who was tracing Lela's route with his finger.

Tallis looked down, nodding almost imperceptibly.

"Lela's mine," Julien said quietly. "The heart wants what the heart wants, *Maman*."

Now Tombeur looked up at Julien, then back at Tallis.

"He's got you there, Tal." He put his arm around her shoulders and she leaned back against him.

"Yes, he does," she said softly, kissing Delphine's head, as Tombeur nuzzled hers.

Jack had no idea just when Julian would figure it out, but he guessed he'd do it the same way Jack had. Tombeur, Julien, and Delphine had the exact same eyes, and they were so striking, there was no mistaking their meaning. With the sort of time Tombeur was likely to spend with Tallis and Delphine, it was just a matter of days before Julien figured it out too.

"You going away, Papa?" Delphine asked.

"I've got to help Uncle Jack bring back *Tante* Lela. You love Lela, right, baby?"

"I love her most of all after you and *Grand-mère*." She looked at Jack and shrugged. "Sorry, Uncle Jack."

Jack grinned and put a hand on her head. "That's okay."

"Well," said Tallis, "I guess you two better pack up."

"We'll miss the tribute…the funeral…"

Tallis shook her head. "You must go. Your father would understand."

As Jack turned toward his bedroom his mother grabbed his arm and mouthed, *Je suis désolée. I am sorry.*

Jack patted her hand without meeting her eyes and turned away.

He was bound to a woman who didn't want him, but the idea that Lela—that *anyone*—could harm Darcy twisted his gut into knots. All of the anger and sadness he felt last night took a backseat to his need—his visceral need—to keep his mate safe. He hadn't meant to return to Carlisle so soon; he'd meant to give her more time to process who he was. But time had abruptly run out.

"You ready?" he asked his brother.

"I'm ready, Jack."

Striding through the cabin door with Julien at his heels, he took a seat, started his car and turned it south.

And even though the immediate threat of Lela and the long-term threat of Solstice should have made him heavy-hearted, for the first time in two days, he took a deep breath. She would still be angry. She would probably still reject him. But in all of the earth, his heart only had one home. The binding was messy, but it had held, after all.

Jack pressed down on the gas.

He was going home.

Continued in...

It's You

Book 2

❧

Coming January 17th 2017

Also Available
from Katy Regnery
via Boroughs Publishing Group

THE HEART OF MONTANA SERIES
Sweet, small-town, contemporary romance

By Proxy
The Christmas Wish
Midsummer Sweetheart
See Jane Fall
Meeting Miss Mystic
What Were You Expecting?

About the Author

NEW YORK TIMES AND USA Today bestselling author Katy Regnery started her writing career by enrolling in a short story class in January 2012. One year later, she signed her first contract, and her first novel, *By Proxy*, was published by Boroughs Publishing Group in September 2013.

Twenty-five books later, Katy claims authorship of the multititled *New York Times* and *USA Today* Blueberry Lane Series, which follows the English, Winslow, Rousseau, Story, and Ambler families of Philadelphia; the six-book, bestselling ~a modern fairytale~ series; and several other standalone novels and novellas.

Katy's first modern fairytale romance, *The Vixen and the Vet*, was nominated for a RITA® in 2015 and won the 2015 Kindle Book Award for romance. Katy's boxed set, *The English Brothers Boxed Set*, Books #1–4, hit the *USA Today* bestseller list in 2015, and her Christmas story, *Marrying Mr. English*, appeared on the list a week later. In May 2016, Katy's Blueberry Lane collection, *The Winslow Brothers Boxed Set*, Books #1–4, became a *New York Times* E-book bestseller.

In 2016, Katy signed an agreement with Spencer Hill Press. As a result, her Blueberry Lane paperback books will now be distributed to brick-and-mortar bookstores all over the United States.

Katy lives in the relative wilds of northern Fairfield County, Connecticut, where her writing room looks out at the woods, and her husband, two young children, two dogs, and one Blue Tonkinese kitten create just enough cheerful chaos to remind her that the very best love stories begin at home.

Sign up for Katy's newsletter today: **www.katyregnery.com**

Connect with Katy

KATY LOVES CONNECTING WITH HER readers and answers every e-mail, message, tweet, and post personally! Connect with Katy!

Katy's Website
www.katyregnery.com

Katy's E-mail
katy@katyregnery.com

Katy's Facebook Page
www.facebook.com/KatyRegnery

Katy's Pinterest Page
www.pinterest.com/katharineregner/

Katy's Goodreads Profile
www.goodreads.com/author/show/7211470.Katy_Regnery

Boroughs
Publishing Group

D ID YOU ENJOY THIS BOOK? Drop us a line and say so! We love to hear from readers, and so do our authors. To connect, visit www. boroughspublishinggroup.com online, send comments directly to info@ boroughspublishinggroup.com, or friend us on Facebook and Twitter. And be sure to check back regularly for contests and new releases in your favorite subgenres of romance!

Are you an aspiring writer? Check out
www.boroughspublishinggroup.com/submit
and see if we can help you make your dreams come true.

CPSIA information can be obtained
at www.ICGtesting.com
Printed in the USA
LVOW13s1548080217
523626LV00010B/981/P